Sunlit Hearts

Meenu Mehrotra

Vitasta
Let Knowledge Spread

Times Group Books

Published by
Vitasta Publishing Pvt. Ltd.
2/15, Ansari Road, Daryaganj,
New Delhi - 110 002
info@vitastapublishing.com

ISBN 978-93-80828-78-7

Layout by Vitasta Publishing Pvt. Ltd.
Printed by Vits Press, New Delhi

Marketed and Distributed exclusively in India & Sub-Continent by:

Times Group Books
(A division of Bennett, Coleman and Company Limited)
Times Annexe, Express Building
9-10 Bahadur Shah Zafar Marg, New Delhi-110 002

For
all the brave & empowered women
who are unafraid to seek their truth,
follow their hearts,
&
celebrate their womanhood

Acknowledgements

There are many to thank for the journey that this book took me through.

My birth town Delhi—where the idea of the book took birth; for the sheer madness of the place that fuelled my passion to write this book; Vineet, for all his love, understanding, compassion, for being in sync with my soul as only he can be and for ensuring that I survived through it all and who made it all possible. Love you; Tamanna C for being my angel, spiritual guide and a great friend. You are a true blessing Tams; Bipin for being a terrific brother and for being around during this journey. Richard Kraweic for reading and reviewing the book—for his caustic comments and honest criticism, for his unfailing understanding of what was in my soul and what I wanted to express. Manoj K Narayanan, for entering my life and restoring my faith in the magic of being connected to the higher self and for letting me experience the Absolute Divine—blessed to have you, Manoj.

Nandita for holding me with utter gentleness always; Sangita, for being emotionally present; Meghna, for making me complete with myself; Vivek saab for that path changing conversation. Many thanks to Richard Crasta, for being generous in reading and reviewing the book and for helping me keep my faith in myself. Special thanks to my kids—Taraash & Tashyaa for their love, patience, understanding and support. A mighty thanks to God and all my angels for this catharsis. And finally thanks to ma & papa for being the reason for my origin. Miss you both loads.

A special word of thanks to my publisher Renu Kaul Verma of Vitasta and to my editor Veena Batra. They trusted my writing abilities and gave it a proper shape.

"There are times when we must
sink to the bottom of our misery
to understand the truth,
just as we must descend to the bottom of the well
to see the stars in broad daylight."
— Vaclav Havel

PROLOGUE

Medha, 1990

I had heard that love makes your soul crawl out of its hiding and wondered if it was ever possible to experience such a glorious state. But the moment my eyes met Nikhil's for the first time in college, I understood the truth of those words. I was not the same anymore.

His intense eyes had arrested me forever, drawing me into them and yet he had seemed so unreachable, like the moon. I seemed to have grown wings, almost overnight and felt I could fly high in the sky without the fear of ever falling down. The faint feeling of trance grew with each day, churning me over as a person. I felt like a mighty conqueror revelling in the knowledge that what I felt for him was unmatched, irreversible and absolute. I started noticing everything about him. Right from how his face lit up when he smiled; how he threw his head back when he laughed; how his clear complexion picked up the colours of his bright t-shirts brilliantly; how his square jawed face looked perfect against the sunlight; how his soft mouth moved like a wave when he talked and how his shoulders seemed so strong on his 6' 2" lithe body, to how his eyes seemed so vulnerable whenever he looked at me and smiled. My whole world had compressed into a single face and that million dollar smile. God! I was in love!

We slowly got friendly with each other and I found out that he had joined only in the last year of graduation because he had shifted from Dehradun recently.

His father had passed away in a freak car accident and he had relocated to Delhi with his mother and an elder brother to live with his maternal grandparents. It had taken all my courage and guts to give him a card for Valentine's Day. I had wanted to tell him what I felt for him. I was sure that he felt the same for me–the same madness, the same skipping of heartbeats when he saw me. But at twenty, optimism is more potent than Viagra. When I handed him the card, my heart had pounded louder than the sound of a dozen horses' hoofs galloping and beating down the racecourse.

"Thanks," he said.

I fumbled. "R-Read it and tell me…"

"Sure." And he smiled.

His cinnamon eyes were liquid and happy and they unstitched me. I had come back home leaving the rest of the college lectures unattended because I couldn't bear to be in the same room with him. The feeling of numbness had rapidly swelled and I did not know how he would respond to my candid expression of love. In the coming few days I had looked for a sign–a special look in his eyes, a stolen glance to convince me that I was indeed special. And then he had called me out from our group of four boys and three girls, sheepishly.

"Thanks so much for the card," he said. "But..."

I felt my world about to crumble somewhere inside me.

He continued. "I...I am sorry... you write beautifully I appreciate your honesty and respect your feelings but..."

I had fervently prayed, Oh no! Don't make him say a no please... God don't please, don't...Nikhil looked at me with immense kindness floating in his eyes, "I don't feel the same for you. I hope you understand... but we are friends." The words came out of his mouth softly, silently, gently like snowflakes falling on the earth.

I stood still, as if frozen, trying to gauge his words that had hit me swifter than lightening and wounded me, perhaps for life. I did not know how to escape. I tried to smile.

"It's ok...I understand," I said, blinking back my tears.

Nikhil stepped closer to me, closer than he had in the past one year, "I... I didn't mean to hurt you... but don't... look I am sorry," he muttered. How I had wished he would just go away and leave me alone. I hated him. I didn't want to see him again. He was heartless and cruel and why the hell did I tell him that I loved him. What a fool I was? I would hate him for the rest of my life damn! I could not even hate him.

When I got back home, I slipped into my room and cried bitterly. How could this be possible? His eyes could not have lied to me. What I saw in them was real, I knew. I had seen something in them, I was dead sure. I could never mistake it. Why did he not see or feel what I did? Why? The questions kept ransacking my peace of mind for the next few days but there was no answer.

Nothing could assuage the anguish of being unacknowledged by the one to whom I had given my heart away. I plunged deep into the ravines of pain the eternal sting of unrequited love.

I, a complete neophyte in matters of love, did not know how to deal with heartbreak and rejection. I did not know how to go about my life as if this had never happened. I cried when I thought of him at home and I had mist in my eyes when I saw him in college. I avoided meeting his gaze directly, as peering into those hazel pools made me weak in the knees. I would steal a look when he was not watching, just to see whether he still discerned my presence or not. I started relishing the sad love songs and became quieter than usual, sucked into my gloomy world. Ma was quick to notice my altered state.

"All ok with you Medha?" she asked one day.

I feigned surprise. "Why? I am fine."

"You just don't seem so, is it some guy you…?"

I winced. "Even if it is, I'll deal with it. You don't need to bother," I said, and walked out of the room. I had every reason to be rude to her because she had been too intrusive of late. And I hated her when she intruded into my space.

The ache of rejected love was sweeter than I had expected; more seductive than I could ever imagine. It defined me somehow and gave me a sense of self-worth, one that I would not part with for anything.

Nikhil surprised me totally though. Gradually he started looking at me a few seconds longer than usual, noticing me, smiling at me more often but he kept his distance, trying hard not to show me what I was yearning to see in his eyes. The insanity, however, only grew. Whenever he looked at me, I felt the warmth of his soft eyes entering me and filling up my heart. And whenever he smiled, I felt drenched in rain. I felt alive and beautiful. I knew he was aware of my intense feelings for him and that was enough for me.

It was late October and the weather was just perfect, neither miserably hot nor unbearably cold. The day was sunnier than usual and the wind was a bit wild as Nikhil came over and sat beside me in the class, catching his breath. "Hi," he said. He smelled of cologne and coffee.

"Hey, how come you are late today?" I asked.

"Mom gave me some work. I had to visit the bank." His eyes trailed my face as if looking for something. The professor entered the class and everyone got up to greet him. We sat next to each other as the lecture progressed. Our hands filled up the blank spaces of the notebooks for the next forty minutes. We never looked at each other, focusing on the lecture.

His presence was enough to sustain me. I sat next to him, smitten and smug. As soon as the lecture was over, it was recess time.

"Canteen?" Nikhil asked.

"Yeah, I badly need tea," I admitted.

And before we knew, the whole gang... Rahul, Sandeep and Sonal were sitting in the canteen drumming their fingers on the rickety wooden table. The breeze was delicious and the sun felt warm on my body. Everyone went up to the counter to place their order but when I got up, Nikhil stopped me. He took out his wallet from the back pocket of his jeans, "I'll get it, don't bother; tea and bread pakora?"

I looked at him. "Yeah…but..." His eyes instructed me not to say anymore and I didn't. Sandeep wolf whistled. Sonal, my best friend smiled at me.

"The story seems to be progressing well," Rahul said looking at Sandeep. Sandeep gave a short laugh. "Of course…it's a rocking story, man," and then he broke into a song "…when you look at me, I can touch the sky…I know I am alive…ye ye ye." Rahul drummed the table to add the required beats. I felt the heat climbing up the ladder of my spine. This was all new to me. Nikhil pointed his finger at them. "Shut up both of you!" and walked away towards the counter.

Sandeep pillowed his head on his arms. "Don't get angry, yaar, we understand…"

"Does your boyfriend also indulge you like this?" Rahul winked at Sonal who was busy biting her nails.

Sonal winked back at me. "Not really...."

I smiled and when Nikhil sat next to me as we devoured the pakoras and sandwiches, Sandeep whistled again. He nudged Rahul to observe both of us closely and Nikhil fixed them with such a hard stare that Sandeep blurted out: "Nik, please don't look at me like that...I am not Medha, yaar."

Everyone laughed and I could see Nikhil's face turn a beetroot red in seconds. How I had felt on top of the world that day and every single day after that! College never remained the same.

***

The last day of college had been memorable. I had worn a blue and white, *batik* print wraparound skirt with a frilled ivory blouse and Nik was in a pair of blue jeans teamed with a white t-shirt. He had driven down in his mushroom coloured Fiat to college and I had given him a rose and a letter. He read out the letter in front of me as we sat inside his car:

"For those endless moments that I loved you, embarrassed you, maybe unconsciously hurt you, caused you pain, I apologize...but I will never forget you all my life and I want to see you happy always and find the love of your life." His voice dipped.

Nikhil held my hand. "I am sorry Medha I couldn't give you what..."

I looked at him, my eyes smarting with tears. "Don't. . I am sorry too for..." My voice shook.

"You don't have to be sorry, you silly girl," he said as he hugged me tightly.

We remained locked for a few seconds as if nothing could part us; as if all this sorry business was a lie; that he loved me as madly as

I did and that we were never going to be away from each other.

I had then torn myself away from him and run out of the car to the basement hall where the party was about to begin. I collected myself somehow and mingled with the rest of the class, pushing my thoughts about him to the farthest corner of my mind. And when the party began and the music played, and the dance floor lit up with a maze of coloured lights, Nikhil had walked up to me and held out his hand. I caught his hand instinctively, feeling his strength and trailed him in a daze. We were the first couple to hit the dance floor.

How we had danced to the cheers and claps of the classmates before everyone else joined us! I had felt truly special that day.

But even months after leaving college, I pined in his love. I remembered him every day even as I undertook a post graduate course, to specialize in Creative Writing; even as I made new friends; visited new places; he just refused to leave me. I wish I had a magic wand to make him go away or make him want me the way I wanted him. I couldn't manage any. You can't forget someone you love as if they never existed and you can't make someone fall in love with you either. The dilemma remained. We were no longer in touch with each other. I wanted to be as far away from him as possible. I couldn't bear to get hurt anymore than I had, but he seemed to be around me all the time...in my thoughts, my dreams.

We discard some memories like an old, tattered coat and we embrace some so firmly, as if in losing them we would lose a part of ourselves. I chose the latter. I kept Nikhil tucked inside me, safe in my heart like a message in my inbox, one I knew I would never delete, lest I might lose him forever. The agony of unrequited love caused me to pine away. It only grew with time until I sealed every corner of myself. And as the days turned into weeks and months, I wondered whether I would ever be able to open up my scams for any other man in this lifetime.

"You never leave someone behind,
you take a part of them with you, and
leave a part of yourself behind."
— Unknown

Medha, 1994

The doctor, a plump lady with short hair and the kindest voice I had ever heard, removed her glasses and smiled at me.

"Congrats, you are pregnant, Medha."

I looked at Rishi and felt a wave of excitement rise inside me. I had been emotionally ready to have a child after I got married to Rishi but nothing had prepared me for this moment, when I would actually realize that there was another life growing inside me.

"Wow! That's great news," Rishi beamed.

The doctor handed us the prescription and recommended a few tests before we left the clinic. As we sat in the car, Rishi leaned over and kissed me. He was happy as a lark.

"I can't tell you how excited I am Wifey," he said.

I smiled. "I can see it…I am so nervous."

"With excitement and joy?"

"Yes, our life's going to change." I confessed.

Rishi turned the car around a bend on the road. "It will all be fine. Don't worry, Wifey."

I felt numb. This was the start of a new beginning; a family, a baby who was an extension of me and Rishi and I wondered what it would be like to have a child of my own. It had taken me a long time to get Nikhil out of my mind before I could think of getting married but he had never totally left me. The more I tried to forget him, to wipe his memories off my mind, the stronger his presence became.

I realized that you could abandon people's bodies but not their thoughts. And that you could carry someone in your heart forever, without even being aware of it. So I took Nikhil with me to my new home when I married Rishi; and there were times when I took him also to my bed. Surprisingly, I never felt any guilt ever. Nikhil had just become a part of me.

I felt the September breeze on my face as I rolled down the car window. I looked at the auburn sky as the sun melted into it and realized how time had passed in the last few years.

Rishi was not all that I had wanted in a man but I had ignored the specifics like so many other women. I knew relationships had to be built over time. Whoever got everything they desired in a spouse? It was an arranged marriage and I had hit it off well with Rishi when we had first met. I still remembered that he had made me laugh riotously. A few more meetings and I had said a yes. After about six months of being engaged, we were married.

***

Rishi fussed over me as if I was a kid throughout my pregnancy. He would take me out for my mandatory evening walks, make me eat even after I had thrown up; remind me to take my supplements on time. I swelled and revelled as an expectant mother.

And then Yash arrived. The moment I saw him, I fell in love with him. He was all that I had not known or seen earlier. He was my little angel and suddenly my life came to revolve around him. He brought all the joys that filled up our world as never before. Our marriage seemed bursting with all the necessary ingredients- love, care, attention, emotional comfort and a child. What more could I ask for?

It was beginning of October and the winter season was about to set in. I could not wait to relish the greens that one got to taste in this season- spinach, fenugreek and many more.

Rishi arrived from office one day. It was six pm and I was feeding a mashed banana to Yash who was about seven months old now.

"Hi honey," Rishi said as he entered the bedroom. Yash yelped in delight as he saw him.

Rishi kissed me on my cheek and picked up Yash in his arms. "How's my rock star? Finish your food and then we will play," he crooned to Yash and placed him gently in his baby chair. Yash gave him a wide grin, his two tiny teeth shining bright. Rishi sat down and began unlacing his shoes. "I have a surprise for you. Guess what?"

I lifted my gaze. "What?"

"Come on, you can do better than that, Wifey?"

I directed the spoonful of mashed banana inside Yash's mouth. "You got a promotion?"

"The review is next month honey."

"Your car loan got approved?" I said.

"Wrong again."

Rishi got up. "We are going for a holiday to Kasauli."

He came closer to me. "For our second honeymoon."

My eyes widened in disbelief. "You must be kidding- Yash is…"

"Seven months old now and I am sure we can manage. He's a sweetheart anyways."

"I hesitated."

Rishi held my hand. "I am there, so what's the worry, Wifey?"

I looked into his whiskey coloured eyes and knew I could trust him completely. This holiday was what I badly needed and he knew it.

***

I watched the mountains from the balcony of our hilltop hotel room. It was early morning and the blanket of mist shrouded the landscape.

"It has been long since we had a holiday," I said, pouring the tea.

Rishi tightened the belt of his woollen night robe. "I know. You deserved one Wifey. Ever since you conceived Yash, you haven't been out."

I smiled. "You are a sweetheart." I reached out for his hand and kissed it tenderly.

"I got up at five to write today," I said excitedly.

Rishi took a sip of the hot tea. "Great! I am glad that you like this place."

I looked at the wide vista stretching out in front of me, and nursed my mug of tea. Suddenly the wailing of Yash broke the train of my thoughts. Rishi got to his feet.

"I'll get him."

He arrived within a few minutes with Yash cuddled like a ball in his arms, socks and cap in place.

I kept down my mug to take Yash in my arms. "Did you...?"

"Yes, Wifey. I changed the diaper," he smiled as he handed Yash over to me

I kissed Yash and grinned. "I am impressed, Mr. Nanda- your services are good."

Rishi looked deep in my eyes. "I hope in all fields, Madam?"

We both laughed out loud, even as Yash grinned and the whole valley seemed to resound with the laughter of our joy. The trip was super and I returned- refreshed and rejuvenated, with a renewed gusto for my writing. I thanked Rishi deep down in my heart for this wonderful break.

ભ❖ဢ

But being married at twenty three had its own (dis)advantages. A new household, new family, looking after the needs of everyone, coping with different attitudes, mindsets (Rishi had many close relatives who often visited and stayed over). I adjusted brilliantly without realizing what I was losing in the process. It never occurred to me and whenever it did, I chose to ignore it. Yash came and life took on a new meaning in which my own desires and dreams seem to get buried. I longed to do something creative and get out of the rut of domesticity. I had been writing articles and had been freelancing on and off with a women's magazine but the urge to do something creative was tugging at my heartstrings for a long time now. And then something magical happened.

It was July and the monsoons had arrived a bit late this year. I looked out of the window of our fourth floor Narmada apartments in the almost posh Alaknanda colony of South Delhi. There was something about the rains that completely seduced me. When the sky poured, it seemed that the earth and sky were making love and I had always found this fascinating. The sky was laden with ink black clouds and the cool breeze wrapped around my body gently. Yash, who was sixteen months old now, lay fast asleep in his cot. I sat on my writing desk, near the huge window and took out my writing pad. It had been a while since the urge to write had been ambushing my thoughts. I picked up my pen and the clouds thundered. I saw a thin, crooked wire of lightning blaze through the sky. And then I started to write and wrote non-stop for half an hour even as the rain beat down; even as the peal of thunder ripped through the clouds and I felt as if this was all I was meant to do... write, wondering why hadn't I started earlier? When I re-read what I had written, I knew this is what I was meant to do for the rest of my life. I started writing a journal and found *myself* in it. It gave me a sense of relief and gave an expression to my feelings. I soon found the wings to fly. The more I involved myself in writing and reading, the more I found it interesting and fulfilling. But life throws us challenges all the time and it did.

***

"Wifey please, I am hungry. Can you give me food?" Rishi called out.

It was one of those rare days when he had come home for lunch. I was busy typing the final draft of a short story that I was planning to send for an online competition. When Rishi landed home, I was deeply engrossed in the story.

"Give me ten minutes Rishi," I shouted back

Rishi switched on the television to catch the news. After a while he strode inside the study. "I have a meeting to catch Medha. Can't you do this later?" he said.

My eyes were glued to the laptop screen. "Why don't you heat the dal and veggies in the microwave- I'm going to make chapattis in a few minutes."

Rishi seemed invisible to me at the moment.

He snapped. "I don't understand this? I mean what's the big deal about a story you are cooking, damn it."

I ignored him. "Please, I have to send this by evening; it's the last day of the contest." My fingers just kept hitting the keypad of the laptop.

"I don't care about your bloody contest. I have an important meeting to attend," Rishi yelled.

I got up from my chair, disgusted, leaving my work. "Enough. Rishi if you can't understand..." I walked past him towards the kitchen. "Don't make it worse," I glowered.

I served him food and as we ate silently, I wondered whether it was ever possible for him to understand me now, when I was charting out a new course for myself?

***

I pillowed my head on my arms and stretched myself. My third short story was ready to be mailed to the editor of a publishing house. Ever since I had won the third prize in that short story contest three months back, I had been freelancing for a few publishing houses. I reached out for a glass of water and drank to my fill. The story had shaped up as I had expected but I needed an instant feedback. Maybe Rishi could do it? Although he had never shown too much interest in what I wrote, he had not been discouraging either.

I called him. "Are you busy?"

"Not really. Just checking my mails…tell me."

I said excitedly, "I finished my story."

"Good."

"Can you read it and tell me how you find it?"

"Just now?"

"If you can, it'll be great. I just can't wait to get a feedback from you."

There was silence over the phone.

"Not now- I am in no mood."

"Please Rishi. I need to discuss the story…please."

Rishi's voice was frosty. "I'll read it once I'm back home. You can then know my instant response."

I felt as if someone had taken the wind out of my sails.

I tried to keep my voice even. "No problem, I'll wait."

I kept down the phone; my eyes glittering with tears and all the joy of creating a story seemed to leave me at that moment. The story was not mentioned when Rishi came home that night. He seemed to have forgotten about it and I did not want to remind him about it. He recalled about a week later.

"Oops! I forgot about your story." he said one evening, cracking his knuckles.

I replied icily, "It's going to be published in the next month's issue."

Rishi looked embarrassed. "Sorry, Wifey..."

"It's ok."

He put his arm around me. "I forgot about it totally but you could have reminded me."

I removed his arm gently. "It's important to share at that moment Rishi. Once the moment is gone, you learn to cope without sharing or maybe you share it with the next available person."

"I am sorry, Wifey, I understand."

"I understand too that you can't be available for me whenever I want you," I said, stung.

Slowly I stopped talking to Rishi about my work. It was a journey of discovery for me which Rishi couldn't completely comprehend. His lack of interest and understanding for my passion for writing left me in agony like a wounded animal. I would tell him what he asked but the joy of sharing and discussing my work with a spouse, painfully eluded me.

Rishi

I watched her as she lay in bed asleep. Her black hair was sprawled over the pillow. Her angular face seemed spread out; she looked almost angelic in sleep. Of late she had been busy with her writing and I knew she loved it more than anything. Her passion for it filled me with wonder sometimes. She wrote beautifully and I had read some of her work, which had been published.

The moment I first met her, I knew she was the one for me. Her exuberance, her zest for life and her laughter. I had taken no time to decide that she was the one I wanted to marry and spend the rest of my life with. And life had been good. There had been no cause for complaint. The arrival of Yash had added a new zing to our lives and I watched Medha blossom as a mother.

I came home rather early one day much to Medha's surprise. It had been raining since morning and the weather was beautiful, really romantic.

"Wow! No work in office today? How come early?" she said.

"Finished all pending work before time, so let's go for a long drive Medha," I suggested.

Medha flashed an innocent smile at me. "Drive? No way, it's Yash's dinner time, then sleep time."

"Please Medha it's been many days- Yash is grown up now."

"Kids love routine. You will be off to office tomorrow but he will be cranky the whole day like it happened last time, nope." She moved past me.

I followed her. "Come on, a slight deviation from a day's routine won't matter."

She fixed me with a stare. "It does I won't do it- we can keep the plan for a weekend, I would be more relaxed."

She made Yash sit up in his chair, buckled him and began feeding him his dinner of dal mixed with crumbs of roti.

"So what do we have for dinner today, Yash?" she started chatting with him like an adult.

I walked inside the bedroom, deflated. The cool breeze hugged me and I watched the rain pour down heavily from the skies. I leaned against the window sill with a heavy heart.

Her total focus was Yash now and sometimes I felt left out when they both seem to be in a world where only they belonged. I felt a stab of jealousy for a fleeting moment. After all another male had managed to catch the attention of my woman.

"You seem to love him more than me," I complained the next day.

She laughed. "Come on Rishi, he is your son. Don't treat him as competition; that's disgusting."

I looked tenderly at her. "He gets all your attention, all your time…probably all your love too."

Medha tucked Yash in the cot. "You are such a kid, how can you?"

"Why?" I stepped closer to her. "I want you only for myself, not for anyone, not even Yash."

I felt her breath on my face.

She smiled. "Try your luck sweetie but Yash will score high."

I looked at her, hurt. She did not even know how much I loved her. In fact it was something I did not know myself and I had never tried to find out. Some things were better left unexplored like the mysteries of the universe; the sunrise, sunset, the wind, sky and earth. All I knew was that I could never imagine life without her.

Medha's writing was slowly consuming her and at times I wondered whether she loved it more than her family.

I asked her one day. "You love your writing more than anyone; don't you?"

Medha stopped arranging the dishes and looked up at me. "Are you crazy Rishi?"

"No, I am not. At times I feel your writing is all that matters to you," I said.

Medha moved towards me. "Writing is like water for me. I need it to quench myself but that doesn't imply that you and Yash are any less."

She kissed me gently on my cheeks and I saw the shining flame in her eyes- the one I had seen so many times and the one that had drawn me to her in the first place. Maybe I was being insecure unnecessarily. She was mine and that was all that mattered, I reasoned with myself.

Rishi, 1998

Yash was four years old and Medha had conceived again. We wanted a second baby and Yash had been coaxing her for a sibling, especially since all his friends had one or were going to have one. Yash had been waiting deliriously for the day when he would be able to hold his little brother or sister in his arms. He questioned us endlessly why are we buying this? Will I get a brother or a sister? When is he going to come? What will he look like? What will I call him? What will he call me? The sparkle in his eyes had been more luminous than all the stars put together.

Medha had learned to embroider during the pregnancy and had put her skills to test enhancing the baby's clothes, bed sheets, bedcovers and the towels. She had even re-painted Yash's cot a brighter shade of blue. As the day of the delivery drew nearer, the excitement in Yash's life grew in multiples.

The memory of that day is as clear as the morning of a sunny day.

Medha woke up as usual in the morning, did her chores and it was when she lay down to rest that all of a sudden she felt the discomfort inside her. She could not decipher it. Her due date was about ten days away and the doctor had told her that the baby's head would engage any day now.

She felt weird and uncomfortable and she wanted to see the doctor immediately. She called me up in office and asked me to come over immediately. It was a wet, wild day. It had been pouring heavily since morning and the weather had become very cool. It was tough driving on the roads. The traffic was bad as several vehicles had broken down because of heavy water logging and to add to it, poor visibility slowed down the traffic, making it crawl. On our way to the hospital, I saw the blanched look on her face.

"All will be well," I assured her.

She opened her mouth and then closed it.

"Medha have faith." I told her but her eyes looked at me blankly.

She had been hale and hearty throughout the pregnancy. There had been no complication. The baby was fine, weighed well, his movements were clear, so why was her face looking like a sunken ship? My heart plummeted. She held on to my hand tightly as we waited for the doctor to arrive. I saw the agony in her eyes and then tears snaked their way down her cold face. I held her in my arms. "Don't worry Medha, all will be well." But I had never seen her so scared.

The ultrasound had confirmed her fears. The baby had managed to wrap the umbilical cord around his neck in the process of engaging his head. Medha had sunk. The doctor called for an emergency operation, but by the time they took out the baby, he had strangulated himself-the cord wound tight around his neck. The baby was still born.

***

There are moments which slow down life to a standstill. You wish time would pass as quickly as it had come, but for that one moment, your life stops as if you have missed a loop in the chain of breaths.

The blankness in Yash's eye was something I would never forget. It had pierced like a sword through me. He had cried aloud, yelling at Medha

"...but you told me the baby is going to come."

Medha had trembled and I had to hold her as she collapsed.

"I feel so empty and useless," she whispered.

I can never forget that vacant look in her eyes as if something had died within her.

The pain had slowly seeped into the crevices of our life and we had found it difficult to banish the anguish that trickled each day. But we both clung to each other, not letting the misery crack the walls of our marriage. And thankfully, the agony had slowly diminished over a period of time.

Medha, 2008

Yash was fifteen now. He had grown tall and fine. Time had flown by and it seemed I had not been able to catch my breath. Bringing up Yash had consumed me completely and my writing had occupied the rest of my space.

Ma had passed away a month earlier after fighting a losing battle with cancer and Papa was learning to cope with life in her absence. He was living with Siddharth, my younger brother, who had shifted base from US just before Ma's health had deteriorated.

Since the past three years, I felt Rishi had been so involved in building his career that somewhere we were losing the thread that connected us in the first place. It all seemed to be breaking apart somewhere.

My passion for writing had grown steadily and I was planning to write a book and engage full time in fiction writing. The freelance assignments, articles, short stories, poetry only satisfied a part of me and not the whole. Every time I had thought of writing a book, it had intimidated me. And raising Yash had occupied most of my mental and emotional space too. Guess I wasn't ready.

A story had been trailing me for a while now, and I wanted to explore the subject thoroughly. But I needed to grasp the finer nuances of writing fiction. And I found the way-writing for contests, getting registered for writers' websites where fellow writers critiqued and commented on your writings and reading the works of other writers, opened my perspective drastically.

But things came to a standstill when Rishi got a lucrative job offer from the Gulf and he decided to shift to Muscat. I was in the kitchen when Rishi dropped the news.

"It's a dream job-General Manager for Acer in Muscat!" The excitement in Rishi's voice hit me hard.

I felt a pang. Moving away from India was not an option I had ever weighed.

"But I don't want to move right now-especially with my work scene."

"Come on Wifey, we are family. We need to stay together. How can you even think of not coming along?"

I added the coarsely chopped onions to the warm oil in the pan on the gas stove.

"Even if I am not happy?"

Rishi took out a bottle of chilled water from the fridge.

"Happiness is a conscious decision. You tell yourself you are happy and you will be, believe me."

"No Rishi," I protested. "I won't be able to shift to another country; I need to be here..."

"But why?"

I added diced mushrooms to the pan and stirred it fiercely. "I have never heard about this place, don't know what kind of people live there and I am just not comfortable leaving Delhi."

Wisps of smoke rose from the pan and the piquant smell of onions and mushrooms filled up the air. Rishi gulped down water from the bottle before he spoke, "It's just that you are not ready to move-you are not ready for change."

"I have worked too hard to start my writing career. I can't forsake it and move to an unknown country."

The argument had stretched for weeks before I had finally relented. Rishi had succeeded in convincing me that Muscat was a beautiful place to live. I had succumbed to his logic of being together as a family and his need to have me around.

"I need you Medha, please don't do this…I love you." His childlike pleading and tears had fenced me in again. I was once again lost for any logic to refuse him.

Thankfully, the change of place gave an impetus to our marriage which was turning lifeless. Muscat was indeed a beautiful place. The smattering of craggy mountains all around overlooking the sparkling sea, the clean, wide roads, the lack of traffic, the ease of life, the material comforts, all helped me in settling down to the new place but the newness of this life soon started wearing off. Slowly my life came to revolve around the mundane; of each day being similar to the next and I began to miss the madness and familiarity of Delhi, the sounds, the traffic, smells of the place I grew up in.

The lack of mobility (I couldn't drive without taking a fresh driver's license) and friends and Rishi's hectic work schedule did their bit in aggravating my bitterness and soon I felt a pebble inside me getting heavy and becoming a rock with each passing day. It had been a month now that we had shifted to Muscat and I still did not feel settled down completely. The mundaneness of life was slowly gobbling me up.

***

I bade good bye to Yash as he boarded his school bus and started to walk towards the beach which Rishi had shown me a few days back. The twenty minute walk lead me to the Ghubra beach. A few men and women could be seen taking their morning walk on the walking track, circling a man made lake with the sea in the background. A white lady in black tights and white sleeveless t shirt jogged, her ponytail swinging like her hips, while an older white man in long shorts and oversized t-shirt walked with his dog in tow. The dog kept pace with his master but would sometimes chase a cat when he saw one. A plump woman in black Abaya with her head covered, struggled to walk fast in her attire, accompanied by a tall, thin man in a white Dishdasha.

I walked briskly and took three rounds of the lake. The sun was slowly becoming harsher but the breeze was cool enough. I finished my forty five minute walk and sat down on one of the wooden benches and collected my breath. I took a few sips from the bottle of water which I carried with me. I moved towards the grey sand beach. I took off my shoes and felt the soft grainy sand beneath my feet. I walked to the sea and felt the cool water circle my ankles. I looked up at the clear vanilla sky and felt its seamlessness. I remembered the dark blue sky of Delhi, and wondered why I felt differently for that sky even though it was the same sky? How tough it had been for me to stay in Muscat during those first few months? It was as if the time had become redundant. I found myself restless with each passing day; I tried to reason with Rishi again.

"I don't like this place, Rishi, please..."

"It's your attitude. If you feel that you don't like this place then obviously you won't," the irritation in his voice had been surfacing more often in our conversations and more so when I mentioned this concern.

I dumped the heap of washed clothes on the bed. "Come on, I am not a kid, I know what I am talking about? Can't we go back?"

Rishi looked at me coldly. "No way! Don't even think about that option. I am NOT going back. I have done enough to accommodate you but now my career is important."

I began folding the clothes clumsily.

"Accommodate? What are you talking about?"

Rishi crossed his legs on the rocking chair he was sitting on. "I didn't relocate anywhere in India because of you. I refused transfers, good job offers all because of you."

"Me? Don't blame me for your decisions. You could have moved without me. Why didn't you? I didn't stop you." I frowned.

"Yes, I was a fool to be emotional, but I won't be now. We stay here and you have to somehow like the place," he announced and walked out of the room leaving me in a daze. I had obviously not expected such an acidic response to my wretchedness. I felt the tears behind my eyes. I felt like a bird trapped in a cage. The decay had begun.

ଓ❖ଛ

Rishi got busy with work while I wrote like a maniac; but inside me, there was a distinct lack of enthusiasm and passion which refused to leave me despite immense efforts. I was scared for the first time in my life. I knew myself well enough to discern that if this continued for a long time, I would reach a point of no return. The fire had begun to wane within me and soon no amount of re-kindling would be able to sustain it.

I tried my best to get involved somewhere else. My movements were restricted because of the absence of a driver's license and to add to at all, the country did not appeal to me on a personal level. Initially I moved out alone, exploring and discovering new places to shop and sightsee but soon became wary. I would go to the nearest mall, listening to unfamiliar Arabic music on the radio in the cabs but soon I started taking my I-pod along just to feel more at home. It was always a delight to spot some Indian faces in the swarm of Abaya clad women and Dishdasha clad men while visiting malls and restaurants and while catching a movie. But what left me paralyzed was the lack of friendliness in the city. It was the perfect place with zipping, shinning cars and even shinier roads. There were hardly any bicycles or bikes to be seen; in fact they were as difficult to locate as the moon in the day sky. The roads were spick and span with no trace of litter or dust. And they shone fiercely under the blaze of the merciless sun. I had even heard that the roads were vacuum cleaned in the night.

The mosques were a common sight and the call of muezzin for prayers (azaan) five times a day, specially the one at four in the morning and precisely at four thirty in the evening were sounds I was getting familiar with.

It was a people, unfriendly city. Even getting out of the house and being able to walk on the street was an ordeal, in the absence of pavements and zebra crossings. To add to the woes of walking on the streets, especially in the not so posh localities, was the presence of labour class expats from Bangladesh, Pakistan or India who would leer and ogle at any female form. The lack of public places limited the outside experiences which was so much part of my life back in Delhi. I missed the Dilli Haat; GK market, Priya complex at Basant Lok; Garden of Five Senses at Saket which hosted many art shows and fashion shows; the art exhibit at the Habitat center and the theatre and interesting workshops at Epicenter, Gurgaon; the hours I spent at the bustling British Council library; the shopping for knick knacks at Janpath and the amazing variety of Indian food…I missed it all.

There was something absent in the city; the human dimension. Buildings and automobiles had overtaken the city and I struggled to feel at home. Everything seemed so mechanical and antiseptic.

Once I had taken Yash to a Malayali doctor when he had fallen ill. "He has viral fever and he should be fine soon," the doctor said writing down the prescription.

"Any precautions to be taken?" I asked.

The doctor looked at me blankly and said," Nothing, just give these medicines and he will be ok in a few days."

"I have an exam the day after," Yash drawled.

"Take rest tomorrow," the doctor got up to go. "And you can go to school the day after." He had been curt and crisp and to the point. How I had missed my family doctor, Dr Paul who had never examined Yash without cracking a few jokes and giving him a few sweets, even now when he was past the age of being offered sweets. Asking about family and work was an essential part of the examination.

The more I compared my experiences with the ones back in India, the more miserable I grew.

I missed the greenery, the colours of Delhi. The traffic, the chaos, the vendors selling their wares on the streets, the smell of street food, the magic of bumping into an old friend at a mall or street, the loud music during festivals, the heated arguments during a discussion, I missed my home town awfully.

I settled down in one of the chairs of the roadside coffee shop in Al Khuwair, famous for Shawarmas and looked up at the cloudless sky. The breeze was a bit cool today. My mind went back to the thundering black clouds in the Delhi sky just before the rain poured. It was the season I loved the most since childhood. My friends and I would drench ourselves when the rain came, playing on the terrace of our houses. I would drag a hesitant Sid, my younger brother, to be part of the fun. How I missed the rains here? The dryness and heat of Muscat had shriveled my spirits totally. The breathtaking beauty of the place seemed to extinguish my eagerness somehow. It had been more than nine months since I landed in Muscat and I still felt like a novice at work.

Rishi ordered two chicken Shawarmas and two glasses of fresh watermelon juice. I looked around. Speeding cars zipped past the eating joint and the huge red plastic road blocks cordoned off the major area of the road where repair work was going on. The majestic mountains overlooked the road. I glanced up to him. "I need to get out of here," I said, the sadness in my voice loud and ringing.

"Please Medha; don't make things difficult for me and yourself."

I reasoned. "I am not making things difficult for you... trust me, things are tough for me."

Rishi cracked his knuckles. "That's your problem. I mean I can only do as much, try to divert your mind to other things. Damn! Try to be happy with what you have and I am sure you will be."

I listened to his argument with a twinge in my heart. The waiter arrived with the Shawarmas. Suddenly I felt very hungry. It seemed that to listen to all that he was saying, I would need more strength, and food could help. I took a bite of the Shawarma.

"You have to realize that this is an excellent career opportunity for me. I can't just let it go."

I picked up the bottle of Ketchup, squirted its content on the plate, dipped the Shawarma in it and ate in silence. Rishi continued with his logic, his endless argument with no understanding of my sensibilities. It made me wonder how I had lived with him for sixteen years. I was more surprised with myself rather than him. He had always been like this; he had in fact not changed in the last so many years. How come I had endured all of this and yet tried to be happy? Driving back home in our Mazda-6, I realized that it was futile to argue or even make myself understood. I had done that innumerable times earlier but now I was tired. The issues were not skin deep. If they were not addressed in time the likelihood of their becoming wounds was very high. There was no point discussing all this with

Rishi when his receptivity was at this lowest.

The quietude continued, wrecking the insides of my emotional world very slowly. I started resenting the place and then one day I realized how disconnected I had become and it scared the hell out of me.

One day when I was writing, something seemed to freeze inside me. I looked outside from the window of my apartment. Far off, the dark mountains stood rock solid, like a perfect picture from the window I looked through. But there was no sensation inside me. I longed to step out onto the wet grass of my lawn in the Gurgaon house and walk barefoot, get soaked in the rain, smell the flowers and watch the butterflies flit from one flower to another. I kept gazing outside fixing my eyes on the mud coloured mountains. The dryness of the hot weather and mute white houses on the street, the deafening silence of the roads, of the apartments and the gnawing silence inside me overwhelmed me suddenly and I dropped my pen. I crumbled like the twin towers of 9\11 and wept.

I wept for the loneliness in my marriage; for being away from my family and closest friends; for being in unfamiliar terrain. I cried for a joyless heart; for trying too hard to settle down; pushing myself daily for it and then failing every time. It was as if the pain of being in a marriage I no longer felt connected to, superseded every other pain. I emptied my heart out and felt somewhat at peace after the storm had passed. I wiped the tears, washed my face and caught a glimpse of myself in the mirror. My eyes were swollen and I looked like a ransacked house and felt bare. I moved my gaze from the almost blank paper to the silent mountains rooted firmly under the piercing blue sky. They seemed to be ambivalent to my pangs and the air around me seemed frigid. They stood tall like stoical witnesses unmoved by my pain. I picked up the pen and felt the urge to write something but the words refused to flow. I needed to cut myself off from the real world and escape. It was the solitary way I could retain my sanity. But my mind refused to budge from the reality staring at me. I was however, adamant and wrote whatever came to my mind and when I had written a page, I felt lighter and much more connected with myself. Tears flowed out and the futility of everything around me became more conspicuous. I felt like a tired, depleted soul, drained of all my physical and mental energies.

I realized that it was the beginning of a shift, identical to the upheaval inside the womb of the earth which precedes an earthquake.

The fault lines had begun to crisscross my marriage too.

Rishi

I had been too busy at work to help Medha and Yash settle down. Although I did all that I could to make them feel at home in a foreign land, I felt they were both missing Delhi a lot. I could sense that Medha particularly, did not like the place; she had started keeping to herself of late. I could feel the resentment growing inside her but I couldn't do much except comfort her through my talks. I could only manage to take them out on the weekends but for the rest, they had to manage on their own, shopping for urgent groceries or stationery, and managing other household chores.

The weather was particularly sultry and warm that day. I adjusted the temperature of the air conditioner to twenty degrees and sat down for breakfast before reaching for the newspaper, *The Times of Oman*, and scanned the headlines for the day- **Teacher cries foul over sacking by Indian school; Rupee freefall fails to spur remittances.**

"I want to go to India for a few weeks. It has been close to ten months now," Medha's voice broke the silence as she served me breakfast.

My eyes were fixed on the newspaper. "Everything costs money dear and we have come here primarily to save for a better life in the future and our kid's education."

"I understand but this place is killing me. You know I can't write anymore."

I diced the omelette, doused it in ketchup and swallowed it. "That's because you have told yourself that you don't like this place..."

Medha fumed. "You know it's not that. I'm trying my best to adjust but..."

I was sick of hearing the same stale complaint of her disinterest in the place. What was I supposed to do?

"Don't worry, people take a lot of time to adjust to a new place, it's not abnormal. I think once you take a trip back home, you will feel better, I will get the tickets done." I realized my tone was business like. I kept my focus on the breakfast and did not probe Medha's mind further. I was in no mood to flare up the issue again. It was an important day at work. I had a few crucial meetings lined up and I did not want to start the day on a sour note. I knew Medha was unhappy but I couldn't fuss over her. She had to learn to deal with this on her own. She could not afford to be like a kid and make a big issue of this. I left as soon as I was through, leaving Medha to deal with herself.

Life continued at the same pace but I noticed that Medha's complaints were slowly fading. Maybe she was dealing with it well or she had totally given up on me? Did she feel I was not fully equipped to handle her problems? I wanted to find out but didn't know my way. Of late she would make sure to come to bed only after I was fast asleep. But one day I surprised her as she slipped into bed.

"Why are you so late, Wifey." I turned towards her. I could sense that something froze inside her.

"Yeah! I have been waiting to crash." Medha turned the other side.

I moved closer and murmured, "You need a massage, you seem tired?"

Medha shuddered. "No, I am fine, I just need to..." I slipped my arm around her waist and felt her stiffen. "Please Rishi." She tried to wriggle out of my embrace. I buried my face in her hair. "Come on now, it's been many days…"

Medha pushed aside my arm and got up from bed. "I can't," she said. Tears glazed her eyes. "I can't." And walked out of the room.

"But why?" I followed her.

She stared back at me. "I don't know, I don't feel like it."

I tried to reason. "Have I done something?"

Medha cried. "I don't know if it's something you have done or it's something that's happening to me, I can't make out but..."

"That's ridiculous. How can you not know what it is?"

"Coz' I am not God, coz' I can be confused as well and I can be lost too," she wailed.

I felt the sting of her words. What could possibly be wrong apart from the fact that she didn't feel settled in this place? She broke down and I felt like a jelly in a mould, shaky and silly, inadequate to handle her pain and so I left her alone. I returned to my bed and closed my eyes, hoping sleep would oblige soon. The soft murmur of the air conditioner filled the room but my heart was crestfallen. Strangely, I hoped there was no one else on her mind.

Medha

I had to bare my heart out to Sonal who was aware of what was going on in my marriage. She was the only close friend I had who understood me for what I was. She asked me to hang in there. She tried to reason with me that marriages go through ups and downs and it's fairly normal for couples to be disconnected. It was in all probability, a phase that we would both outgrow. She, of course, wanted me to give it another try but I wasn't ready for more pain. She listened to my woes, trying to fathom the depth of my misery. She had always thought that I had adjusted well in this marriage, in spite of the major divide in my temperament and Rishi's. My frustration was probably the tip of the iceberg. There was more to this marriage that was demolishing its sanctity. I continued with my rumblings and Sonal probably realized then that things were far worse than what seemed on the surface. I needed to get out of here and needed to get back to my writing.

My much anticipated visit to Delhi, finally happened. Yash and I were happy as a pair of birds on their flight back home. The mere thought of meeting my family and friends had elated my spirits and I had soared like a balloon in the sky.

Papa looked much better than last time. Yash rushed forward as he saw him and touched his feet. I hugged him tightly. He seemed more emotionally stable now than what he was after Ma's death. He joked with Yash and asked him about his school. When Yash had left his room, he turned to me. "All well between you and Rishi?"

My heart sank. "Of course Papa," I said "What made you think otherwise?"

I felt the warmth in his eyes. "I could sense something from the way Sid has been talking to you of late."

I looked away. "Nothing to worry, Papa. All's well."

A wave of relief seemed to wash his face. "Marriage always involves a lot of compromise and once the kids arrive, any adjustment is worth it," he said.

I nodded. "Yes Papa."

Argument was not on my mind at all. I had realized over the years that sometimes not getting into a confrontation with your parents was sensible. It saved you a lot of heartache.

I wanted to reach my Gurgaon house at the earliest. What had actually taken me by surprise or rather shock was that as soon I had landed, the urge to write had overwhelmed me completely. It sort of drove me to reach Gurgaon earlier than expected. Papa and Sid, both tried hard to make me stay longer but the urge to be home was too strong. As soon as I sat at the writing table, a rush of emotions besieged me totally.

I had already zeroed in on the story; a woman to woman relationship, a deep bond, a far cry from the complicated man-woman relationship. The present misery of my marriage was enough ammunition for me to fire up a book on a woman centric subject. I wished it would take me away from my present, even if for a while, and make me delve deeper into my own self. I had scanned many sites on the internet, gathering information and had even interviewed a few lesbians through email. I was all set to begin.

I went through my notes and the interviews, and began to write. I felt the tears as they blurred my vision but the writing journal filled up. Yash was surprised to see me get involved so intimately with writing.

"All ok, Mom?"

I dabbed the mist around my eyes with a tissue. "I am fine, just writing after a long time..."

Yash stepped closer. "Are you sure? I mean why you are so emotional?"

I lifted my gaze to him. "Guess I am emotional, can't help it." I tried to smile.

"Yup! I know but just chill ok. I don't like to see you weepy and all. Relax."

I gave a wooden laugh. "I'll be fine. Don't worry."

Yash nodded his head and smiled. "Get back to your book

now; you need to finish it fast."

"Yes, sir." And we both laughed.

I was surprised at Yash's maturity. He was so clued in to my mood and understood how crucial it was for me to write. But he had always been a sensitive kid and wasn't maturity hand in glove with being sensitive?

When I began to write after Yash had left, it was as if a frozen sea inside me had thawed and I just couldn't stop. It seemed I was trying to fill up a chasm that had grown wider and deeper in the last few months and if I didn't, I would lose a precious gift forever. I wrote and felt the stone lift from my heart. The pain which had accumulated in the recesses of my soul, soon found its way out. I became totally oblivious to my surroundings.

Finally, when I emerged from my study, I was physically and emotionally drained. But I also felt a cord of relief threading its way through my entire body for the first time in close to a year. It was joy all around, something I hadn't experienced in Muscat at all.

❧❖☙

I was finally at peace with myself and called Sonal over for dinner. She came in directly from her office, where she worked as an assistant to a fashion designer. She looked resplendent in her bright red top ,in a geometric pattern, matched with black trousers. Her face still held the same charm and attraction that had arrested many guys' imagination and left many a broken heart in school. Although she had put on a few extra kilos and appeared more bulky because of her not so tall frame, the delicate beauty of her features still managed to burnish through the plumpness and her face glowed.

We both hugged each other. It had been a long time since we had last met.

"Hey! Good to see you," Sonal gave a broad smile.

"I am so happy to see you sweetie."

Sonal surveyed my face. "You look so worn out and pale."

"Arre! baba I am fine, just a bit tired."

Sonal slumped on the sofa. "Yeah I can see how tired you are. Why are you such a kid?"

"Don't be my grand mom now." I grinned.

"As if you will let me be."

"I began work on my book...can you believe it?" I chirped like a teenager.

"Great," she said and looked closely at me.

"You have no idea what it feels like to write after a drought of ten months," my voice shook.

"I can imagine." She got up and put her arms around my shoulders and suddenly I was trembling.

She wrapped her arms around my shaking body. "You are such a brave soul. I admire you for it."

She let me weep. These last few months had been tough. Sobbing, I said, "I don't want to be brave, I am tired of it. I can't anymore."

"Relax now. You will be fine. You don't have to be miserable anymore. We will find a way out of this," she said tenderly.

My crying soon mellowed and Sonal helped me to the sofa and put my feet up. She went into the kitchen and arrived with two mugs of steaming coffee.

I took the mug from Sonal. "I feel so disconnected with Rishi; I wonder what's going to happen?"

Sonal bit her nails as she looked at me. "I am not surprised. He had always been like this, insensitive and callous."

I stared at the blue flower on the mug.

She continued, "I am sure you will sail through this. After all you have lived with him for so long, there must be something that has held the relationship till now. I feel you have spoilt him completely."

I shifted uneasily and stretched my legs. Sonal had never really liked him right from day one and now the dislike was more conspicuous than ever. I did not know how to receive it. Whether to appreciate Sonal's bluntness in the face of my crumbling marriage or ignore her strong dislike for him, since I was myself experiencing the same emotion? Whatever it meant, it discomforted me a great deal somehow.

"To tell you frankly, I don't feel the need. These ten months have emptied me somewhere. And Rishi's attitude has only added to the problem. I was taking all his idiosyncrasies with a pinch of salt all these years, but now they have become too conspicuous to ignore," I argued.

"But has he always been like this?" Sonal countered.

She was faintly appreciative of him at times but at other times she would rip him apart as if I was not present in the room or he had no purpose in my life whatsoever. Was this what best friends were supposed to do? I wondered why I felt ill at ease when Sonal ran down Rishi. I cradled the mug tightly in my hands. "I thought that by stretching myself a little, I would be able to buy peace in the house, but I guess..."

"You were wrong," Sonal remarked as a judge and surveyed her nails.I took a sip of the coffee. "I didn't even realize how much I had pushed myself tolerating his short temper, constant snapping, I resented these but in spite of my resentment, he never cared. I thought time and age would blunt their impact but..."

The evening was warm. The sweet smell of Rajnigandha's which Sonal had brought, wafted in the air. A vegetable vendor shouted out the names of vegetables in the street outside.

"I still can't believe how all this happened to you?" Sonal reflected.

"Even I can't."

***

I got up and walked towards the door which opened on the lawn outside. It was dark now and there was a faint breeze that stirred the plants gently. Sonal had left immediately after dinner. It had been a relief touching base with her. I realized that phone calls could never suffice for the warmth and joy of meeting a friend face to face, especially when it came to sharing pain.

I admired the green grass that glistened dimly under the translucent moon and stepped out of my slippers to feel it. The touch of the slightly damp grass under my feet was comforting. Yash joined me.

"I thought you were sleeping." I said softly.

"I was playing XBOX. So how was it, meeting Sonal aunty?"

I smiled. "Great as usual."

The nippy breeze brushed against our bodies. We both walked together, mapping the little lawn.

"How was your day?"

Yash's face beamed. "Good. Catching up with all my old friends. We even played and won the match today; I took three wickets."

"You like it here, don't you?"

Yash looked at the sky above. "I do wish dad was here too."

I let the silence take over for a few seconds.

"I know- I wish things had been…"

"No, you don't have to explain, I understand but I want both of you."

I felt the pain stab me from behind my eyes. "Sometimes wishing is not enough." I muttered under my breath.

The chirping of the crickets was brimming over the silence of the night and the ivory moon moved in and out of the clouds. It was a beautiful night but I felt a weird emptiness consuming my spirit somewhere inside me. Only God knew where all this was leading to.

Rishi

Medha and Yash had been gone for a week now to India and I was missing them already. The weather was hot and muggy and the sky was bare of any clouds when I stepped out of the office. I went home, and after a shower and an insipid dinner of buns and eggs that I managed to cook, I decided to call Medha. It was about 9.30 and 11 PM in India.

"Hi Wifey, you seem to have taken to Delhi; no worry about husband." I grumbled.

Medha yawned before speaking. "You are old enough to take care of yourself."

"Of course I am but wouldn't mind if someone told me that she was missing me."

Medha drawled. "Come on Rishi, grow up…"

I felt a thud inside my heart. Why didn't she long for me as I longed for her? Maybe the culprit was the number of years we had been married? Maybe that spoils all the fun and kills the spontaneity in a relationship and makes everything so predictable.

I found my voice somehow. "Leave it, you won't understand."

Medha leapt to her defense. "Yeah I won't- how can I?"

I ignored her remark. "How's Yash?"

"He is good, enjoying himself thoroughly."

"What about you?" I asked peering at her photograph hanging on the wall in front of me.

"I am good. Busy with my book, have been writing a lot."

There was a hazy excitement in her voice and I could sense that it was all thanks to the writing. I felt good for her. Thank God she was happy. The trip would do her good, recharge her spirits and equip her well to settle down back in Muscat. I couldn't have been happier.

"That's great. I am happy for you," I said.

"India is just the right place to write and experience. So much is happening here. The publishing industry has begun to bloom. I don't want to miss a single opportunity…I wish I could stay back forever."

I was sure my heart skipped a beat when I heard that.

"I understand but…." I said slowly.

"No you don't. Anyways, got to go now, catch you later," she announced coldly.

I kept the phone down and felt the moistness in my eyes. Suddenly my mind rewound to the small town of Kanpur, where I had grown up. Life had been so simple and carefree. I vividly remembered those narrow, paved lanes where I used to play as a child with my friends and then mummy would shout out for me from the terrace to come back home. That house had been huge with five terraces and it was the biggest one in the lane. She would invariably be removing the washed clothes from the clothesline. And when I would refuse, she would sometimes tempt me with the promise of making my favourite onion bhajiya or papri chaat and I would come running over, leaving my friends behind. Suddenly I missed the warmth and security of my mother's lap and her hug. I felt a tremble rise in the pit of my stomach and die down somewhere.

The coldness between Medha and me seemed to be growing and I felt it very strongly today. I wish she had not gone to India but then that wouldn't have changed things drastically. I wondered what had begun to go wrong and where? I wish someone would tell me the way to fix this coldness that was creeping rapidly into our marriage. I wanted her to come back as soon as possible.

I would work things out. I would pay her more attention, give her more time. I had been too busy at work, I realized. She had been struggling to settle down in a new country. I should have been more understanding and compassionate. How could I be so stupid so as to leave her alone to manage? I reprimanded myself daily for my inadequacies, promising to make it up to her once she arrived back.

The day she was to arrive, I was happy as a clam in high water. I was longing to be with her and share the wretchedness of her absence in the past four weeks. I knew she would have missed me too and couldn't wait for her to admit it.

Medha

I opened the windows to let in some fresh air. There was not a single star in the sky and the moon seemed a bit dull too. The night was still smoldering with the heat of the day and the traffic on the road below the balcony had died down considerably.

When Rishi climbed into the bed, I shifted uneasily. Why were things becoming so tough? I knew what he wanted but I did not want it the way he desired and that was weighing a lot on my mind. If I did not want it after a month of separation, was it a cause for worry? I was not sure whether it was the physical act that I was getting averse to or the thought of getting intimate with him, although both were a part of the same. But I needed to know what was what?

Rishi looked at me. "So how was India?"

I met his glance. "Great as usual..."

"How's the book coming along?" he moved towards me.

I crossed my legs. "Perfect."

His eyes were all over me. "I want to..."

All I wanted was not to talk, not to hear what he had to say. All I wanted was to see whether I could survive being physically close to him. I caught hold of his hand.

"I know you want to," I murmured. He took me in his arms and moved his hands all over me. I felt my body stiffen with every move. Why couldn't I flow, damn it?

There was a deep hunger tucked away somewhere as his mouth arrested my lips in its grasp. Suddenly I pushed him away.

"I can't, Rishi..." I withdrew abruptly.

Rishi was stunned. "What's wrong Medha?"

"I don't like it anymore. Don't ask me why?"

He snapped his mouth shut and moved away from me with a wounded look on his face. I felt the tears rise in my eyes. How could I hurt someone so much? But what could I do if I had begun to get disinterested in him? I tried to be intimate in bed with him a couple of times for the sheer fear of isolation ; of moving away from him if I didn't but it made me feel even more miserable than ever and so I decided against it. My focus was now to complete the book, so I would wake up earlier than usual and after sending Yash to school, would resume my writing. The maid would arrive after an hour and would get the lunch ready, set up Rishi's tiffin for office and serve him hot breakfast. Rishi would invariably get up to find me engrossed in my writing. He tried distracting me a few times but gave up after he found it ineffective.

***

I managed to finish the book over the coming months and felt euphoric. It was an act of courage especially under the present circumstances. I was proud of my accomplishment. Completing the book had added wings to my dreams and I couldn't wait to fly high. I knew that getting the book published was a tough and tedious project. I immersed myself in selling the book to various publishers and also began making notes for the second book.

Time flew and I forgot for the time being that I was in Muscat except when I was with Rishi. At that time my loneliness sneaked in from somewhere and stood right there in front of me, staring me in the face. The more I got engrossed in my writing, the more I grew distant from him. I could sense my need to be with him diminishing in the light of my self discovery as a writer. I was delving deeper into my own self(after all writing was all about confronting one's inner self) and I was discovering newer shades of myself.

"So what's up with the book?" Rishi asked me one day.

I looked up from the book I was reading. "Searching for a publisher."

"You never offered me to read the book or some initial chapters?"

I removed my reading glasses. "Do you have the time? You are always busy."

"You didn't feel I was sensible enough to understand, didn't you?" he bemoaned.

I replied woodenly. "I never said that; you are presuming as always."

Rishi motioned me to keep shut. "You feel, how this insensitive bastard can understand the complexity of my book, its depth and emotion…isn't it?"

"What kind of behavior is this?" I said.

He kept lashing out. "He doesn't have the intellect or the sense…."

"Rishi STOP IT."

I walked out of the room. His insensitivity and bitterness was becoming hard for me to deal with. How I wished I was in Delhi, away from this maddening marriage that was threatening to hijack my sanity.

***

The inertia of my life broke after about eight months. I opened my inbox to find a mail from a renowned publisher informing me of the acceptance of my manuscript for publication. I shrieked with joy and the first person I thought of was Sonal.

I knew this was the moment that would change everything for me. Sharing the news with Rishi did not give the temporary momentum to our relationship as anticipated and I realized that we were heading into a scary territory.

When I opened the door for Rishi that evening, I smiled. "My book has been accepted for publication."

I opened my arms and felt him walk into them in a robotic manner.

"I am so happy for you," he managed but I felt the coldness of the hug seep into me.

"Thanks," I said evenly before we withdrew from each other. All I could manage was a dry as a dust smile. If a delirious piece of news couldn't make me express my joy in front of him or glue our hearts momentarily, then what else would, I wondered.

Rishi

She moved inside the house as if I never lived there. There was a spring in her steps as she did her chores, oblivious to my presence. She would pass me by in the living room where I read the newspaper and would have her tea after I had had it. She started avoiding breakfast with me as well. I could sense the distance that was growing like a gulf between us. Her total lack of interest in me and her lack of need for sex were driving me insane. What had happened to bring us to this crossroads? I had always loved her and I hadn't changed much since I married her so why this transition from her end? Maybe she did not love me? I was not going to beg her for sex, never. She could go to hell and enjoy herself. If she did not love me then even I wasn't going to wag my tail behind her like a bloody dog. No, I would never!

The frenzy of having her first book published sustained her amazingly. Our marriage sucked but she went through it all or rather ignored it all in the face of the upcoming book. It was clearly the big moment of her life and she focused on it, diverting the rest of her energies to the next book. The next trip to India was planned to coincide with the book launch and this time I also travelled with her. I wanted to be with her in her special moment. I was proud of her no doubt, maybe a bit jealous too. She had managed to achieve what she had set out to, inspite of the tough time in our marriage and I admired her for this trait, although I would never admit this to her, lest the arrogance went to her head. I knew it was very tough for me to have such unwavering focus towards my work.

The book launch was scheduled at Habitat centre. Medha was as excited and nervous as a pregnant woman about to deliver.

"Rishi I am having goosebumps, see." Medha stretched out her arms for me to see.

"You will be fine." I said.

She could surprise me at times. Sometimes she became this cold, heartless woman and sometimes she could be like a child- open and vulnerable, trusting and easily wounded. I wondered why this side of hers was so rare to experience, or rather why she did not show this side of hers very often?

She gulped down two glasses of water. "I hope all goes well."

I tried to placate her fears. "All will go well. Is your speech ready?"

She took out the sheets of paper from a file and began reading. "Oh! yes but let me revise again. There's still time before I start getting ready."

I got up to my feet. "Let me get Yash." I said, and left the room.

Medha

I was extremely edgy as I went through the speech. I wondered whether my book would be appreciated or even considered worth reading. As I took out my cream and gold anarkali suit I had specially picked up from an exclusive boutique in Delhi, Sonal tried to appease my doubts. "You have done well to land this contract with a big publishing house as a first timer; you will rock."

I rolled my eyes. "You are being kind coz' you love me."

"Well then, you are really bad and shouldn't be having this book launch at all." Sonal bit her lips as always.

"Thanks for the encouragement," I said winking at her. I eyed a pair of gold earrings with a large drop of pearl looping at its base that I had chosen to wear. "I just hope it all goes well. Yash is more excited than I am."

I fumbled with the piece of paper in my hands. "Let me go through my speech again. My God! I am so nervous."

***

The Habitat Centre was splashed with huge posters announcing the release of my book. THE BURNT ROSE by Medha Nanda, it read and I felt a ripple in my heart. It was the day I had waited for with much earnestness. I walked in with Yash and Rishi and felt a surge of emotions inside me. It was too huge to be contained in a single word or expression. I squeezed Sonal's hand. Sonal felt the coldness of my hands and told me to relax.

Soon, I mingled with the crowds and met all my friends and some close relatives who had come to encourage me. The energy of the place was amazing and I felt as if I was in my skin for the first time. I basked in the glory of the moment. It all seemed unreal- some kind of daze that would take a long time to sink in. I was glad to be alive.

"Medha." I heard my name being called. There was a distinct familiarity in the voice and certain warmth that baffled me somehow. Who could it be? I turned around, curiosity flooding me.

And there standing before me was a man I had thought I would probably never see again in this life. Was it a dream? I was probably too excited today and had started hallucinating. There he stood, tall as ever, his body more filled out, his face broader, his cheeks fuller and the moustache more bushy. His cinnamon eyes had the same tint they had twenty years back and when his face exploded into a smile, it reached his eyes as always. It couldn't be true. I froze.

"Medha," he called out again. Gosh! I had forgotten how his voice sounded. His name tumbled out of my mouth. "Nikhil" and we both rushed towards each other. I realized that I had uttered his name after twenty long years. We hugged and I felt the warmth of his body engulf my senses.

"How come you are here and you look the same," I said.

I felt the tremors all over my body as he released me.

"Oh! I called up Sonal, found her number somehow, after I came to know through a common friend that your book was getting released."

"Sonal never told me."

Nikhil's smile was warm and luscious. "I requested her to let it be a surprise."

I disengaged my eyes from his face.

"Old habits die hard. You haven't changed, have you?" I said.

"You bet."

I found myself drawn to his eyes again. "I can't believe it's you Nik."

"It's my ghost," he said tilting his head towards me.

I laughed.

He continued. "I am mighty impressed, writer and all. I am not surprised though. You always wrote well."

His eyes were on me. "Remember the card and the letter you wrote to me?"

I smiled. I had even forgotten how his eyes softened when he looked at me.

"You still remember that one? I thought you must have forgotten about it long back." I tried to sound casual.

"I don't forget easily. I still have that card and letter...both."

The tremors hadn't stopped. Was this all true? No, it couldn't be. I wished Sonal was near to pinch me.

"Hey Nikhil, what a pleasant surprise!" Sonal's voice reached me through the trance.

Nikhil hugged her. "Hey! How are you?"

"You never told me?" I said.

"You were not supposed to know dear," Sonal said with a slow smile.

"Ma'am I would like a bite for our newspaper so can you please..." I heard someone address me and I turned around to see a young girl, with a notepad and a pen in her hand, looking towards me.

"Oh sure," I said and stepped aside gesturing to Nikhil and Sonal. "I'll be back." I left them to find a quiet corner to talk to the journalist.

The formal launch followed soon thereafter. It was a lucid affair. The celebrity guest, Eima Azmi, a well-known actress of the small screen, tore open the wrapping to release the book amidst loud cheers and claps. Her brief introduction to the book was followed by my well-rehearsed speech.

"Thanks to all of you for being here this evening," I began. "Many friends have asked me why did I write a novel about two women in a relationship? What inspired me? The answer is that stories pick up the writer and not the other way around…"

Nikhil sat in the last row and I felt a pang of excitement threading its way through me.

"This story trailed me for a long time, occupying my mental space, making me restless before I was compelled to write it down. I remember a quote which sort of sums up what the book is about- Happiness grows at our own firesides and is not to be picked in strangers' gardens. THE BURNT ROSE is a story of two women who are not afraid to look inside themselves and answer the call of their souls. So the book is a celebration of the spirit of womanhood... the power, the resilience, the energy of being a woman; of exploring the inner self and revelling in that discovery…" Sonal and her husband Rohil sat in the front row while Rishi was busy shooting the video and Yash was clicking the photos.

"…the book reiterates that love empowers you, uplifts you, liberates you and helps you to be yourself. And when love moves beyond the metaphysical- it doesn't matter whether the person you love is a man or a woman…"

I caught my breath. "This book has been a journey of self discovery for me, as a woman and as a writer. I'm glad I took this journey. It was worth all the pain. I believe life shrinks and expands, in proportion to one's courage and I'm glad I took the courage to write this book."

I fleetingly glanced towards the paper I was holding. "In this room are gathered some of the finest souls I know. You have influenced my life in many ways. I cannot thank you all enough. I specially want to thank my publishers, Vani, my editor and a very big thanks to my family and friends for making this journey easy. Thanks for joining me tonight. I hope the book makes you proud. I want to end with a quote from Richard Bach, 'Whatever enchants, also guides and protects. Passionately obsessed by anything we love, an avalanche of magic flattens the way ahead, levels rules, reasons, dissents, bears with it over chasms, fears, doubts. Without the power of that love, we're boats becalmed on seas of boredom'. Thanks."

The room resounded with claps and cheers. And it finally sunk into me at that moment that my book was now out. After a brief question and answer session, I was soon crowded for signing copies. It was only when Nikhil asked me to sign his copy that I fumbled with words. What to write…there was so much I could but all I could manage was his name and with all my love, Medha. He must be a married man now, I presumed, but did that matter to me? It probably didn't.

I just looked into the hazel pools of his eyes as I handed him back the copy of the book and found myself struggling with what I myself didn't know. Was I opening up myself deliberately to him or did it happen without my even realizing it? Sonal called out just then. I was thankful for the intervention. There were many guests to attend to but his presence in the room made everything so special. It was like a fragrance that had spread all over the place. I felt myself drowning in it. I introduced Nikhil to Yash with an unusual pride and felt the surprise in his eyes.

"He is so grown up. I never knew you had…"

"I married young, remember-" I said.

Yash smiled and rushed to be with his friends whom he had called for the occasion. When I introduced Rishi to Nikhil, there was more surprise in Rishi's eyes this time.

Rishi extended his hand for a handshake. "Oh! So you are 'The Nikhil'. Medha has told me about you."

Nikhil shook hands with him and smiled. "All good things I hope."

"All good."

Nikhil's face burst into a delicious smile. "I am so glad I could make it."

Rishi smiled back.

"Hey! Let's all go out for coffee after this; join us Rishi," Nikhil suggested.

Rishi must have caught a glimpse of disappointment in my eyes. There was something in him that just flattened out.

"Sure, we need to catch up," I said and looked at Rishi. "Yeah! You come along too."

Rishi nodded. "What about Yash?"

"Puru's dad can drop him," I said flatly.

My face drooped. Maybe I was expecting him to decline the offer. Maybe I wanted to share the moment alone with Nikhil. Rishi felt the uneasiness as he shifted the weight of his body from one foot to another and the way his narrow mouth curved at the corners. I felt a slight knotting in my heart. My helplessness was justified. Rishi could not be there when Nikhil was with me. I wanted to be alone with him. There would be too much that Rishi could notice and I was not ready to handle any more chaos in my life right now.

❖

I felt Nikhil's eyes on as we settled on the sofa at Barista in Connaught place. Although the weather was not warm, I felt the slight dampness of sweat at the back of my neck. Rishi sat next to me while Nikhil and Sonal sat opposite us. The place was cozy and snug. Attractive lights in overturned cup shapes hung over each table forming interesting patterns on the square tables. The rich aroma of coffee filled my lungs. Outside, the bustle of the people returning home from work was fairly audible.

"I have become a coffee addict, you know," Nikhil said.

"College mein to chai-chai karte the," Sonal quipped with a naughty streak in her voice.

Nikhil rolled his eyes. "Preferences change with times."

"Oh yes they do!" Sonal agreed.

Rishi smiled as he flipped through the menu.

"So what's the book about? I read the jacket cover, seems quite bold." Nikhil said looking towards me.

"It's a story about two women in a relationship, who discover each other through their bond."

Nikhil scanned me with his soft eyes. "You have always been brave, I am not surprised… you must have done a lot of research for the book?"

Rishi got up on his feet. "I'll order the coffee. Any preferences?"

"Cappuccino," Nikhil and I blurted out together and burst out laughing.

"I'll come along with you," Sonal said, biting her lips.

I turned my attention to Nikhil, happy at last to have him alone. "What were you saying about the book... yes, it was a challenge to write it."

Nikhil kept his eyes on me. I continued. "I know someone who was in a similar relationship. Also did a lot of research, spoke to psychologists. I wanted to explore the subject as an outsider."

Nikhil grinned. "Lesbianism, very interesting, daring as always."

I met his gaze and felt his eyes pierce right through me. Nikhil moved his hands through the thick crop of his hair. "Honest, fearless- you have been unlike any other girl I have met Medha."

I lowered my eyes. "Come on now, don't." I always went beetroot red when he praised me. Somehow he was the only guy who had seen this side of me, all coy, shy and girlie.

"I agree with you hundred percent Nikhil," Rishi gave me a start as he said this, sitting down on the sofa. I felt my hands go cold and I saw the colour of Nikhil's cheeks turn a shade pale.

Nikhil fumbled. "Ya, ya of course. Ask Sonal?"

Sonal saved the awkwardness of the moment. "And Medha could talk endlessly without a break, my God! we sometimes wondered what she had for breakfast."

We all laughed.

I felt confused. Why did Nikhil ask Rishi to come along, damn it? I couldn't even talk to Nikhil the way I wanted to. Rishi's presence had spoiled it all. He was already aware of what I felt for Nikhil way back in college. I had confessed it all on our honeymoon. Rishi was sharp enough, I knew, to catch any fleeting glance or word that rose between me and Nikhil. But did I really care?

"So are you married?" Rishi asked Nikhil.

"It's been ten years now. I have one daughter."

The coffee arrived and the aroma floated in the air around us. Rishi passed the wide mouthed cup to me.

"Who's the lucky one? I mean her name," Rishi said.

"Priyanka."

My gaze was fixed on Nikhil as he uttered her name. The name hung in the air like a drop of mercury- thick and unshakeable. It all seemed so weird. The boy I had fallen for in college was now all settled–happily married with a daughter.

"Nice name. What does she do?" Sonal's voice filled up the space and I came back to my senses.

"She's a housewife," Nikhil said.

Nikhil took a sip of the coffee. "What do you do Rishi?"

"I head Acer's operations in Muscat…and you?"

"I run an advertising agency."

I shifted in my place and tried to reach for the sachet of sugar kept at a distance. Nikhil reached for it instead. "Let me," he said, and tore open the sachet to drain its contents in my cup. His gentleness was trapping me surely. I suddenly felt great to be with Nikhil. To sit opposite him after all these years, in a coffee shop, seemed so dreamlike. Rishi's presence was a hurdle but I chose to ignore it.

"Big clients? How's business these days?" Rishi enquired.

I watched Nikhil speak. I watched the words tumble out of the soft corners of his mouth. I watched how his smile collected at the rim of his eyes like a pool. How I wished Rishi was not there. If only I could speak to Nikhil alone without being chaperoned by Rishi's eyes…it would be heaven.

Nikhil turned to Sonal. "How's Rohil? I met him about six months back at the trade fair that's how I had your number."

"Oh yes, he told me. He is fine," Sonal said.

"I was quite surprised when I heard you and Rohil had got married," Nikhil admitted.

"Even I was," Sonal said and winked at him.

My eyes met Nikhil's. "Love paralyses us all," I said.

I felt my heart thumping louder than the drums roll at the Republic day parade. I could feel the goose bumps all over my body. This was too silly.

"I am still paralyzed, ask me?" Sonal got up from the table, biting her nails. "I am hungry…sandwich anyone?"

"Not for me," I said.

Nikhil stretched his long lcgs. "Not for me either."

"Well let me help you." Rishi was on his feet again.

"Your husband's a sweet man," Nikhil said turning towards me after Rishi had left. The word *husband* sounded so strange from his mouth. It seemed as if we both did not know each other at all- that we were strangers who had met long ago on a train journey and years later had now bumped into each other all of a sudden.

"Where do you stay?" I asked.

"Gurgaon" My eyes opened wide. "I don't believe this. We too have a house there. Whenever we are in Delhi, we stay there."

"Really! We are at Boulevard II, DLF III and my office is in Mega towers."

"We are at Nirvana. Your office is hardly ten minutes drive from my house."

The world seemed to be getting smaller for me and I took a long sip of the coffee.

Nikhil looked at me with fondness again. "When did you get married? I wasn't even invited?" His tone had a hint of resentment.

"Do you think I would have been able to get married with you around?"

His eyes rested on me again. "Come on." I found him struggling for the right words.

Sonal and Rishi arrived after ordering the sandwiches. There was so much to talk. There was no sense of time left. I went back in time. I had not expected to meet Nikhil after all these years and specially on the day of my book launch. There sure was a divine plan at work. After about an hour, Sonal announced that she was leaving. It was fairly dark by now. The streetlights shone brightly and merged with the headlights of vehicles mapping the road outside. Nikhil ordered another round of Cappuccinos and Rishi's mobile buzzed.

As he walked out of the coffee shop, Nikhil lifted his gaze towards me. "You got married quite early?"

My voice dipped in scale. "Yup! There was no reason to refuse Rishi so I said a yes."

The coffee arrived and I averted my eyes from Nikhil. Nikhil stirred the sugar in my coffee again and I felt something stir inside me as my eyes followed his hands, unabashedly. The conversation flowed like a soft, mellow river finding its way over hills and plains. It was a smoothness I had not experienced in a long time. I felt like a teenager experiencing the first flushes of love. I was buoyant and light as a kite, finding its place in the sky.

"Medha, Medha…" Nikhil was calling out to me.

"Yeah," I said, recovering. I had been lost in my thoughts totally.

Nikhil sat down. "Where are you? I finished a call and came back and you are still lost."

"Oh! I was just remembering."

"College?"

Nikhil stirred his cappuccino gently and spooned the creamy froth and swallowed it. I observed him brazenly. His sensuous, soft mouth curved a little as the spoon went inside his mouth.

"How do you know?" I asked.

"I know you." Nikhil smiled at me and I wondered when the spell would end?

"No you really don't," I admitted.

Nikhil smiled again. "You will be surprised but I do."

I heaved a long sigh and looked around but Rishi was still outside the cafe, on his call. The conversation drifted and it was time to leave when Rishi entered and announced that we had to leave. Nikhil insisted on paying the bill even though Rishi was adamant.

"Let him pay Rishi," I intervened and Rishi obliged.

Nikhil looked at me with a disarming smile. "Next time, you pay."

I felt the wallop in my heart. So he wanted to meet me again? We walked down to the parking area where both the cars were parked. My eyes wouldn't leave him just yet. The softness in his eyes had melted my heart yet again. We hugged each other and I knew Rishi's eyes were on me all the time.

As Rishi pulled out the Silver Grey Santro from the parking, Nikhil waved to us from his peacock blue Toyota. I felt a lightness that could lift me up in the sky. My life in the past more than a year had been empty as a rainless cloud hanging precariously in the sky. It seemed different now. I felt good and alive and hummed a song as I switched on the radio smiling. I just wanted to be in the moment, without fear or doubt of where it would lead. Rishi's presence didn't seem to matter to me at all.

I had not felt so much joy in a long, long time.

Rishi

Throughout the drive back home, Medha sang and hummed to herself. She even caught herself smiling in the rear view mirror. There seemed to be music all over the place, in the air, in the sky above her. All her senses were drenched in melody. The evening was about to set and the sky was a cocktail of all the hues of red, pink, orange and gold.

I broke into her thoughts "Nice guy."

"Yeah!"

I tried to read her face. "No wonder you liked him."

"I still do," she murmured.

I smiled, trying to downplay my reaction. "I can see that."

Medha kept quiet and looked out of the window. Silence was the best weapon when there was no answer to anything. She reached home and the enchantment hung in the air, refusing to leave. She was quick to put together a meal for everyone. But when she sat down to eat, she realized she had no appetite.

"I am not hungry anymore," she said.

"Too much coffee I guess," I said, cheekily.

She gave me a look. "There's no harm in having more of what you absolutely love."

I was taken aback by her answer. "Sure, no harm."

"The launch was great mom," Yash said.

"Yes it has been the most awaited day of my life," Medha spoke with a gay abandon. The smile reached her eyes. I was becoming slowly aware of the effects this evening was having on her. Suddenly she seemed more distant from me than ever. I also knew she was happy and it relieved me somehow. When she lay down beside me in bed, she was still humming. It seemed as if she was in her own world where I was not privy but I wanted so desperately to be a part of it. I wanted to know what was happening inside her. The smell of carnations, lilies, rajnigandha rose from the bouquets that were gifted to Medha at the launch. I was dizzied by their heady scent but wanted to inhale Medha's fragrance inside me. I moved towards her encouraged by her happy state of mind.

"The launch was great. You were superb," I said.

She shifted a little in her bed. "Yes I am glad it all went well. I hope the party tomorrow also rocks."

"I am sure it will," I said trailing the sides of her arm with my fingers. She squirmed uncomfortably.

"Rishi I am very tired…please." She turned her back.

"But it's a special day, we must celebrate."

"Please I want to sleep," Medha's voice was dry.

"Can't you forget everything for a day, let's just…"

Medha looked at me. "It's not about forgetting. It's about wanting and desiring and that I don't."

I felt the fall of her words like stones on glass. I turned my back on her and I heard a sigh of relief escape her lips. A prick of pain pierced my eyes from behind and suddenly I felt the tears. I never seem to give up on her in spite of her coldness. Why? Why was I ready to make another effort to have her, to make her come around? Maybe I loved her too much but of what use was this love if she did not understand it? I got out of the bed and headed straight for the bathroom.

Inside, I let the tears flow out and cried silently. I seem to be losing her and I did not feel good about Nikhil entering our lives at this point. I had seen the inevitable in his eyes and I had seen the same light shine in Medha's eyes too. They both seem to be connected as if by some unseen force. But I didn't want to think about all this now. I splashed cold water on my face and dried it to remove any traces of my vulnerability. I was never going to show her how much I wanted her in my life. *Never.*

Nikhil

I looked at myself in the mirror and sprayed a whiff of Bvlgari on my wrist's, behind my ears and on my armpits. My blue check shirt matched well with the dark denims. I was eager to be a part of the party thrown by Medha–as a child all excited for a picnic. I hummed as I dressed. I had not felt such exhilaration in a long time. Medha had also invited all our other batch mates too for this celebration and I was looking forward to meeting all of them after many years. I felt numb and in a daze. I still couldn't believe that I had met her, had spent more than two hours talking to her, soaking in her presence and savouring the special place that belonged to both of us and which had remained intact after twenty years-almost in a pious way. I picked up her book from the nightstand and felt it in my hands. Such thoughts were sure to do me more harm than good. We were both married now and it was best to let things be where we had left them years back. Priyanka entered the room and cast a suspicious glance at me.

"Are you going somewhere?" she enquired.

I kept the book back. "Yes, I am off to a party."

"I thought we were going for a late night movie show!" she said.

"Some other time. Medha has invited me over for her book launch party."

"Medha?"

"Oops! I forgot to tell you yesterday. I had gone for her book launch. We were together in college. Now she's a writer and today she has thrown a party; my old batch mates are also coming," I said.

She surveyed me like a detective. "Great! The least I expect is to be informed where you go and with whom. I was under the impression that we are going for a movie..."

"I am sorry, I forgot."

She gave me a dirty look flopped on the bed. "That's a good excuse, I forgot."

I whipped around.

"Excuse for what? I forgot, simple. Don't make mountains of molehills please," I snapped.

I was already getting late and here she was bent upon spoiling my mood. But this was nothing new. She was a pro at the game of screwing my happiness and I didn't really care. She looked at me with helpless rage. "Screw you," she said fiercely and walked out of the room.

The moon hung like a lantern in the pitch black sky, spreading its sheen all over. I pulled down the window of the car and felt the breeze on my skin. Medha's face loomed large over my mind. There was complete mayhem in my heart right now. Meeting Medha had taken me back in time and I was surprised at myself, that even after twenty years, she could still make me sit up and notice her without her making any efforts. I still remembered the Valentine's Day card she had given me shyly and I had till date, saved it as a proud memory.

It dawned on me why all this had happened. Maybe we were destined to meet again and pursue a relationship that had not even begun in the true sense of the word? Suddenly the car behind me honked as the light had turned green and I found my foot on the accelerator. My mind was still entangled in Medha's thoughts. The letter that she had given me on the last day of college, before the farewell party began, was still fresh in my mind. How she had apologized for her feelings, the red rose she had given me... how it must have broken her heart to feel sorry for loving me? What an ass I had been? It hadn't really hit me then as strongly as it hit me now. Yes, I had fancied the honour of being pursued, wooed and loved the attention and affection I had received from Medha but the depth and genuineness of her true feelings had eluded me somehow. I had not realized it then, at twenty two. Maybe I had not been mature enough to handle such emotions. If I had responded to her feelings back then, things would have been different. But then it was not meant to happen and it didn't.

Medha looked arresting in her flowing red top matched with a dark blue pair of denims, and high heels. Her legs seemed longer somehow and her body was more filled out and curvy than what it was twenty years back. I rested my eyes on her expressive, kohl lined eyes. There was a light that shone in them. She flipped back her hair as she spoke to a friend and then saw me and moved towards me. I felt instantly drawn. What the heck was wrong with me? She greeted me with an endearing hug.

"So how are you?" she asked.

I fixed my gaze on her face. "All well... a big day for you."

"Just an excuse to get drunk and dance," she said, winking at me. She gave me a broad smile. "I've waited long for this day. It's like I feel I have finally delivered the baby, now I can relax."

"You can't dance if you delivered yesterday, its not recommended," I teased her.

She fixed me with a soft look. "Lots of things are not recommended... still they happen, don't they?"

I felt the adrenalin rising somewhere inside me.

"Medha," Rishi called out from behind. "Oh! Hi Nikhil, good to see you," he shook hands with me and turned towards his wife. "Wifey, I need to talk to you. Will you excuse us Nikhil?"

"Of course, she is all yours," I said.

Something sparked in Medha's eyes for a millisecond and then died down. I reached for a drink and felt calm as the liquid flowed down. The party was soon in full swing. The music played and soon everyone was on the dance floor. It was fun meeting up with old batch mates. Some had grown fat and were unrecognizable; some bald and some still looked the same. I watched Medha dance, her body swaying rhythmically and she had a gay abandon about her which I had seen at that farewell party but today she was more chilled out.

Medha, Sonal, Rohil, Rishi, Sandeep, Rahul, all tapped their feet to the music and I joined them. It must have been ages since I last danced.

Soon it was Medha and I dancing together to 'yeh mera dil pyaar ka deewana- aata hai mujhko pyaar mein jal jaana- mushkil hai pyare tera bach ke jaana…'(my heart is mad for love. I know how to set myself on fire in love…its tough for you dear to escape now). We danced unmindful to the world around us. It was only when Rishi joined us on the dance floor again that I realized I had been dancing very close to Medha. I withdrew on the pretext of filling up my drink. The atmosphere of the party was all charged by now. I was sitting with Rahul and Sandeep when Rishi came and requested me to open the chilled bottle of champagne. I got hold of the bottle. Rishi called out to everyone on the dance floor. "Guys and gals, your attention please. This is a toast to the first book written by my lovely wife, Medha. I am very proud of her. Many more books to come. Yippee."

Medha stood next to me as I shook the champagne bottle vigorously and uncorked it amidst cheers. As the champagne popped out of the bottle, I directed it towards Medha.

Medha was stunned. "Nikhil," she yelled as most of her blouse got soaked in the frothy liquid.

I burst out laughing. "Come on, it's a great day."

Rishi moved swiftly filming the whole show.

"Good show Nikhil," his voice was fairly boisterous.

I had never been so expressive about my fondness for Medha so unabashedly. And I didn't know what came over me but I saw the look in her eyes. I knew she loved every bit of it. I had surprised myself more than Medha.

I had begun treading into a forbidden territory and I knew it.

Rishi

I tried wooing her in bed after we came back from the launch party but Medha was cold. I had sensed the vibes between her and Nikhil and it had upset me but I preferred to keep silent. I was quiet the next morning. The coldness between us could be felt by both but we chose not to discuss it as Yash was around.

"I want to stay here for a few more days," Medha said as she buttered the bread.

I looked up from the newspaper I was reading. "But why?"

Medha reached for the kettle on the kitchen counter and poured the hot water in the mug. "I need to promote the book signings and probably a radio show."

I folded the newspaper clumsily. "What about Yash?"

"He can travel as scheduled next week. I'll follow a week later."

I walked to the counter and put my coffee mug in the sink with a bang. "But how will I manage without you?"

The sunrays filtered into the room, blazing the granite counter like a black jewel. The morning was cool and fresh. The faint rumble of kids leaving for school, floated in the street outside. I heard the thud of the newspaper as it fell on the grass outside, delivered by the vendor rolled in an elastic band.

"I am sure you can manage," the finality of Medha's tone was very forceful. I was not prepared for this. I threw my hands down.

"I can manage of course, but..."

Medha chose to ignore it. I found it sensible to give in without any further argument. Medha could not be stopped now. Her book had opened new doors for her. Her journey had begun.

So it was decided that Medha would stay an extra week or ten days depending on the situation and Yash would fly all alone, the coming week. My grumpiness invaded the air. This was most unexpected. I had been waiting for her to return home and the change of plan at the last moment was most unwelcome. I could not bring myself to accept it. I withdrew. I was mostly on phone till the moment it was time for me to leave for the airport.

The parting was crisp and formal. I was expecting her to express what was clearly not there and the disappointment on my face must have revealed it all.

"Take care beta. I'll miss you." I put my arm around Yash's shoulder.

"I'll miss you too. Don't forget the finals on Sunday. Arsenal versus Chelsea."

Medha fidgeted with her sunglasses and looked distracted.

"Hurry up Yash. We will catch traffic on the way," she said stiffly.

I gave a quick hug to Yash and moved towards her.

"Take care and all the best for your book," I said.

She looked at me coldly. "Thanks," she said, then shifted her eyes to Yash. "Come on Yash- move your butt now," she ordered.

I pushed the trolley inside the airport and soon my face merged in the sea of faces. I guess she must have been relieved to see me out of sight.

Medha

The phone rang. I defocused my attention from the laptop and picked up the mobile. Nikhil's voice soothed me instantly. "Hi! How are you? Yash has gone back?"

"Yes I left him at the airport about an hour ago."

"All ok?"

"The house is so quiet without him! I am feeling a bit lost…"

He cut me short. "I can understand but you are a brave girl."

I felt a pang cut through me. I wish he had listened to me and allowed me to vent my feelings. I would have felt better. Rishi would never have minimized my emotions this way.

"When are we meeting? We can meet at eight today." he said.

"Seems fine. Can you pick me up?" I said, slightly deflated.

"No problem. I'll pick you up by eight."

I went back to my writing. The house was hushed except for the whizzing of the fan and it allowed me to concentrate better on my work without any distractions. It felt good to be all alone, with only my thoughts for company.

Suddenly I found myself short on concentration for my writing. I shut down the laptop and figured that reading a book was better at this time. I was distracted. The thought of meeting Nikhil in the evening flooded me and I pushed myself back to the pages of the book I was reading.

I looked at myself in the mirror as I hummed a song. I had chosen to wear my black jeans with a fuchsia crepe blouse with huge white flowers printed on it and matched these with black and silver slippers that I had picked up a few days back from GK market.

The weather was cool and there was a hint of rain in the air. It was pitch dark by now and the street outside my house had gone quiet. Children and their mothers had returned home from the park. I did my eyes–kajal, mascara and left my hair untied. When the doorbell rang, my heart pounded. I opened the door to see him standing there. He looked dapper in his pista green shirt worn with blue jeans. His salt and pepper hair suited him perfectly.

The drive from my house to the restaurant was short and as we stepped inside, the stylish ambience, the smell of food made me hungry suddenly. As we settled, I found my eyes trailing Nikhil as usual. I turned to leaf through the menu.

There was joy in my heart. An ordinary thing like ordering the food seemed so special today... all because I was with him.

Our conversation picked up from where we seemed to have left it last time. There was just too much to share and talk. There were things we didn't know about each other... our families, siblings, about our work, our spouses and soon we were engrossed in our own world.

The waiter arrived with the Pizza and Spinach Lasagna and the aroma of food was irresistible. Nikhil sliced the pizza and placed a triangle on my plate. I watched him indulgently. I didn't want to stop him from spoiling me, not even as a formality. It felt good to be taken care of. He listened and then he spoke and I listened. There were clouds outside and I saw a flash of lightning through the window.

"I wish we had tried to know each other more back in college," I said with a lament.

"I wish we had but I guess..." he said and I caught a feeble longing in his voice.

His eyes rested on me. "I never realized that you were so serious about me?"

I opened my mouth and then shut it.

"I was so damn stupid, an ass," he added.

I gazed at him. "But it had to be about us... not about me alone so I couldn't do much, apart from telling and doing what I did."

"True. Guess sometimes things just escape us," he reflected.

I merely smiled. "That was past. It's gone. What matters is now, the present."

He took a sip of water. "To live in the now is what life is all about, isn't it?"

I returned my attention to the food. Maybe life was all about the present but then didn't the past carry the present in its womb? Wasn't my getting drawn to him, a result of what I had felt in the past? Wasn't my past shaping my present, right here and right now?

My eyes lingered on him; he averted his gaze from time to time.

We ordered coffee after dinner. It began to drizzle. The smell of coffee, when it arrived was strong and fused with the smell of the wet grass rising from outside the window. Nikhil emptied the sachet of brown sugar in my coffee and stirred it. I watched him treat me like a queen. It was the way he looked at me with the slight tilt of his head, that overwhelmed me. His total attention towards me when I spoke and when he spoke made me like him even more. There was so much enchantment in everything he did. I felt the sexual attraction between us. We had never gone out like this in college. I was contented knowing that he had been thinking about me often all these years; that he had wanted to be at my wedding; that his smile reached up to his eyes now; that his eyes softened and turned a shade lighter when he looked at me; that his hug made me feel so secure and that there was a side of him which probably Priyanka hadn't discovered. I felt the strong pull that was slowly disarming me and I checked myself.

The conversation carried on and we realized it was closing time for the restaurant. He opened the door of the car for me and I slid in. He switched on the radio. I looked out of the window and felt the cool breeze on my face.

"Where is this going to lead to Medha?" he said after a while.

I stared at the moving road outside. "I don't know Nik nor do I want to." I had called him Nik after years. I turned my face and looked at him. I couldn't bear to meet the heat of his gaze and lowered my eyes. He pulled the car over and killed the engine. He tucked a strand of hair behind my ear. "Why don't you want to know?" he murmured.

The touch of his fingers sent a tremor through me. I shuddered.

"My marriage is on the rocks Nik... things are not the same anymore." I could feel my lips trembling. "I... I have begun to feel very lonely in my marriage." The tears welled up in my eyes and they fell swiftly. Nikhil wiped them with his hands and held my hand.

"Don't please," he said softly. "Give it time... marriages go through their worst phases."

I looked at him and saw the same pain in his hazel eyes.

"Yes I know but I feel I'm losing myself steadily, and that scares me." I said.

He hugged me and held me close as I broke down. My defenses simply crumbled in his arms.

He smelled of after-shave and coffee and I inhaled him, filling up the spaces inside me with his fragrance.

Rishi

I came home in the evening to find Yash studying, wearing his cotton jacket. It was pretty cold inside his room. No one could ever imagine that the weather outside was a total contrast, sultry and very hot. There was a deafening silence in the house which unnerved me. His head was bent over the study table and he was not even aware of the unlocking of the main door when I entered.

"Hey son what's up?" I said.

Yash looked up. "It's you?"

I smiled and noticed his sleepy face. "Tired?"

"Just got up from sleep."

I loosened my tie. "Had your lunch on time?"

Yash flipped through the pages of his book. "Of course dad. It was pathetic though."

"Why? I had it too, it was fine."

"Your standards have gone down surely," he said. "I don't like dosa, idli sambar anyways and this cook…"

"Come on. Once in a while you can have," I defended our cook. Jyoti had been with us ever since we had shifted to Muscat and she was a kind soul who was looking after the house well in Medha's absence. It was a blessing to have her around. It took away a lot of my headache.

I walked back to my room and unlaced my shoes. It was close to ten pm. The tiredness was creeping into my body and I craved for a hot cup of tea. Medha would have obliged, if she was around. I had no appetite left for dinner. I pushed myself to get up and warmed dinner for Yash and served him in his room before I got into the kitchen to make myself a hot cuppa. Medha's absence loomed large. The house was not the same without her and as the steam rose from the boiling water, I felt a pang. There was something that told me that things were not the same anymore. Ever since she had met Nikhil, Medha seemed a different person to me. From the way she had looked at Nikhil in that coffee shop, the way they both had spoken and shared things, the way Nikhil's eyes had been drawn towards her and how they had both parted, I knew I was an intruder somehow.

I poured the tea through the strainer and hoped that what was crossing my mind at the moment would turn out to be untrue. I dialled her number. I knew it was late and she might have slept by now but I couldn't stop myself.

"Hi," her voice rangout.

I took a sip of my tea. "How are you?"

"I am good. How's Yash?" She sounded chirpy.

"He is fine, studying right now. When is the radio show?"

"Day after at 5 pm; listen I have to go; talk to you later," she said hurriedly and before I could respond, the phone went dead.

I stared at the tea, its faint smell floating in the air, as if looking for an answer to my dilemma. The hush of the night spread around me like a web. I felt trapped.

Medha

I entered the house after disconnecting Rishi's phone. I was in no emotional condition to converse with him at this hour. There was too much happening.

I soaked in the peace and quiet. I felt completely in sync with my home. Oh How I loved it! I stepped into the shower with a thousand thoughts bubbling inside me. As the tepid water caressed my tired limbs, I felt relaxed. For the past six months, I had not felt like this. Getting intimate with Rishi had been an effort but today I had experienced a sexual thrill with Nikhil that I thought I had lost. The water trailed over my entire body, wetting me, soaking me and all I could think of was Nikhil. I had never experienced such exhilaration of the mind and body together. I didn't know how to handle it. Strangely there was an acute restlessness too that I had not experienced earlier. My heart seemed to sink deeper in myself and I felt as if someone had been able to touch me deep inside. Perhaps the closest I had felt to this was back in college, probably the moment when Nikhil had reached out his hand to me in front of the whole class and asked me to dance with him. This feeling was stronger and crazier. Could I resist it? Should I even attempt curbing it and detour its way? Did he feel more strongly for me now?

He was a married man. Would he risk his marriage for me? Many questions flooded my mind.

It was a profound moment for me and I felt the divinity of the present moments as if God had blessed me. I hugged myself and smiled as I slid into the bed with a book. I felt the warmth of my body spread inside my night gown and I was soon in another world.

I woke up to the chirping of the birds. The sunlight peeped through the windows, as I pushed aside the curtains, and fell on the framed picture of Ma, enlivening it as I settled down to relish my first cup of tea for the day. The picture showed her in her favourite purple sari splashed with tiny white flowers, her hair gathered in a bun. Her smile was sweet and she had the kindest eyes I had ever seen. The skin of her roundish face was pale and smooth.

A sigh escaped my lips. Ma had been through so much in her marriage. My father's insolent behavior, hot temper and lack of empathy had pushed her to her limits. But she had coped with her husband's frailties with extreme patience and tolerance. I had not even inherited half of it. There were times she would retaliate but most of the times, she would just slink away into a hole- where she stored away all her bitterness, anger, frustration which would spill over into our daily lives, once the jar got full.

I had been astonished by her dignity and grace but her eyes

sometimes could not hide the pain. She had truly lived up to her name, Mayil–full of grace and beauty like a peahen.

I had not been able to mourn her death properly. The chaos in my marriage had rendered me frozen and had deadened some part of me. Ma's death had only made it worse. There were times I used to howl wanting her to re-appear and tell me what to do with my life, but only silence echoed back. And yet most of the times, I felt her close, when a sudden gush of wind would move the curtain or when she would come in my dreams and smile at me. I felt Ma deserved more mourning than what I, as a daughter, had given her. The weight of this guilt was still lodged inside me like a splinter of glass.

***

I was nervous and excited for the impromptu interview of my book on Meow.FM, a radio channel exclusively for women. I spent the entire day preparing for it. I curled up near the window with a steaming cup of coffee, looking out. The sky was overcast with heavy clouds and the plants swayed to the cool breeze like an intoxicated bunch of revellers. I went through my papers on the book and others on homosexuality, rehearsing for the show. In no time it started to pour. My heart swelled with joy.

I drove through the crowded roads of Delhi with the rain beating over the roof of the car. Papa always spared his extra car for me when I was in Delhi and nothing could make me feel more at home than driving in the city I grew up in. I realized how much I had missed the rains back in Muscat. The air was redolent of the smell of wet plants and grass and I inhaled lungfuls of it.

I reached the studio much before the scheduled time. The moment I sat before the mike, I felt a different person.

"So what inspired you to write the book?" the radio jockey

asked. She was a plump girl with a sweet face and voice.

"An acquaintance who was going through a similar phase in her life… the seed of the book was sown then," I answered.

"There is no hint of the characters being lesbians in the first hundred pages or so; in fact it comes as a surprise."

I moved closer to the mike. "Of course it's foreshadowed earlier on when Barkha makes love to her fiancé and feels something is amiss…"

The RJ moved to the next question. "Your novel does not provide the cheap thrills normally associated with a lesbian novel. Was it deliberate or was it a natural outcome of the story?"

"It was deliberate," I said. "I wanted to explore the subject from an outsider's point of view and probably highlight that it's all about love at the end of it. The gender is simply co-incidental."

The radio jockey bombarded me with all sorts of questions and I answered them quite convincingly. By the end of it, I was happy with the way the interview had panned out and I was inundated with messages from my friends who felt I was real and amazing on the show.

The best compliment came from Nikhil. "You were incredible Medha- such clarity on the subject is amazing and your voice sounded so well over the radio."

I felt something shift inside me. I knew the universe was aligning me to a new force. It was one I could not stop, even if I wanted to.

Nikhil

The breeze caressed me as I drove back home. I was in a mood for a drink or two, to sit under the sky, in my lawn and watch the stars. The traffic was not as mad as it normally was during peak office hours and I drove at a leisurely pace, not aware of what awaited me back home.

"You are late again." Priyanka said crossly.

I unloaded my laptop bag on the chair. "Last minute meeting."

"You had to take me for shopping, remember."

I swallowed. "Sorry! I forgot. Seriously, I am so sorry sweetie."

Priyanka snapped. "This is your regular excuse. I am sick of it. I have been waiting the whole damn fucking day...it's the last day of sale."

"Give me a moment. I have just entered the house and you take off? Be reasonable, I am dog tired…" I tried to keep my voice even.

"The least you could have done was to call me. I wouldn't have got ready like an idiot?" Priyanka grumbled.

I looked past her and reached for the jug of water and poured myself a glass. "You could have called me to check." I gulped down the water.

"Your phone was unreachable," Priyanka raised her voice.

I folded the cuffs of my sleeves. "I was in a meeting."

"I had to take Neha for her dress trial to the tailor."

I moved closer to her and cupped her face with my hands. "You could have taken her dear. Why did you wait for me? Now don't be angry and give me a hug."

Priyanka pushed my hand away angrily. "You don't even remember that my car is in the workshop."

I felt the heat around the collar of my shirt.

"I...I am sorry...I forgot. It's just that..."

"There is no need to explain. You have everything else on your mind except us." Priyanka gave me a furious look and left the room.

I slumped on the sofa, burying my face in my hands and wondered how careless could I get? Was this the way to deal with pressures at work and demands of a family? How could I find a balance somehow without losing my sanity?

I walked out onto the lawn with bare feet. The touch of soft grass relaxed me instantly. Bano, our housemaid was watering the plants. She was a thin, frail woman with an equally thin face. But her agility mismatched her physique and she smiled all the time as if life had given her enough to celebrate. She smiled as usual when she saw me.

"I'll do this," I said.

"Sure sahib," she said handing me the water pipe. "Should I get your tea?"

I nodded and directed the flow of water towards the thirsty plants and trees.

Bano had been our housekeeper for the past five years now. She and her husband had been taking care of the household and Neha quite well and their presence had been a blessing for us. Since the couple was childless, they poured all their love and affection on Neha and I made sure to reward them with extra money, a day off or presenting them with lavish gifts from time to time. I knew that would keep them charged enough to stay put in the job and push them to take good care of Neha. People could only be won by love and care. Why this didn't work with Priyanka was a mystery I had yet to solve though?

I liked the sound of water; it soothed me. The blue Jacaranda and the Gulmohar trees shaded a corner of the lawn. The vibrant orange Zinnias, the yellow Sunflowers, the turmeric coloured Marigolds and the paprika coloured Roses...all smiled at me. I inhaled their sweet fragrance and Medha's face flashed before my eyes.

The last rendezvous with her had shaken me to the core. I could not even imagine that she was going through a bad marriage. I had not seen this side of her...this vulnerable, softer side. I had always known her to be a bold, strong girl but she took me by surprise yesterday. Medha's tears had moved me immensely. I couldn't bear to see her cry. How could a vivacious, spirited girl be in so much pain? How could things be so wrong in HER marriage?

Suddenly I felt the water soaking my feet.

I heard the rustle of feet on the grass and turned around. Priyanka stood, watching me.

"You seem to be lost. See, your trousers are half wet," she said calmly. All her anger seemed to have vanished.

"Oh! I didn't notice," I said.

Priyanka cast a doubtful glance at me. "Nothing seems to affect you these days? Not even my bitterness or coldness?"

There were many questions in her eyes. I did not want to answer a single one of them.

"Come on now, that's presuming. I have just grown sick of your complaints," I explained. "And I am dead tired too. It's no big deal if I came home late and couldn't take you to the damn market?"

I turned my attention to watering the plants.

"It's no big deal Nikhil but the worry is, it no longer even matters to you how I feel," she said evenly and moved inside the house, leaving me flummoxed.

꧁❖꧂

It was a Sunday and I was more relaxed. I took a sip of my morning tea as I sat in the lawn and surfed through the newspaper. **Twelve killed in a bomb attack in Jama Masjid. People damage police jeeps and the minister's car to protest against rising terrorism in the capital.** Reading such depressing news, first thing in the morning was now becoming a trend. I moved to the Sunday magazine section. The sweet smell of zinnias and marigold rose in the air along with the smell of just-watered grass. I looked up at Priyanka who was busy reading the newspaper as well.

"I am planning a picnic for the staff on Sunday to Neemrana fort. I want you and Neha to come along," I said.

Priyanka looked up from the newspaper. "I have already made plans for a movie and lunch with my friends."

I folded the newspaper. "Please Priyanka. I promised Neha."

"I can't. I have already committed. You can take Neha," she replied tersely.

"But don't you want to go out as a family?" I tried to reach for her hand.

She withdrew. "Things don't move according to you, Mr. Chopra. I cannot come along."

"Don't be juvenile. You have a problem with me, we can discuss it? Why deny Neha the joy?"

"Neha is sensible. She will understand. I can't come and that's final."

"How can you be so unreasonable?" I shifted close to her. I could almost hear her breathe.

Priyanka scoffed, moving away from me. "Don't you dare Nikhil. Stay away from me. I am glad you know now what it means to be on the other side of the fence."

"So you want to prove a point, isn't it?"

She gathered her hair in a bun. "I am not like you."

My voice softened. "Please, I want you to come. It will be lot of fun."

"I am sure it will be but I can't. I have already promised Ekta and Gauri. I have to be there."

I took the last sip of tea. "Don't blame me later for not making enough efforts to work on this marriage."

"I won't Nikhil. I stopped blaming you for it long time back. Marriage is more than a stupid blame game anyways!" Priyanka said flatly and walked away. I watched her step inside the house. We didn't enjoy being with each other anymore. All we ended up discussing were bills, chores, social commitments and Neha- her school, education, and extracurricular activities. We both seem to have found a comfortable hole where we had tucked away our marriage so it didn't cause us pain.

I wondered what had linked us in the first place. I had stopped making efforts when all I got in return for my sincere overtures was icy coldness and callousness from her. My advertising agency was climbing up the ladder. Age was catching up with me; chasing money and success seemed the only way to survive.

I vividly remembered the day when Priyanka had made a big fuss when I had met Shilpa- a close school friend who had migrated to Canada and whom I bumped into after ten long years. I avoided conflict at any cost and that day had been no exception. My lack of anger baffled me at times but I had always been peace loving and most people had taken this trait as my weakness.

I no longer told Priyanka about meeting Shilpa. Peace was priceless. I could pay any price for it.

Suddenly my eyes caught two squirrels chasing each other, nibbling something from the grass, climbing up and down the branches of the tree.They seemed to be so joyful and free. I smiled as I watched them play. Medha's face flashed again before my eyes and I winced.

Medha

I flipped over the last of the onion paranthas on the iron griddle with a spatula. The aroma of fresh onions rose in the air. I unlocked the kitchen door which opened onto the backyard and felt a rush of air and loads of sunshine flood the kitchen instantly. The sight of my kitchen garden was a feast for the eyes and it smelled great too. I relished the touch of breeze on my face and bare arms. Rishi had called in the morning and yes, I hadn't felt guilty about *not* sharing Nikhil with him. Our relationship had even ceased to be a friendship long ago. As I had realized lately, there was a sheer lack of understanding and intelligence in comprehending what made me a person, a writer. All this contributed towards making me withdraw more into my self. I somehow sustained my intellectual and creative side. He slowly got edged out of my life and I felt a bit numb with this realization.

The doorbell rang and I rushed to open it.

"Hi what a surprise," I said, greeting Sonal at the door.

"I thought of stopping by. I was here for some grocery shopping."

We moved inside.

"I have been waiting for you to return. How was Mauritius?" I asked, switching off the gas stove and unloading the parantha onto my plate.

Sonal sat down on the sofa. "It was marvellous...clear blue waters, open skies- I loved it."

"Tea?"

"I don't mind," she said with a smile. "How's your book coming along and how was the signing?"

I placed the pan of water on the gas stove and ignited it. "Signings have been good; good crowds but the book is still at the research stage but coming along fine."

"That's great. You sound a bit different today? What's up?"

"I met Nikhil." I rolled the parantha and took a bite.

"Met?"

"We went out for dinner."

"No wonder there's a spark in your eyes."

I drew in a deep breath, adding the milk to the boiling water.

"We just decided to meet and it was divine. I can't tell you how it felt. It was going back in time." I found my voice reach a different decibel.

"Are you sure of what you are getting into?" Sonal asked.

"I feel good after meeting him, that's it." I added the tea leaves and the sugar.

"You know what I mean. You feel so strongly for him and you will be sucked into this before you even realize it...so just be careful."

I grew silent, soaking in her words like a sponge. I had myself realized that my emotions had been running very strong ever since I had met Nikhil. But I had not been able to stem their course.

Twenty long years...I had remembered him fondly at times, a flashing memory that shone and died like a meteor in the sky.

"Medha-the tea is boiling over," Sonal called out.

I quickly turned off the burner and grabbed the strainer to pour the tea.

"All I know is that I am just flowing in the present and relishing every moment" I said softly. I took a few more bites of the parantha and offered some to Sonal, who refused.

She took the tea from my hands. "Of course do enjoy it but remember you are playing with fire. It can burn you…"

Sonal had been in the preaching mode ever since I had met Nikhil. She had just not able to reach out to me beyond her logic. Of late, I had a growing feeling that Sonal was just not emotionally adequate to understand my deepest feelings.

We moved from the kitchen to the living room.

"As long as you are merely enjoying the experience, its fine but don't forget he is a married man." Sonal continued.

"So married people can't have special relationships?"

Sonal took a noisy sip of her tea. "The word is *affair* my dear , an extra marital affair."

I stared at her. "I know what you mean but we do not choose to fall in love …it just happens."

"But you can always stop yourself in time?"

"Were you able to?"

Sonal bit into her nails before she clarified. "Rohil was not a married man."

The silence was long and pregnant.

"Would it have made any difference?" I took the last bite of the parantha.

Sonal took a deep breath. "Yes, definitely. Listen, please don't be naive. As per my reading, Nikhil is a coward and he is spineless. He wouldn't ruin his marriage for you."

I wrapped my fingers around the tea cup gently. "If falling in love means being naive, I frankly don't care."

"I understand. Not many people are able to experience the beauty of love at this age but just use your head for God's sake?"

I sighed. "If it's not madness, it's not love. I am sure of this; I can't deny myself what I feel for him."

"This feeling is so immense Sonal…almost like an ocean spread in front of me. I can't ignore it."

Sonal swallowed. "Do as you please Medha. I am just worried about you getting hurt and I …"

I spotted a beautiful orange and black butterfly hover around the flowers in my lawn. I smiled slowly. "I will deal with the pain, sweetie, I really will."

Sonal looked at me, unsure and shifted her focus to her tea. I guess she realized that nothing could stop me now.

Holding myself back was not an option anymore.

Nikhil

The full moon peeped through the sheer beige curtains of my bedroom. The air conditioner hummed the usual, familiar sound and I couldn't wait to sleep. I brushed my teeth and tiptoed to the bed careful not to awaken Priyanka. Medha had been busy with her packing and since she could not meet me today, I had fixed up a drink and dinner session with Rajan and a few other friends.

Rajan and I had been thick as thieves back in school, inseparable but Priyanka had not been able to understand this closeness and had grudged his presence in my life. She had made every effort to squeeze Rajan out of my life but I had kept my friendship going with Rajan, who was perceptive enough to gauge Priyanka's attitude towards him. Her insecurity, probably her need to have me all to herself had led to lots of showdowns. The inability to openly share my friendship with her had however pushed me to withdraw into my shell. Silence was my escape route. Somewhere I felt a door closing on me which I knew I wouldn't be able to open again in front of Priyanka. A kind of inertia had hit our marriage ever since I had realized that she was militant in her efforts to push Rajan as far away from me as possible.

I had barely closed my eyes, when Priyanka switched on the light.

"So you had a great time?" The sarcasm in her voice was evident.

"C'mon now. It was such a pleasant evening, don't spoil it please."

"Friends, friends and friends, that's all there is to your life."

I turned around. "Why do you grudge me my friends? I mean you have friends too. I need to chill out as well. "

"What about me? Have you ever bothered that I need to chill out too?"

Priyanka's eyes were wild without a trace of sleep in them and it was as if the words had been well rehearsed and planned before being uttered.

"I have never stopped you from meeting your friends."

I was losing my patience now. The last thing I wanted was an argument, especially after the drinks had mellowed my senses.

"You are a man; you can move in and out anytime without any worry but I have to think about a lot of things before Igo anywhere , the servants, home, Neha ..." She said as she glowered.

"I move in and out because of my work and not ..."

"You are trying to tell me I don't work?" her voice was gruff, loaded with bitterness.

I cried, "Oh my God! You are impossible," and moved out of the room.

Priyanka followed me. She was in no mood to relent.

"What do you think of yourself? You think I will put up with your disgusting behavior...No, I won't," Priyanka screamed.

I was shocked. What had warranted such a reaction from her–Just a mere evening out with friends? No, it had to be something more. She had been behaving weird lately. Was it Rajan? It was better to ask.

"I don't understand this. What's your problem? I was just out with a few friends, damn it."

"Go anywhere, why should I have a problem? I am a bloody housewife. You enjoy yourself with your girlfriends."

I stared at her, "Do you think I was meeting my girlfriends?"

"Your phone calls, smses and e mails tell the whole story." Priyanka's resentment was slowly closing in on me.

"So you have been spying on me. Disgusting! I am not going to justify or clarify anything. I went out with Rajan and if you have a problem with that, too bad," I said without a trace of emotion.

Her voice was frosty. "You are not bothered how I feel, what I go through?"

I shrugged. "Of course I am bothered but why are you making it out to be such an issue?"

"I am tired of being a mother and a housewife. I also need to find my own path…"

"Then do, you are a free bird. Have I ever stopped you from doing anything?"

"You haven't stopped me but you have not encouraged me either."

I watched and listened as Priyanka let loose her tongue and heart, steering all her acrimony in my direction. She accused me of being self-centered, selfish and careless and how I was totally focused on making money. I could not understand what caused her more anguish–her own inability to find a focal point in her life or my focus on my work.

I was in no mental and emotional state to stretch this further, I reached for my car keys and stepped out of the house.

About two weeks later Priyanka announced that she had got a job in a lawyer's office.

❦❖❦

By the time her departure was round the corner, I met Medha two more times. I had told her that she didn't know me very well and that I had a lot of negatives which she would eventually discover if she came closer. She had laughed and asked how did it matter? If she had a darker side, would I feel differently if I found out? I had replied that the moment people discovered the real you, they didn't love you the same. We embraced as we parted. I wanted her to stay.

I drove back home feeling a bit weird. Saying goodbyes was not my cup of tea. The evening had turned a bit balmy and the breeze flew right over my face. For the time that she was around, Medha had made me feel so alive. I wondered how life would be minus her?

The radio crooned-aage bhi jaane na tu, peeche bhi jaane na tu- job hi hai bas yehi ek pal hai (you don't know what lies ahead…you do not know what you left behind…whatever you have is this present moment and nothing else) and I smiled.

I was soon humming the song. Life seemed good. I was certainly basking in the attention heaped by Medha but it also dawned on me that I was getting drawn towards her as well. Her loud, throaty laughter rang in my ears and I hummed aloud, trying to drown my thoughts in the song. Was it so easy?

I entered the house and turned the mobile's ringer to loud. I had set it to mute when I was with Medha. There were three missed calls from Priyanka. I hoped all was well.

Priyanka was watching television. "It's useless to ask, what took you so long?"

I sat down beside her on the sofa. "Why?"

"Neha had to be taken to the doctor this evening...she had an appointment."

"Oh God! It just slipped out of my mind, sorry."

Priyanka took a long sip of her iced tea. "Try something new next time," and shifted her attention to the television program she had been watching.

"We can go now...there's still time," I said.

"I came back early from office and took her...your phone was switched off." She rose from the sofa. "You are no longer dependable, my dearest hubby," she said, and walked out of the room.

I felt the words smack me right in my face.

Medha

As the plane took off, I felt a dull pain invade my entire body. I knew I belonged here and leaving only made this fact more conspicuous than ever. When I had said goodbye to him, our eyes had met and in those few seconds, I saw his desire shining forth. I felt his grip on me growing strong. He was invading my being slowly. It would help me survive in his absence I knew.

I looked out at the kingdom of white clouds rising magnificently in the sky and felt their beauty seep into my soul. They looked immensely beautiful. I guess their beauty lay in their proximity; the closer you were to them, the more appealing they were. I promised myself that I wasn't going to be miserable but would make the best of what life had to offer.

The stewardess arrived after a while.

"Juice or coke, Ma'am?"

"I would like a scotch on the rocks please."

I caught a faint glimpse of surprise in her eyes and I smiled to myself.

She handed me the drink in a clear plastic glass along with a packet of peanuts. I took a sip and felt the whiskey trail the walls of my throat like fire. The flight was almost full and the murmur of voices floated in the air. The inside of the plane was quite cold and I gathered myself tightly within my shawl. I flipped through my mobile pictures, clicked during my stay. Papa's face flashed through a few of them. I observed how old he had grown since the last time I saw him.

Papa had had a tough life, having lost his father at the age of five and bringing up his family of three sisters, all on his own, getting them married and settling them down. He lost his childhood in the process and grew bitter and Ma realized that she and her kids paid the price of it. I felt overwhelmed as I regarded his photo.

Ma's illness had mellowed down Papa over a period of time. He had grown more patient, more compassionate and the mere thought of her slipping away had made him insecure. I remembered he would drive her to the hospital for her chemotherapy and radiotherapy sessions, which left her brittle both emotionally and physically. He would trust no one else with it. I had offered to help but he had always refused. He was a changed man towards the end of Ma's life- a far cry from the husband who had been a pushover all his life.

Maybe serving his wife was a form of his penance.

He would fuss over her with food and medicines. Ma's illness, ironically, bonded them in the last phase of their marriage. Their love had been uncelebrated and private and rose from the recesses of the deepest layers when the need arose. But what they never realized was that as parents they needed to celebrate it in front of their children in order to awaken and restore their faith in love. I took a swig of the liquor and felt my senses relax.

Suddenly Ma's photo flashed on my mobile as I surfed. I had taken it just days before she passed away. She was frail and unrecognizable. I had been shocked to see her. She had deteriorated beyond recognition. Her body had shrivelled, reducing her to a mere heap of bones. Her skin had turned dry and dark and wrinkled. Cancer cells had eaten into her body and spirits. She was barely able to stand and worse, she could hardly talk. The breast cancer had slowly spread to her lungs and uterus. Surgery was not a wise option and all we could do was ease her discomfort and pain through medicines. I felt the river of tears rise from the rim of my eyes. I gulped down my drink and asked for a refill.

Siddharth had been adamant in shifting Ma to the hospital. He had wanted to give her the best always but this time we found her slipping away from our grasp. I knew it was Sid's way of making up for the time he had not been able to spend with her. He had been abroad for the past fourteen years and had shifted only six months back with his wife and a one-year old daughter. Luckily he had found a lucrative job as a Finance head with an MNC.

Ma had been delirious with happiness on his return. She had

always missed him like a hungry child misses food. She fought back valiantly in celebration of her son's return and the joy of a grandchild prancing about the house, but I guess it was already too late. Her spirits remained unvanquished but her body gave in.

She was gone within a year of Sid's return; gone when I needed her the most; gone when my marriage had begun falling apart. And I had gone cold as a stone.

Rishi

I looked at my watch once again. The airport was bustling with people and Yash stood near the arrival lounge, waiting for Medha to emerge. The place was redolent of shawarma and coffee that was being sold at the nearby café. It was a particularly windy day and I found it hard to keep my hair and clothes in place when the wind rushed in through the open door as people walked in.

"Why is mom taking so long?" Yash asked, clearly bored.

I smiled. "Patience, son. She is alone and managing the luggage is not easy."

"Why does she have to shop so much in India?"

I gave out a hearty laugh. "Remember this on your next trip."

Yash gave a broad smile. "There she is," and rushed to greet her. She looked happy.

I moved towards her. She hugged Yash tightly and gave him a kiss on his cheeks, much to his awkwardness.

"You seem to have been fasting in my absence." she complained as an indulgent mother.

"What did you expect? With the rotten food the cook made, my appetite would have grown?"

Medha gave him an angry stare. "Yash..."

She faced me now. Yash took care of the trolley and pushed it ahead of us. The coldness between us seemed to hover above us. I hugged her lightly and she merely allowed it.

"Good to see you," I said.

She smiled dryly.

Back home, I felt she didn't feel at home somehow. The house was in a bit of a mess and what put her off was her own room and writing table, that was in complete disarray. She set about cleaning the room. I tried to help her but she shunned me totally.

I watched her, hurt. I walked out to the living room and switched on the television, wondering what was wrong with her now? She was clearly looking for an excuse to run me down and deviate from the core issue that needed to be sorted out. Fussing over the cleanliness had just been a pretext to move away from me and create more distance. I soon lost myself in the television program, trying to come to terms with her erratic behavior.

When I walked into the room after about an hour- the room was dusted and cleaned. The night lamp was at its dimmest and she lay on the bed with her eyes closed.

I called out to her but there was no answer. I closed the door behind me and walked out of the room.

For the first time I was scared.

"The only business of the head in the world
is to bow a ceaseless obeisance to the heart."
— William Butler Yeats

Medha

The night was still and dark. It was September end and the weather had started to turn pleasant. I closed the book I had been reading, took off my glasses and drank from the bottle of water kept on the night stand. The tiredness of my stay in India was coming to the fore now. I slipped into my quilt, yearning to catch some good, sound sleep and reached over to switch off the night lamp. Rishi entered the room just then and switched on the night lamp. I turned my face away from him. Rishi slid into the bed and moved towards me. I could sense him near me and felt an acute discomfort. Rishi came close. We were a breath away.

"Tired?" he began.

"Yeah, I am sleepy."

He brushed his hands on my hair and I felt cold.

"Please Rishi, don't." I withdrew into my quilt.

"What's wrong, Medha?" his voice was irritated. I felt the tension rise within me.

"Please, I am not interested," the curtness in my voice was deliberate but Rishi was determined.

"Please, Wifey, it's been so long." He tried holding me.

I pushed his hands away and shouted, "Don't do this for heaven's sake. I don't like it." I pushed him away, kicking him in the process.

Rishi was stunned like as a child stung by a slap on his face in front of his classmates. I marched out of the room wondering if anything could warm up the cockles of my heart ever again.

I walked up to the huge window in Yash's room where he was fast asleep. I stepped lightly and opened the window. The air came rushing in and I saw the city lit up before me. From the third floor, the view was beautiful. The silver crescent moon hung from the black sky illuminating the grand Sultan Qaboos mosque. It's lofty, four pencil shaped, fluted minarets surrounded the huge, golden dome in between, jutting out like a glittering gem against the low white buildings, which were covered in a translucent haze in the dark, making it almost surreal. Although the darkness had concealed the mountains in the background, their presence still lurked in the backdrop and their visibility made this entire view look so breathtaking during the day. The faint glow of the street lights filtered through the curtains and cast a pale glow on the ceiling. I hugged myself. I was slowly losing the inclination to make any effort in this marriage. I wanted to be away from Rishi, as far as our marriage would be resilient enough to take the brunt. I closed my eyes and Nikhil's face flashed before me, his smile and the softness of his eyes. He was all around. I had not planned this. Never in my wildest dreams had I expected to meet Nikhil and have my buried feelings rise like a phoenix and threaten to resurrect my life and overpower me absolutely.

I shifted on my feet, crossing and uncrossing my legs. I had tried my best to resist them but then there was little one could do to stifle feelings that had taken birth twenty years ago. It was all coming back from the past to shake my present and future forever. The more I would resist it, the more it would persist, I was aware of this.

I had not experienced this beautiful emotion ever in life. What I had experienced with Rishi was something I couldn't quite define. It was surely not love. It was a comfort zone. He had become my habit, an everyday body function like brushing one's teeth. I couldn't deny myself this beauty and ecstasy that I was experiencing with Nikhil. The mere thought of being in love had sent me into raptures. I had not been able to fathom the darkness in my married life till the time I met Nikhil.

I wanted to go back to Delhi.

Muscat seemed like a prison I wanted to leave forever but it was not going to be easy. I needed to talk to Rishi and thrash the issue. How would he react to my decision to move permanently to India? He would try his best to convince me to stay back.

I kept gazing at the dazzling lights for a long time. The tears fell on my hands–delicate and soundless.

Rishi

I pursued her once more after a gap of two weeks. I came home early one day and after an early dinner, I asked her to accompany me for coffee. I knew she would not refuse. She loved coffee.

The seaside Caribou Coffee cafe at Jawaharat Al Shatti was her favourite place. It overlooked the vast sea and the sound of the crashing waves in the background formed the perfect soundtrack for conversations.

Medha chose a Turtle Mocha while I settled for a hot chocolate. I wasn't really a coffee person but gave company to Medha whenever she was keen to make a trip to the coffee shop. The late evening breeze was refreshing. I looked at Medha. She was lost somewhere faraway.

"Medha I want to talk to you about what is happening between us of late," I began.

She looked at me. "It's something you really can't do much about."

I skipped a heartbeat.

"But we can talk about it?"

"No there is nothing to talk about."

The waiter arrived and placed our beverages in front of us.

"Enjoy your coffee ma'am," he said with a smile.

The rich aroma of coffee engulfed my senses.

"But why Medha?"

Her eyes were focused on the coffee. "I feel it's beyond you to understand me as a woman, as a person and I am tired of explaining myself to you."

The waves crashed against the shores once again. I felt the pain inside me.

"If you do not tell me, how am I supposed to know?" I said.

"I am not supposed to tell you each and every thing. Some things have to be understood, without words being uttered, empathized with."

"You are not some kind of a Queen,Wifey, that I am supposed to read your thoughts and predict your whims and moods?"

She looked away.

"I told you- you can't understand."

I sensed the gulf that divided both of us. I took a sip of my drink.

"If you have assumed already that I can't understand, then what can I say?"

"It's better if you leave me alone to myself. I'll sort out things that are bothering me," she replied coldly.

"The problem is, it's not about you alone. It's about *us*."

She looked through me as if I did not exist. "Yes it's about us but if I don't sort out the *me* in it then the *us* might not exist."

"Listen, I can't understand your jargon and your so called intellectual talk. Why can't you be simple with me?" I said irritably.

I saw the light go out of her eyes. "I am damn complicated."

I opened my mouth to say something but snapped it shut.

We finished our respective drinks in silence and were soon on our way back.

I looked at the road ahead as I drove and wondered why some paths only lead you to a dead end?

Medha

It was midnight and sleep was playing truant. I had read for more than an hour but as I lay down, sleep vanished.

Yash had been busy with his project work and had slept late. Rishi was still at work. The darkness outside wrapped the world like a lover's hug. I tossed and turned in bed wondering what to do. Suddenly I heard the key turn in the lock of the front door. Rishi was home. I closed my eyes. I heard the sounds of the shoes being taken off, the bathroom door being shut, the running of water, the splash on the face, the flush being used and the slight squeak of the bed when Rishi lay down beside me.

I shifted in bed. He came closer to me. He smelled of liquor and mint. I froze inside my body. He had been relentless in his pursuit throughout the week but had met with no success. He was clearly growing restless and I could sense it but found myself at a loss. I felt a faint nervousness as he touched me. I thought of Yash. He could already sense the stiffness between us and I did not want him to harbour any thoughts that his parents' marriage was going downhill.

I let him move closer to me. It all seemed sterile; the switching off of the lights, the undressing, the murmur of breath, the cold brushing of the bodies, the lack of hunger and the hush that filled up the room. I resented everything about him. The way he touched my body, the way his hands moved over me, the way he reached for my breasts and swallowed them ...the tentativeness of his touch, the anxiety in his eyes, I detested it all. I was merely allowing it. Merely allowing him to feel the familiarity of a naked body; merely allowing myself the hope that my feelings might go through a shift.

When he was on top of me, with his eyes shut, he was totally unaware of the deep loneliness in my heart and my total disconnect from him. And when he entered me, I closed my eyes hoping in the process that I would be able to shut out his existence for the time being.

As I felt him grow harder and warmer inside me, my mind brimmed with thoughts of Nikhil and I realized that in the process of fulfilling my conjugal duties to the best of my abilities, there was something that was dying inside me. As Rishi rolled off me, I turned my back towards him and felt the prick of tears in my eyes. I was becoming dead somewhere inside me.

☙❖❧

Life moved on but my world had undergone a sea change. I hated myself for that night. I realized it was a blunder that had exposed the crevices of my broken marriage sharply. How could I go against my grain to keep my marriage intact or please Rishi?

Writing became my survival in Muscat. My journal became my armour to protect myself. I would pen down thoughts that infested my mind throughout the day. Talking to myself about what happened during the day was a big relief.

Sonal surprised me one day by announcing that she was arriving in Muscat for two days. She had specially planned a visit to meet me, on her way back home from Dubai, where she had accompanied her designer boss for a fashion show. I hired a cab and met her at Holiday Inn where she was staying. We chose the open coffee shop that overlooked the blue ocean. The heat was bearable and the sea breeze made the weather really pleasant.

"But you must try and communicate with him… I am sure once the ice is broken, things will move," Sonal said as she settled on the cane chair.

"You think I don't know that but I feel he is plain dumb at times… he doesn't even attempt to understand." my voice quivered.

"Maybe you have held him responsible for uprooting you, so you are sort of blaming him- unconsciously."

"I don't know but maybe. I do feel that I am here because of him, in this boring, insipid place."

Sonal passed me the sandwiches. "Yes and maybe you are punishing him by denying him the affection and caring…"

I sighed. "It's not that I'm punishing him, that never crossed my mind but seriously I don't feel the pull anymore."

"Just relax Medhu; leave it for a while. I am sure things will be fine. It's just a phase, it'll go away. Don't stress yourself too much." She took a bite of the sandwich.

I felt the lack of solace in her words. Probably what I needed most was a friend who could understand my pain and show me the way to heal it. My voice cracked with agony.

"I hope so…I just can't force myself to do things. Why the hell do I feel nothing for him?"

Sonal sipped her coffee. "Is it Nikhil?"

I looked past her to the vast blue, glittering ocean. "I don't know. Maybe if I hadn't met him, I would not have realized what I was missing in my life."

"Medhu...where will all this lead to, have you thought about it?"

I cradled the cup in my hands. "If it wouldn't have been him, it would have been someone else."

"I understand but don't mix both the issues...you will become a wreck."

I gazed at the bunch of fresh lilies on the table. "But these things are intertwined?"

"No they are not. What you feel for Nikhil has nothing to do with what you feel for Rishi. You need to sort out your feelings for both separately."

I blinked my eyes. "Yeah! As if it's that easy?"

"It's not, but focus on your marriage right now; forget about Nikhil for the time being. He will never have the courage to love you even if he knows you do. Don't ruin your life for him."

The words stung me like a bee.

"It's not as black and white as you say but I'll try. I need to get out of here first." I said.

"Be calm. Think before you decide." Sonal bit her nails.

"Don't worry. I'll survive."

We sat for long, chatting about other stuff...her work, my book, her family. We had lunch together before I returned to the scary silence of my house.

Rishi

I came out to the dining area. Medha had called twice for food already. Yash was at the table. I cast one look at the laid out table and my appetite suddenly rose.

"I am damn hungry, Mom," Yash said.

"You guys can start. I'll get the chapattis." Medha called out from the kitchen. She had made her son's favorite shahi paneer and capsicum aloo. I served both the veggies to myself and started munching the salad.

Medha arrived with the casserole of hot chapattis and served Yash and me before she settled down. I tore the chapatti with my hands and dipped it in the curry. Suddenly my face knotted up.

"What's wrong?" Yash asked.

"Nothing," I said.

Yash persisted. "You don't like it. Do you?"

I muttered under my breath. "As if I have a choice..."

Medha gave me a dirty look.

"It's absolutely fine, Dad, just a bit hot but I am enjoying it." Yash tried to lighten the tension a bit.

"I don't understand why you can't pay more attention while putting in the spices. You know I can't have chillies?" I said upset,

It was as if I had given her the perfect fuel to flare up.

"This is the best that you'll get from me. You can keep a cook if you want. I've had enough of this and you."

"That I will since you can't even manage this much." I snapped.

Medha took a bite of the chapatti. "No, I can't manage anything. You know very well that I have lost all interest in cooking after coming here. Back in India I had a lot of help; here I just don't enjoy it anymore."

"That's because you don't want to," I countered her.

Medha made a sullen face. "Whatever, there's no point in arguing."

Yash shifted uneasily in his chair.

Damn! Why couldn't she cook properly? Sometimes it was excess of salt, at other times it was excess of chilies. This was becoming a regular feature now. The least I expected was good food, considering good sex was rationed now. I sulked as I ate and she scowled at the sight of my grumpy face.

Yash stepped in, "Come on Dad. Mom cooks well and..."

I yelled. "Keep out of it." I could feel the air going out of my lungs.

"But you can't talk to mom like that," Yash said.

My eyes burned with anger and I was in no mood to be preached by a child.

"You are a child remain one. There's no need to butt in," I shouted.

"But you can't speak to her like this, I am sorry." Yash stomped out of the room.

I turned towards Medha. "So you have begun turning my son against me?"

"I don't need to. He has eyes to see and brains to understand. If you misbehave with his mother, he won't witness it like a spectator."

I banged the plate on the table. "I'll see to it that you don't achieve your evil designs you bi…"

"C'mon say it, BITCH. That's what you are supposed to call the mother of your child."

Her eyes were as cold as marble. I was trembling with rage and wished I would hurt myself to get rid of this frustration somehow. I got up and moved towards my room, knocking a chair on the way. I slammed the door of my room and drove my fist into the wall. Blood spurted out of my knuckles and I felt a searing pain slice through me. Yash had never spoken to me like this before.

I could sense the chaos that the breakdown of our marriage was bringing forth yet. I was not ready to accept Yash's insolence at any cost.

Medha

Each passing day in Muscat strengthened my resolve to go back to Delhi. The claustrophobia inside me was like an impending storm that threatened to engulf me.

I thought of Nikhil with fondness and joy. Although our phone calls were not regular but we kept in touch through text messages. I realized that I was letting him in while concurrently shutting the doors on Rishi. It was extremes that I was going through–abundance of love for Nikhil and chilling coldness for Rishi. I was going through complete chaos and needed to find a balance somehow.

I focused more on my writing. That was the only way I could survive this turmoil. Moreover the pain and rage were emotions to invest in the writing–to enrich it and make it more intense, sensitive and real.

I had begun to totally withdraw from Rishi.

"I want to go back in Delhi," I told him one day.

"Come on Medha' this is such a beautiful place.

I folded the laundry into a neat pile. "It is but its dead. I can't live here anymore."

Rishi stammered. "But-t its perfect...t for your writing...the sea, the mountains, er...the picturesque beauty..." still unable to believe what he had just heard.

"Its only when you live here that you get a feel of the real place. And why should I pretend to be happy in this environment when I am not?"

"But I don't understand..."

My voice was frosty. "I think you need to soak this in."

He got up without saying a word. The weight of my words seemed to crush him and I knew the impact of my decision on Rishi. It was not going to be easy. He followed me inside the bedroom.

"Understand what?" he glared at me.

I arranged the pile of clothes in the almirah. "That I don't want to live with you anymore."

His jaws dropped. "You can't do this?"

"If I don't, our marriage will be over and done with."

"It's dying anyway, your going away will ruin it forever."

"You decide...you want it to die right now or you want to give it some time to breathe so that maybe it can..."

I glanced at him. "Don't shut all the doors Rishi. Let me go in peace; leave some doors open. You never know which one may open and give way to which one."

He looked at me. His mouth drooped. I lowered my eyes and focused on tying the laces of my worn out Reebok sneakers and stepped out of the house. I needed to escape. The half an hour walk did me good. I felt comforted and more in tune with myself. The rest of the day passed in peace.

I was trying to deal with his presence in the house without being openly hostile but it somehow spilled over. I would avoid sitting in the same room with him. I would finish my meals earlier or quietly, if we ate together. I would retire early to bed with my book so that when he came to bed, I was in another world. Maybe I didn't really love him enough otherwise why would I find things about him so incongruous and out of place? They were perfectly normal things for any happily married couple but for us they had become larger than life issues, like his need for physical intimacy.

Nikhil

I drove out of my house for the office. The weather was getting a bit nippy. It was a big respite from the killing heat that Delhi had experienced in the past few months. I turned on the radio and focused on the road. It had been more than two months since Medha had gone but she seemed to have never left my mind.

My mobile beeped. I clicked to find a message from Medha– *Life is almighty's novel, let him write it. We've got to relish the turns and twists provided by him. Have a great day! hugs*

I smiled and felt a wave of excitement wash over me. Our bond was growing. I had found new hope in my dreary life with the arrival of Medha. My marriage had run into predictability and lack of passion and was bordering on boredom. Priyanka was neck deep in her full time job and looking after Neha. I felt like a lonely soldier posted in a tough terrain.

"You know my life is so full of daily chores, it doesn't leave time for anything," I had told Medha once.

"You have to find time for what you want to do," Medha said.

"I know but I don't seem to find time even for myself."

She had smiled. "That's an excuse we give ourselves; time has to be taken out, it's never available easily."

I had taken a deep breath. "Maybe you are right;"

"Don't park things–act on them."

My voice had suddenly grown softer. "Let me begin with you then…"

"Yeah try your luck, who knows?" she quipped.

"Who knows what?"

"You know your antenna is quite weak, doesn't catch signals too easily."

I had whispered. "Oh! Really, the day it becomes stronger, you will have a problem, you will run away."

She had caught the desire in my voice.

"I won't, I promise. Try it," she had whispered back.

The words had filled up the spaces between us bringing us closer than ever.

And we had both laughed.

Rishi

I entered our bedroom and searched for Medha's journal frantically. The weather was fairly cold but I was sweating. I took off my blazer and loosened my tie before I drew the curtains away from the windows. Reams of sunlight swamped the room. I felt a bit better. Medha was out with Yash shopping and I had entered the house using the spare keys. I knew it was a lemon coloured spiral bound journal. I ransacked her study table and book rack but couldn't find it. I tried the nightstand drawers and found it tucked under a few books. I picked it up without a sliver of guilt and hid it in my laptop bag and carried it back to my office. I had been eyeing this journal for some time now and had felt a strong desire to know the workings of her mind. Stealing seemed a fair option.

I settled myself to read the journal. I pulled away the blinds to get more light to view the wreckage of my heart, I guess.

I read and the words fell on me like boulders –

It's like having three-four pegs of scotch on the rocks and gloating in the intoxication of being drunk. A conversation of one and a half hours can take you to such heights of bliss is unimaginable. But it does. It's like having a mental orgasm. I soar, lifted by him-unafraid and fearless, even if he removes the ground beneath my feet. It's all worth it; worth every second that he is with me; worth every fibre of happiness that my heart weaves; worth every drop of heavenly nectar that seeps into my soul.

And I discover a new side of him, hitherto unknown. Those moments have become eternal, never to die, to be always alive in my heart. I laugh openly as I never have in so many years. He brings alive a part of me that had been buried deep inside me. I laugh my heart and soul out and we laugh together like souls attached to each other. Nothing matters at that moment...neither my past, nor the present nor the future. The bliss of the moment transcends everything and becomes a pearl to be cherished and hidden within me. Everything is light, buoyant, full, complete, meaningful, beautiful and perfect, like the sunrise on the faraway horizon, spreading the blush of happiness all around.

He is a powerful light in which I can see the darkness of my world clearly. The light attracts me, pulls me towards it and I follow mesmerized, unquestioning. The light is the reason my eyes are blinded and my soul dances. I am not ashamed or regretful of anything. It flows like a river taking all in its stride; delirious in its own self discovery. I revel in the joy of being alive and kicking.

I reached for a glass of water and gulped it down. My throat was dry as if coated with sand. The words seemed blurred and indistinct like the houses seen through a fog. I turned over the pages again, going back and forth trying to assess the damage they had done to me.

Alas! I knew I could not even fathom the depth of the piercing of this nail in the coffin of my marriage.

Medha

It was ten in the night. I switched on the night lamp and opened the drawer to take out my journal. The weather was a bit colder now, being October, and it was the best time to be in Muscat and enjoy the flowers blooming along the roadsides and roundabouts as also the cool breeze, especially by the sea side.

The journal was not there. I looked anxiously for it, overturning papers, searching on my writing table and the book shelf. I ransacked every possible corner of my room but it seemed to have just vanished. I knew it was Rishi.

Rishi peered into his files, pretending ignorance.

"I know it's you, just return my journal to me," I commanded.

"I don't have it and why will I have it?" he said. I knew he was telling a lie.

My eyes burned with anger. "Don't lie to me. It didn't grow wings overnight and fly out of the window? You have it and it's a shame that you stole it."

"I haven't got it. If you don't believe me, then it's your problem," Rishi said and walked out of the room.

I felt the tears stinging my eyes. I felt violated.

I sank on the bed and hugged myself tight around my knees. Anger seeped out of every pore of my body. It was hard for me to believe that Rishi had breached my faith and intruded my privacy. I was hurt and deflated as never before. I could not keep things lying around my own house? I had to lock things like my journal too? This would kill me–this fear of being intruded. I decided to talk to him calmly the next day but to no avail. I explained that it contained my manuscript notes for the second book but he wondered at my desperation for a mere journal. His eyes had a glimmer, as if he had laid his hands on a treasure. I pleaded with him but he was unmoved. He completely denied having seen it or even touching it.

I was sure that he had read everything that I had penned down. Then why didn't he have the balls to confront me? How could I live with such a man? His own pain was most important and he wanted to revel in it. Was this love? This was being plain selfish. I knew it would be hard for me to forgive him ever.

I grew restless and angrier. For the next three days I begged him each day to return my journal but he dodged the question. My persistence to get the journal back continued and Yash questioned his father sensing the matter was becoming unbearable for me. Rishi feigned ignorance but offered help to find it. He had to appear good in his son's eyes. I knew the journal would appear the next day and it did. Rishi found it under the almirah where I had already searched at least five times. I preferred not to react. But I lost all respect for Rishi after that day.

My marriage was now like a bicycle running downhill and it was impossible to apply the brakes. The tension between us was aggravating. There was nothing more painful than this everyday spectacle of emotional degradation of a sixteen year old relationship. And the last thing I wanted was to expose Yash to the ugliness of our marriage. But could I avoid it? The strain between us brewed and blew into shameless fights. The icy coldness that followed the fiery fights was making me lose my mind. It further fuelled my longing to go back to India as soon as was possible.

***

"So why don't you understand?" I yelled.

"Because I am not as intelligent as you are," Rishi shouted back.

"Don't expect me to sleep with you just because I am your wife." I banged the book on the table.

Rishi laughed. "Don't expect me to beg you for it too, Wifey. You think I can't survive without it?"

"Of course you can't. Find yourself a hole, damn it." The words burned on my tongue.

Rishi looked at me, his eyes raging red. "You are full of filth."

"I wonder how I lived with a person like you for sixteen years." I ranted.

"Even I am surprised at myself."

"Mistakes can be rectified," I shrieked.

His mouth stiffened. "Yes that's the easiest solution you can find...bloody coward."

"Don't you dare bloody me," I yelled. "The least we can do is to stop fighting in front of Yash."

"You think about it. You start it always. Poor kid, what he must be going through?"

"What do you mean, I start it? It's all my fault, right? You are innocent.... Am I the only one to be blamed?"

Rishi got up to leave. "I don't want to argue with you. I am sick of your shouting."

"Yeah and I am sick of *you*."

"Then why don't you leave me?" Rishi threw up his hands.

"Yes I guess that's the best option. At least the kid will be spared some misery." I slammed the door on him and stormed out of the room.

I rushed towards Nikhil with more intensity and hope. Nikhil's thoughts soothed me. It seemed the only way to save myself and survive. I needed time to sort out my emotions and living here could never help. Rishi had been behaving very weirdly after reading the journal and expecting him to be mature and calm was foolish. But I had to try for Yash's sake.

"Please get our Gurgaon house vacated. I wish to move to India," I requested him one day.

"Why? So you can be on your own- absolved of all responsibilities?" Bitterness oozed from every word.

I straightened out the cushions on the sofa. "Don't be foolish. It's for the sake of my son. Our daily fights are affecting him terribly."

"So you want to be left alone to pursue your relationship..."

I stared back at him.

"Look...Nikhil and I share a beautiful friendship. I have already told you I liked him a lot back in college so..."

"And now he's back in your life."

"Come on Rishi...try to understand."

"Of course I do. It's plain and simple cheating. You are cheating on me, you adulterous woman."

I felt the punch hard on my face. I looked at him crushed, soaking in the shards of his words. "Do you even realize what you are saying?" I asked.

"I know and I am right. You are cheating on me."

"You steal my journal, read what was not meant for you and then decide that I am cheating on you? Splendid Rishi!

"Look at you. Guilty aren't you?"

I could feel the tears springing in my eyes. "You are disgusting. You have insulted my status as a wife and..." the words got stuck inside my throat and the tears flowed out. I ran out of the room.

Adulteress...the word echoed in my ears like a brilliant abuse, burning up my insides.

"Every conquering temptation represents
a new fund of moral energy.
Every trial endured and weathered in the right spirit
makes a soul nobler and stronger than it was before."
—William Butler Yeats

Medha

Landing in Delhi was as refreshing as soaking in the monsoons after being in a desert. I smelled the air as I stepped out of the aircraft. It was January end and quite cold. The warmth of the sun kissed my skin as the chilly breeze whipped at my clothes. I realized I had been missing the Delhi winters badly. A deep calm seemed to descend on me immediately. Places can do wonders and I sensed it today more than ever.

Papa was waiting for me as I strode out with Yash. I had been reluctant for him to pick me up from the airport but he had been insistent and I had given in. I had reasoned with myself that these are the joys of being a parent and should not be denied. I saw him standing outside his car. Our driver, Rana stood near him. Papa's lean, straight body looked limp and soft. His face had added more years since the last time I saw him. His complexion had grown darker too. I rushed to meet him. There is no purer joy than meeting your parents after long. Yash pushed past me to meet his grandfather.

"How's Rishi?" he asked me.

"He is fine Papa," I replied.

He caught hold of my hand as the driver reached out to open the door of the car. I sat next to him. Once we had reached home, he called me to his room.

"Why this sudden decision to move back?" he asked.

I had rehearsed the answer several times.

"I just don't like Muscat Papa and it's not good for my writing. Moreover Yash has also not settled well; the education is not great you know."

He took a deep breath. "How will Rishi manage alone?"

"He will, Papa. And we will keep meeting every now and then."

He looked at me. "It's not easy to manage alone. You are a woman."

"I am your daughter. I will never say never."

He gave me a slow smile. "Still, life's a bitch, beta."

"I have you and Sid and Yash," I said.

He caught the mist in my eyes and held on to my hands tightly.

"Yash needs his father as badly as he needs you; maybe a few days here and you will know what it is to keep your son away from his father."

"I know but I had no other choice," I said.

"There's always a way out in tough situations. We sometimes choose the easy one."

I shuddered. Maybe he knew that all was not well in my marriage but I was in no emotional state to discuss my marriage with anyone.

Yash entered the room and started narrating his anecdotes. Papa was soon lost in his talk. I looked around the room. Ma's face peered from a photo frame- healthy and smiling. Suddenly her ghost like face flashed before my eyes and tears sprang into my eyes. How beaten her body and spirit had been when she neared death? How helpless and broken. I wish I could have saved her for some more years. Coming here had made her absence more obvious. I missed her a lot now that I was going through the worst phase in my life. It was a phase that wouldn't eventually last. It couldn't. The law of the universe would come into play.

By the time I reached my house in Gurgaon in the evening, I

was tired. It felt nice to spend some time with Papa, Siddharth and his family. Back home, the house had to be cleaned and Yash lent a helping hand. The furniture, curtains, Fridge, Microwave, Air conditioner were all a part of the house when we gave it on rent and the ex-tenants had taken good care of them. Unpacking was major work and it took us a few hours before everything was in place.

I finally settled down with a cup of coffee and a book and my thoughts returned to Nikhil. The desire to see him had grown stronger after landing in India.

I looked at the watch; it was 10 pm. It was rather late to call him so I decided to wait till morning. Rishi called in the meanwhile.

"Oh! I forgot to call you. I have been busy settling everything."

"How can you be so irresponsible? I was wondering what happened. I tried your number and Papa's too several times but the call didn't get through."

"I just forgot to call you back," my voice was cold.

"I just got out of a marathon meeting. Why are you so cold always?"

I took a sip of my coffee. "Rishi please not again- I am too tired."

He gave a short laugh. "That's what you always wanted–being alone."

"Yes, that's what I need right now," I said.

"Have you ever thought how it will affect Yash? Being away from his father?"

I was silent. This was the last thing I wanted to discuss at the end of a bloody hectic day.

"For your own whims and fancies, you are putting the child through hell," he continued.

I took another sip of the coffee. "How come your paternal instinct never awakened before this moment? You should have realized where all this was leading to?"

"I never thought that you would go to this extent." Rishi's tone was caustic.

"I am glad you know now. This was the last thing I wanted to do but you left me with no option. I had to be a mother first and protect Yash from witnessing the ugliness of our marriage day in and day out. Call me a bitch for that, I don't care." I disconnected the phone.

I got up in disgust and stomped out into the lawn, the mug cradled in my hands. I sat down on the concrete ledge that bordered the grass and felt my lips quiver. I sat there for a long time, letting the chill of the night soak into my bones. I tightened the shawl around me and felt the coldness of my life engulf me. After the showdown that day when Rishi had called me adulterous, he had apologized later, breaking down in front of me but I had been unmoved. We had become complete strangers, living under the same roof.

I took a deep breath. My marriage seemed to be a big lie at the moment and I couldn't believe I had lived it for sixteen years. I just wanted to be myself now, without being a wife to someone. I had to take control of my life. I felt that Rishi, by stealing the journal, had created a wedge between us without even realizing it. His curt and unreasonable behavior had had unlocked the gate for my exit.

When I saw the blanched look on his face at the airport, I knew it would be tough for him but I was not moved by his pain anymore.

After a while, I rose to my feet. It was too cold to sit outside anymore. I locked the door and sauntered inside the house, switching off the odd light here and there. Yash was fast asleep and I adjusted his quilt, tucked him tightly and kissed him softly. It was not going to be easy for him as well. He had come with me but he was deeply attached to Rishi. I hoped he would be able to deal with this separation and that it wouldn't hit him hard. I knew I had to help him grow into a strong, courageous, sensitive boy who would be unafraid to love, in spite of his parents' unhappy marriage. That he would still have faith in the goodness of life.

As I slid into my quilt, I felt intensely lonely and craved for a human touch. I knew it was much more than a need for physical intimacy.

Nikhil

I got up to the sound of the chirping of birds and looked out of the bedroom window. The day was warm and bright and the sunrays filled up the room with a gay abandon. I checked the time on my mobile. It was half past eight. I knew Priyanka would have left for her office.

I changed and left for Medha's house. She was only a fifteen minute drive away. I rang the doorbell, yearning to catch the surprise in her eyes.

"Good morning, still sleepy?" I said as she opened the door.

She rubbed her eyes. "Nik?" her voice melted in my ears.

She smiled as we embraced each other.

I wandered inside the house. "Where's Yash?"

"Fast asleep," she plonked herself down on the sofa. She looked so desirable in her pink and white night suit showing her curves distinctly.

She interrupted my thoughts. "I thought you forgot."

"That you were arriving?" I combed my hair with my fingers.

Medha gazed at me. "And I kept waiting for your phone...never mind."

"What...never mind. You have to pay for your negligence," I teased her.

"You were supposed to call me." she said.

"But you could have, too."

Medha smiled. "What do you want me to do?"

I looked into her eyes. "I will think and let you know but you can't refuse whatever I ask."

Medha drawled. "Depends…I may." She played with the cushion in her lap.

"No way...a punishment is a punishment."

She threw the cushion at me. "You are such a swine."

"I thought I was a cheapster?" I said.

"Oh! You remember that?"

"You bet. How can I forget that? Nobody called me that except you in college."

I drew nearer. "I love it," I whispered.

She untangled her gaze from mine and got up. "Tea?"

I nodded.

"It feels good to be back, Nik," she reflected as she switched on the kettle. I watched her over the kitchen counter.

"Here there's a lot to stimulate and motivate me."

"People or places?" I asked.

She poured hot water over the tea bag and added milk and sugar. She stirred it gently and handed me the cup.

"Both."

"You know that's what I admire in you- your clarity of thought," I said.

She smiled.

"No I mean it." I let my glance move over her. "So when do we go out?"

Medha teased. "You are asking me out at last!"

I laughed. "Better late than never."

We both laughed. It was a delicious start to the day.

I drove back home with contentment in my heart. The mobile buzzed; it was mom. I had not spoken to her for a week now, ever since she had gone to Dehradun with her sister to stay with my grandmother. She asked about me, Priyanka and Neha, telling me she was missing Neha a lot. She told me she was fine and enjoying the lovely weather and catching up with her old friends in Dehradun. The call was short and sweet. Suddenly I realized, I was missing her too.

She had refused to stay with me or my brother; Instead she chose to stay with her mother, who had been her pillar of strength ever since Dad had expired but who was really old now and needed her more. Living life on her own terms , that was what my mother was all about and I admired her for it. She had been a bubbly, chirpy mother who would always be ready with a smile on her face. I had never seen her sad while I was growing up. She would always find excuses to celebrate little, seemingly insignificant moments of life and I had come to value every moment in life. She would make us smile all the time. It was either baking a cake for us, taking us for picnics and rides, watching a movie together, teaching us to cook , dancing with us, playing poker on Diwali when we were grown up...life had been a never ending party for us. But I had seen the sadness engulf her after Dad passed away. She never remained the same. Something died in her, I guess. Although Dad had left enough money in the bank and she put our Dehradun house on rent, she started embroidering cushions, bed covers, table linen to make some extra bucks. My grandparents were a great support but it saddened me to see her lose a part of herself. She never lost her grace and courage and I simply adored that in her.

Rishi

I looked at my watch again. It was only eight. I had already sat an extra hour in office without much work. My colleagues had already left for home but I still could not gather my energy to get up and proceed towards home. There was however no other option but to leave. I had to get back to at least eat and sleep in that lonely place that had ceased to be home.

I shut down my laptop, put back the reading glasses in the leather case, arranged the strewn papers in a file, put back the half eaten bag of chips in my drawer, locked the cabinet, collected my car keys and mobile, switched off the lights of my cabin and left quietly.

I had come to this country hoping to have a peaceful, comfortable life with my family and here I was, alone in a foreign land with not a soul to call my family. I remembered the narrow, cobbled, dirty, smelly lanes of Kanpur-my home town and realized I was missing it all today.

I called up Medha as I pulled over.

"How are you? How's Yash?" I asked.

"He's fine, enjoying himself."

"I guess even his mother is enjoying herself."

"You have a problem with that?"

"Of course not. It's your life." I replied stiffly.

"Stop fooling yourself. You always grudge me my happiness."

"I have no grudge. You decided to move away from me. It's not a cakewalk for me either."

"Look Rishi, I don't want to get into this mess again. You have to accept it and move on …but … I feel sorry for you."

"Why should you feel sorry for me?"

"Because you have got to understand that sometimes too much effort can ruin things. You have to let it go. Sometimes things don't work if we try too hard."

" Yes of course, I am trying too hard to understand what went wrong between us but how much difference does it make to you- hardly any."

Medha kept quiet for a few seconds. Maybe she did not want to converse with me at all? Maybe she was getting weary of my phone calls?

Medha steered the conversation towards Yash.

"Yash got selected into the cricket academy; he's damn excited."

I tried to sound happy. "That's great."

Medha kept her tone even. "I have to shop for his shoes and clothes."

I could sense her hurry to finish the phone call.

"Where is he? Let me talk to him."

"He's just gone over to a friend's house down our lane."

I sighed.

"He has promised me he's going to work hard once he gets admission and give it his best shot. But I am not pressurizing him too much-."

"I'll talk to him."

Medha continued. "Also guide him on how to shave. He's getting a stubble now but he is adamant that he won't shave. I tried to reason…"

"I will, don't worry."

The conversation carried on a bit more, I realized that we could have a cordial conversation as parents not as spouses.

I breathed deeply and started the car's ignition.

Nikhil

I sat down besides Priyanka attempting to strike a conversation with her. It was around eight pm and I had reached home earlier than usual. I thought a little warmth would help.

"Mom called. She was asking about you and Neha," I began.

Priyanka asked,"How's she?"

"She's good, enjoying her stay."

Priyanka called out aloud, "Khana lagaa de Bano."

"How are things at work?" I asked.

"Since when have you started asking me things that do not concern you?"

I caught her bitterness.

"I just asked a simple question. if you are not interested in talking then..." I said.

She got up and started folding the newspaper strewn across the dining table.

"I am interested if you really want to talk, not if you are on a guilt trip."

"What do you mean guilt?"

"I can sense what you don't even tell me Nikhil. Don't forget we have lived with each other for ten years and that's not a short time."

I felt the sweat on my forehead. What did she know? And why was she behaving so weirdly? I had only wanted to strike a conversation and loosen her up a bit. What the heck was wrong with her?

I walked out of the room. My marriage had been getting dull and lifeless for the last few years and connecting with Medha was like escaping to a fantasy land- a world where I could be who I really was without the baggage of who I had become. It was a state of joy where I reconnected with myself. The emotional distance between me and Priyanka was becoming an obstruction in our marriage.

I walked out on the lawn and sat on the swing. There was no breeze but the weather had begun to turn colder and winter was just a few weeks away. Bano arrived to announce that dinner was served.

That night I lay in bed surrounded by Medha's thoughts. I met her for coffee the next day. She looked fetching in a white salwar suit matched with a blue and white printed dupatta. I could not take my eyes off her face, the big blue round bindi on her forehead was distracting me.

I looked at her. "I feel marriage restricts you as a person, I mean the right to develop other close relationships."

Medha adjusted her dupatta. "Depends on what you are as a person. I feel once you are open to relationships, the rest follows without any conflict. Being married doesn't come in the way."

I stirred the sugar in her coffee. "You end up becoming a robot, fulfilling the wishes and demands as a father and a husband and your own desires go for a toss."

Medha looked deep into my eyes. "I too felt handcuffed as a mother and wife and had to break free. Either be true to yourself and confront it or accept whatever is there without complaining."

I took a sip of the coffee. "I know. The humdrumness of life makes it very challenging."

Medha tossed her hair.

"The moment we define someone as a spouse, sort of label them, everything falls flat. It's the sheer dynamics of marriage."

I drew in my breath. "Yes we get so caught up in making the whole damn thing work…"

"That it doesn't flow like a river anymore," Medha completed my thought.

"That is why nameless relationships are more beautiful. We don't put them in boxes or bracket them in chambers to stifle their flow," she said.

"But they are not easy to nurture either," I ran my fingers through my hair.

"They are, if you need them. We can let go of our wants but not of our needs."

I rummaged for an answer. "Again depends and sometimes it takes us a long time to realize what is it we need and what is it we want."

Medha looked at me. Her eyes seemed to light up something inside me.

There was silence.

Silence, we could listen to and feel its echo in our souls.

It filled up the emptiness between us, cushioning the hardness of our rocky marriages somehow.

❧❖❧

I saw Medha step out of her car and proceed towards the Costa Coffee outlet in Greater Kailash II, where I was waiting for her. The street was buzzing with traffic and cars were honking as she weaved her way through. The sun had just set and the glow of sunset still remained. I quickly looked at my watch. It was six on the dot. She was on time as usual. She looked a bit different today though. I had never seen her wear this beautiful shade of purple before. It suited her wonderfully and I liked the way her hair cascaded down softly on her shoulders in gentle curls.

"Hi," Medha beamed.

We stepped closer and hugged.

"Did I make you wait?" she enquired.

"A lot."

Medha smiled at me- her eyes warm and soft.

"Let's order something" I said rather abruptly and proceeded towards the cash counter. Medha followed me. We ordered two caramel lattes and a rockslide brownie. Once we had settled on the tan sofas, Medha prodded me. "Are you ok? What's bothering you Nik? You are not your normal self."

I fixed my eyes on the poster behind her.

"Oh! Nothing."

"Please Nik, tell me."

"It's become a daily routine now- these arguments at home."

She crossed her arms. "What happened now?"

"I lost my cool today."

"What happened?"

"You know how busy I am; I hardly get time even for myself; running an agency is no joke."

"I agree," she nodded her head.

"And late night is a common thing. I've been reaching home late for the past two weeks and yesterday..."

I continued. "She took off that I don't care for the family. I am a workaholic, selfish and self centered."

I ran my fingers through my hair. "I know my personal life is not the same. Time constraints have taken their toll. I understand this but..." my voice broke as I looked away.

Medha held my hand. "If you understand her pain, you will be able to deal with it."

"We had a major argument and she hasn't spoken a word to me since yesterday. I mean how am I supposed to know what's going on inside her? She has to talk, damn it!

I felt the kindness in Medha's face.

"I can't take this coldness...I am sick of making efforts and she has got to understand that this Advertising Agency is my baby. How much effort I had put in after Nalin back stabbed me and took away the entire business from me? I had to start all over again." I said.

The road outside was very crowded now and the street lights

had come alive shattering the ensuing darkness of the coming night.

"Your coffee ma'am." The voice of the waitress intruded.

Medha stirred. I saw her skin glow under the dull lights of the coffee shop. The waitress kept down the coffee and the brownie in front of us. Thin wisps of smoke rose from the cups. Medha listened as I spoke about how my brother Nalin had cheated me and usurped the Agency. The court battle that lasted five years and how I finally won, got my share and started my own Agency. Medha watched me with tenderness as I poured my heart out. She remained silent, patiently listening.

"I have never seen you so angry before," Medha spoke after a while.

"I don't know- I have felt like this after a long time–you know… sorry I..." The words just left me.

"It's really ok. You may not realize it Nik but maybe you are focusing too much on work, you need to balance it out."

"My work is my worship; she has to understand it and if she can't then too bad…"

Medha took a sip of her coffee and gazed at me. I gazed back at her.

Many seconds later she murmured, "Your eyes are much softer now. I like them this way, without the anger."

I felt my heart squeeze.

She leaned closer to me. "But I still see a lot of pain in them which I want you to give to me, forever."

I felt the heat rise to my face.

I whispered, "You are not meant to take my pain." I turned my eyes away from her. I couldn't bear to look into her eyes anymore. I reached out to her and embraced her.

Medha

I stretched myself and moved my eyes over my bed. The sun's rays had set the tiny pink lilies ablaze on the bed sheet and the white lace curtains were soaked in yellow sunlight. The winter chill sieved through the window and caressed me. I soaked in the glint on the grass and gazed at the plants swaying in the early morning breeze. This was heaven.

Nikhil had called in the morning and we had a long chat. It was becoming a regular feature now- to start and end the day with his voice. I got out of bed lazily. His voice still lingered in my ears. Whenever I spoke to him, there was a deep, unconscious part of me that seemed to sing. It was better to get down to the humdrum life in order to bring myself back to my senses. I tied my hair and headed towards the washroom.

I felt all charged up to face the day and go back to my writing. When I was with him, I always felt something deep that seemed to lift me instantly. I wanted to soak myself deeper in this feeling.

It was rather strange how I had blamed myself for the coldness I had felt towards Rishi, I had begun to wonder if I was becoming sexually frigid. But today I had felt the desires rising inside me, tiny waves appearing on the surface and I knew the storm was inevitable.

I opened the window and felt the brush of breeze on my cheeks. I had not seen this side of Nikhil earlier and this vulnerability seemed to draw me towards him almost seductively. The warmth of his embrace still remained and I shivered with a desire I hadn't felt in ages.

***

Nikhil and I had not been able to meet for a week now, and the restlessness to be with him had mounted high. I craved for his presence and realized I was getting addicted to him very slowly. I looked at myself in the mirror. The long mint green skirt that I wore seemed to match well with the sleeveless, crème, crochet blouse.

The doorbell rang and my heart jumped.

His eyes trailed me from top to bottom as we sat in the corner seats of the dimly lit restaurant, so that we could get the requisite privacy.

"You look good," Nikhil said.

"Thanks," I tried to look away from him.

"So how was the book signing?"

"Good. There was a decent crowd and lots of questions, all very interesting."

His eyes engaged mine. "Good."

We sat, aware of our desires reflected in our eyes. Our hands grazed each other and I felt my body flutter. We didn't say anything and Nikhil shifted next to me. The warmth of his eyes sliced through me as I held his gaze. He reached for my hand and moved closer to me, aware of the effect he had on me. Our cheeks brushed even as our lips barely felt the softness of each other. Nikhil's mobile buzzed, shattering the sanctity of the moment. We both withdrew abruptly. Nikhil collected himself in an instant before answering the call.

"I am busy in a meeting," he fumbled. "Anything urgent? Let me call you back."

The urgency in his voice was tinged with restlessness. He threw his head back and closed his eyes.

"All well?" I asked, sheepishly.

"Yes, the usual domestic stuff it was Priyanka."

Our hands had disengaged by now and before we could move towards each other, the waiter arrived.

"Your order sir."

I saw the longing flash and die in Nikhil's eyes. I felt my own desires crashing silently.

We ordered the food and filled up the spaces between us till the arrival of the food, talking of Nikhil's travel, my book signing and writing. The incompleteness of our encounter lingered like the taste of a half eaten chocolate.

As I sat next to him in the car on our way back, I felt the dizziness take me over and just being next to him today made me nervous. Nikhil drove as it didn't really matter who sat next to him. I marvelled at his nonchalance. We spoke to dispel the silence, deliberately. Words were needed to fill up the crevices between us, and still they were not enough to close the gap, that we had become acutely aware of in the restaurant. It had to be closed, completed. It was a need waiting to be fulfilled.

The car screeched to a halt outside my house. The street was dark with not a soul around. The night was cold and the silver disc of the moon floated amidst the clouds. Nikhil switched off the lights of his car and I watched him. Against the faint blue moonlight, I saw the light in his eyes as he reached for me. I felt his fingers, light as a feather touch my cheeks and then circle my mouth. He moved closer, his breath all over my face and I smelled him...inhaled him for the first time. My lips trembled as I saw the light in his eyes growing brighter. Suddenly he seized my hair and locked his lips over mine, tasting me, drinking me like a thirsty traveller.

This kiss had been suspended in the air for twenty long years. It was a kiss that had been lost on so many occasions; a kiss I had longed for all my life. It was like the bursting of fireworks in the sky and for the first time I felt I had risen and expanded a bit, just like the river that climbs down the hill and spreads itself wide on its journey.

We both relished the deliciousness of the kiss like a feast and when our lips parted, I knew we had crossed the line of friendship forever.

Nikhil

I settled myself on the garden swing and opened the newspaper. The sunlight streamed through the trees and fell all around, warming up the chilly winter morning. Bano arrived with my morning tea. The ribbon of smoke rising from the hot milky tea soothed me instantly.

"Has madam left for the office?" I enquired.

"No, not yet," Priyanka said, walking towards me.

Bano started walking back.

I shifted wondering why Priyanka was still at home. She usually left by 8.30. I checked the time on my mobile. It was 8.48 am.

She sat down on the cane chair, facing me. "Wondering, why I am still at home?"

I caught the sarcasm in her voice but trained my eyes on the newspaper instead.

"Come on, ask me?"

"I am not interested."

"Why would you be also? Life's one long holiday for you. You come in as you please, you take off as you wish. There is no one to question you or hold you responsible."

I chose to be silent.

Priyanka poured herself a cup of tea.

"Bloody coward," she muttered under her breath.

"Excuse me." I said, falling into the trap.

"I know how busy you are. You expect me to believe its work?" Priyanka yelled.

"It's work and if you don't trust me…"

"As if I don't know you. You just need a reason to be over friendly with people," she said tersely.

"That's the way I am; you need to understand this."

"I am supposed to understand everything about you. What about you." She spat back.

"Listen I am in no mood to argue with you."

Her eyes widened. "Yes, you can only argue with your girlfriends."

I threw up my hands in despair. "You have a problem with everything in my life. They are good friends for God's sake."

"Friendship between a man and a woman is not possible?"

I felt my face flame.

"Grow up please. Widen your thoughts. You have a one track mind so you will think one dimensionally only. You can have a healthy friendship if you know where to draw the line."

She paused for a while before she spoke. "And if you don't?"

"If you don't, then that's destiny and whatever has to happen will eventually happen but things would go far worse if one is pushed towards it," I said and got up to leave.

Her face twisted. "You mean I am pushing you towards it."

"You may not realize that you might be doing exactly that Priyanka. Look at the way you talk. Sometimes you don't converse with me for days and then when you do, you pick up fights."

She slammed the cup on the glass table. "Oh! What do you expect me to do? Wait for you to make an effort to talk to me, share your life with me or bloody fuck me?"

I looked away. This was becoming tough.

"Two people can be right at the same time and still can be wrong for each other. Maybe we both are…" I felt the words leave my mouth.

"You mean we are both in a wrong marriage, then what next Nikhil?"

I seemed lost for more words. "I don't know." I started to walk back to the house.

"Run, escape...that's all you can do. Bloody bast…"

I walked on without looking back, relieved at escaping her. I was in no mood for an argument or an emotional dissection. The problem was, I never was. But as of now I had to escape.

To Medha. She was the only one who understood my pain and who loved me in spite of me being me.

"I have spread my dreams under your feet;
Tread softly because you tread on my dreams."
—WB Yeats

Medha
March 2009

The evening sun was setting far away streaking the sky with hues of gold, ruby and topaz. It appeared like a painting–perfect and seamless. I looked at Nikhil. The smell of grilled asparagus with blue cheese salad rose in the air. It had taken us so many months to reach here. We had demolished every excuse that had come in the way of our desires, determined to quench our thirst for each other and decipher the codes of our happiness. And here we were, in Mumbai.

The sixteen years of my married life with Rishi seemed non-existent at this moment. I felt like a twenty year old in a forty year old body. I found it hard to take my eyes off him even as I raised the glass of Shiraz to my lips and took a sip. The night glowed under the stars; relishing a meal at the seaside Italian restaurant of a Mumbai hotel with Nikhil, seemed perfect. The black, red and white interiors made the place elegant and a live band crooned a seductive number in the background. I adjusted my streaked chiffon dupatta over my short charcoal kurti. I felt the softness of my tresses on my bare arms. Nikhil was sitting, his head thrown back. He looked more like an aspiring model than the owner of an advertising agency. My heart was in my mouth and I wondered whether this was just a dream.

Nikhil attacked the pan, seared scallops and penne and swirled it briskly in roasted pepper sauce, stuffed it inside his mouth and washed it down with a gulp of the wine. The sound of waves, punctured the stillness of the night.

His whiskey coloured eyes were focused on me and there was no escape from them.

"You wrote that love scene?" he asked.

"Oh I did! technically it's a sex scene."

"So what happens in the scene?"

"They make love, what else?"

"Thanks. I didn't know that a love scene meant that?"

I laughed.

The storm in my heart had been deafening for the last few days. I had perhaps never waited for any moment as this one. I could clearly feel the world around me collapsing, disintegrating and becoming formless. Nikhil's eyes were locked with mine. I felt drawn to him like a moth to a flame, fearless and flirty. I knew I was living out my fantasy exactly as I had seen it.

I polished off the asparagus, wondering if the appetite for food was a mere camouflage for my emotions and Nikhil's scorching presence. The sea roared.

***

"Come on tell me," Nikhil pleaded.

"It's better if you read it. Writers don't discuss their work-in-progress."

Nikhil's eyes turned warmer. "I can guess what you must have imagined."

"It would be a little tough for you to imagine what I can."

He grinned. "Really! You doubt my potential."

I winked at him. "The protagonist is wild and restless."

Nikhil leaned closer. He smelled of wine and talc. "You still don't know how wild I can be?"

"I don't mind a bit of an education…" I murmured.

I could see the hunger in his eyes. I drank unabashedly but the thirst seemed far from quenched. It had only grown manifold. My eyes begged him to leave me but he was unforgiving. The wine was sipped only as a ritual. I felt the desires intensifying. I felt the moment Nikhil would touch me, I would disintegrate. I wanted to slow down the moment just like the slow motion of camera in movies, unhurried and sluggish. I wanted to capture each tiny speck of its existence and cocoon it in my heart forever.

The mobile rang Nikhil disengaged his eyes and I was thankful for the intervention. It was hard to resist him damn! I was with him. I had never hoped to see him again, let alone be here and be desired by him in ways I had always dreamt of. I turned my eyes towards the sea. The water shone with the glint of the silvery moon. Nikhil finished his phone call and returned to his chair. He sipped the wine and I watched his soft mouth curve. His eyes rested on me again. I knew this was destined.

I circled the rim of my glass with my finger. "Don't look at me like that. You make me nervous."

"I thought that was an art you had," Nikhil said, with a teasing smile.

"Come on you are better at it than me," I said.

The wine was delicious and I sipped it slowly. His eyes were undressing me and I felt as if he could see every throbbing fragment of my being.

"Can I ask you something?" he said gently.

I tilted my head.

"Tell me your wildest," he whispered, leaning closer to me "sexual fantasy."

"You tell me yours first."

"Come on, let's hear it," I dared him.

He leaned back in his chair. "Take a guess."

"That's not fair…out with it."

He held my gaze. "I am the master, she is my slave. I drive her wild with prolonged foreplay. I instruct her and she obeys my commands, doing what I tell her."

Nikhil continued. "She tries to resist me but I overpower her. She is ready, begging me to enter her but I don't. I tie her to the bed as she struggles, begs me profusely…she's on fire and then as I enter her, she calms down."

I felt the heat rise between my thighs. I looked at Nikhil... dazed and drunk.

Nikhil raised the wine to his lips. "It's your turn now."

I looked away. I was slipping into an abyss that I had always wanted to drown in, and now that the moment was approaching, I somehow couldn't help but feel helpless. What a strange twist of fate? I could hear my own heartbeat loud and clear. I felt paralyzed, unable to move.

"I need to leave." I said to myself.

"I don't tell my fantasies." I whispered as I moved closer to him. "I prefer to play them out."

His eyes probably saw the raw desire on my face.

"I am game," he said lustily.

His eyes had already made me drunk with desire. My eyes invited him as I entered the glass elevator.

❧❖❧

I closed the door behind me as I entered the room and flung my dupatta on the chair. I was restless to take a shower. I looked at myself in the huge mirror. I had never felt so beautiful. I smoothed my hand over my face which was full and round now, not thin and angular like it had been when I was younger. I noticed my pale, wheatish complexion appeared glowing today. I traced the lacy, skin coloured bra, faintly visible under the cotton kurti with my hands and felt a quiver run through my breasts.

I smiled dimly and reached the huge French windows, pulling aside the soft crème curtains. I opened them, letting the breeze in. The dark sea roared in the background, lighted up by a lonely ship somewhere deep in the middle. I turned around to see the shell shaped lamps, that lit up the yellow and white roses on the bed sheet. The smell of the fresh, long stemmed amethyst lilies, kept in the crystal vase next to the bed drifted in the air. There was a flutter inside my heart, like a restless storm was about to break me.

I moved towards the bathroom. My physical exhaustion was at its peak yet there was a weird peace that had descended on me. As I turned on the shower on my tired body, I felt a tingling. I could feel the adrenaline rising. The cold rush of water rejuvenated me instantly. I hummed a song and relished the delicious fall of water on my body. The doorbell rang. I knew it was him. I drew the plum coloured robe around myself and rushed to the door. Nikhil stood in front of me, scanning me as I dripped water, my wet hair coiled just above my breasts. I was suddenly aware of the softness of the purple and crèam carpet below my feet. The breeze rushed into the room, curling around my wet body and I shivered. I knew then what it meant to be weak at the knees. I tried hard to avoid his intense gaze. I have you, his eyes seemed to say.

"I...I'll jj...ust change and ..." I stammered.

Nikhil's eyes instructed me not to move and my feet were glued to the carpet. I was slowly losing all sense of myself. He locked the door behind him and moved slowly towards me. His eyes were locked with mine. He reached for me and pulled me close to him. As we stood close to each other, I inhaled his rich and intoxicating fragrance. I felt his breath on my face. There was a sense of déjà-vu... I had seen Nikhil make love to me, with the waves crashing in the background in my dreams many times.

He brushed his lips over mine. His tongue reached inside the hollowness of my mouth. The last time that Rishi had made love to me was eight months ago and these months had left me feeling like a virgin. I had forgotten how it felt to be touched. My body tightened as his lips became hungrier, responding to him.

His hands untied the string of my bath robe and as the robe fell in a heap, I could no longer look at him. I found myself melting, within the confines of his strong arms. The hunger was at its peak and I ripped his shirt off his body and felt him for the first time with my bare hands. I buried my face on his hairy chest, moving my mouth over his nipples and kissing him with all the tenderness I never knew existed inside me. My damp body still smelled of the shower gel and my wet hair was still dripping. His hands moved all over as if they knew each and every contour of my body, as if he had always belonged there.

I watched him undress with a complete lack of self conscious-ness. His tall, supple body looked so vulnerable. He picked me up with a single sweep and laid me gently on the bed looking deeper into my eyes. I felt the mist rise in my eyes and flow out. He kissed the tears and my face all over in acknowledgement of the pain that we had been through. I gazed deeply into his eyes. He moved his hands over my breasts, kneading them gently. A sigh escaped my lips. My body rocked like waves on the sea. I watched the softness in his eyes, the tenderness embracing me and taking me over.

He closed his mouth around the nipple and I felt his hunger for the first time. It wet me instantly.

He moved lower. He opened my legs and stroked the insides of my thighs, grazing the triangular matt with his lips. As his tongue searched for the moistness inside me, I let out a loud moan. I felt an unexplained frenzy rise within my body and accumulate at the exact spot where his tongue was. His tongue tasted me...the pink, moist insides of me and I writhed in ecstasy. His appetite seemed to grow and my moans grew louder. I felt as if I would disintegrate into a million pieces. I was slowly merging with him. Where I began and where I ended, I was myself not aware. Nikhil nibbled at my ears and moaned "I love you…oh! I love you."

The endearment drove me crazy. I moaned. "I love you too" and moved my hands around his inner thighs. He stiffened and grew hard. I brushed my lips on the insides of his crotch and took him inside my mouth. My body trembled and shivered. I felt the soft, fleshy part of him growing hard and erect. He cried out loud. I moved above him stroking him and caressing him. As he moved beneath me, his moans grew stronger and he pulled me up with his strong arms. The winds whipped at the curtains and the room resounded with the crashing of the waves outside.

When he began to enter me, the frenzy was at its peak. I rose and fell like tides in the sea with every thrust that moved inside me.

All fear seemed to leave me. It was as if my fear had suddenly found wings and had flown away, never to return. I was no longer afraid of losing anything- anything at all.

My moans became his; my cries became his; and all that mattered was for me to merge with him. I wanted to scream but all my sensations were muted by the profundity of the moment. He looked at me and I knew he caught the unmistakable triumph of once unrequited love in my eyes. He hugged me firmly, crushing me and then he whispered, "I love you Medha." and at last, I felt completed and sewn–stitched to the last seam.

Medha

The morning sun filtered through the curtains and flooded the room. I turned around to see it illuminating the small, round birthmark on his shoulder. His face was calm and he slept content as a child. I kissed him on his lips careful not to wake him up from his deep sleep. I kept caressing him with my eyes as if that was all there was for me to see. We had only been able to sleep by half past three in the morning. We had talked and then made love again and I had wondered from where the hunger for love arose?

I knew he had reclaimed a part of me forever. I needed only *him* to claim me, own me at this point in my life when I was hungry for an emotional anchor to ground me. We had been two ravenous souls who had fed on each other without any constraint, pretense or regret. And that it had been so pure and beautiful, so untainted and divine.

I walked towards the window and pulled aside the curtains. The blue sea was calmer than last night but one could still glimpse a residue of last night's restlessness. The sunlight kissed the water and turned it into a sheet of silver. The sky opened up in front of me like a seamless canvas.

Mumbai would always remain special for me, I thought. Here in this city we had found each other and the anonymity of the place was somehow seductive. I smiled, tempted to wake up Nikhil but decided in favour of a shower instead.

I let the water cascade down my body. The water traced its way over every part of my body and I recalled everything about last night. He had finally possessed me. I had seen in his eyes that I was all that he had in this world. All I ever wanted was to feel him, to find the twenty two year old boy in this forty one year old man; to feel the dizziness and sweetness of intimacy; to experience a connection that would skyjack my soul, mind and body. All I wanted was a part of him and I had it now.

But it had not merely been a night of raw passion for both of us. Our bodies had merely been a means to reach each other's hungry souls. I realized that sex was a life force that determined one's perspective of a lot of things. I had heard from others that it was a spiritual energy but had only felt it last night. I understood what I had missed with Rishi till now. I could sense it clearly...the yawning gap between having sex and making love. How was I supposed to go back now to a marriage which had emotionally expired and had gone sexually dead? I shuddered.

I began humming an old song and finished my bath. I patted myself dry and stepped out of the bathroom, wrapped in the king sized towel.

"Good Morning" Nikhil drawled.

"How come you got up so early?"

"Who wants to sleep when you are around?" he murmured.

I sensed the heat rise inside my damp body.

"You..."

"Why not?"

He moved closer to me.

I held on tightly to my towel and smiled. I walked towards the other side of the bed to reach for my clothes but he lunged towards me and yanked off my towel before I could save myself. He gathered me in his arms and kissed me.

I was too smitten to resist.

***

I turned the key in the lock and pushed open the door of my Gurgaon house. There was a lightness in my step and elation in my spirits. Nikhil had departed at the door after helping me with my bag. His kiss lingered on my lips and I smiled to myself. I sank on the leather sofa in the livingroom. The evening was fading away and there was a certain mystery in the vanishing remnants of the day. My eyes however moved inside the room and trailed everything that occupied it. The brown ebony Cuckoo clock that I had bought at an exhibition a few months back, the grass green sofas with raw silk cushions, the wrought iron corner with glass shelves with various curios. My eyes rested on a photo frame- Sonal and me framed in a mother of pearl frame. I hugged a cushion.

Sonal and I had not spoken to each other for many days. And to imagine that there was a time when I could not hide even a sliver of my feelings from her. She was always the first to know what I was going through; whether I was happy, sad, dejected, disillusioned, angry or irritated, she knew it all. She was my friend, philosopher, and guide. We had shared countless special moments and had been inseparable. And then somewhere we lost the thread that connected us. It was not the same anymore. Sonal's marriage to Rohil changed a lot of things between us. She became more guarded...perhaps faintly resenting the things that she admired in me earlier...my outspokenness, honesty, childlike trust in everything, my chilled out attitude. My marriage and motherhood also changed me and our lives somehow didn't seem to fit into each other's as it did earlier.

I picked up the framed photograph and regarded it, my eyes glassy with tears. Maybe we had outgrown each other but I still loved her and missed her, specially today. Will Sonal ever know what I experienced today? Would I be able to tell her: "Sonal you were wrong when you told me, don't follow a mirage...Nikhil will never have the courage to love you..."

My lips quivered and I cried. I wandered out with bare feet to the lawn outside. Why did the pain of the past catch up with the happiness of the present sometimes? The feel of the wet grass soothed me. A tiny red and yellow butterfly fluttered about and settled down on one of the flowers. I smiled. The garden was beautiful like my life felt at the moment.

I sat down on the grass, flooded with the contentment of having been touched at last; of my entire being illuminated to the core. I sat still for a long time. The house was quiet. Yash was away to Muscat and although I knew it was imperative for father and son to spend time alone with each other his going away seemed destined somehow. But I was missing him now.

The mobile buzzed.

"I was thinking of..."

Nikhil cut me short, "Don't think too much of me or you will find me around."

I smiled. "So who's afraid of having you around?"

"Are you sure? Have no regrets later?"

"You know I'm not the kind to regret."

"Then open the door, I'm standing outside."

"Nik...you can't be serious? I mean you just left..."

"Open the door," his voice was unnerving.

I rushed to open the door and there he was standing with a bunch of beautiful red roses.

"You never went home, did you?"

He tilted his head "No I didn't, I couldn't in fact." and entered the house. I closed the door behind him. He handed me the roses.

"This is for giving me the most beautiful night of my life and the rosiest morning ever," he said.

I looked at him with disbelief. I took the roses from him and kissed them. Setting them aside, I moved into his arms. Our lips locked with an urgency and passion that only seemed to belong to new lovers. It was hard to let go of each other.

"I never knew you could be so romantic!" I declared.

He smiled, tracing my face with his fingers."Well you still have to learn a lot about me babes."

"I guess so," I said.

He reached for my hand. "What's wrong? You fine?"

"I have never felt so special ever in my life."

Nikhil hugged me. He murmured, "I better get going. Neha must be waiting for me."

I felt the warmth inside me evaporate. Why did he need to mention Neha at such an intimate moment?

"You spoke to her?" I asked.

"Yes I did and she said she'll wait for me."

I rubbed his arms tenderly. "Then you better get going."

We stepped out into the evening hand in hand. The daylight had already faded. We kissed each other goodbye. As Nikhil's car pulled out from the parking and moved away, I noticed a flock of birds dotting the sky. Their urgency to return home showed in their flight. The car was swallowed by the bend in the road. The evening was warm and the stillness of the night was fast catching up with the evening. I stood there longer than usual then retraced my steps inside the house.

Nikhil

As I drove back home, I combed my fingers through my hair. The wind blew hard and I loved the way it brushed against my face. It had been a good idea to park the car at the airport before we took that flight to Mumbai. This had been a day that had come in my life unplanned and in the most unexpected manner. I had wanted to soothe the ache in Medha's heart and to feel desired and wanted. I had not touched Priyanka in the last six months. I had almost forgotten what it felt like to be naked next to a woman. I felt my heart beat faster than usual. How could I possibly tell my wife now that in the arid land of my emotions, I had finally found an oasis? That I was happy and felt loved at last.

I increased the volume of the CD player. Bryan Adam's voice crooned–summer of 69 and I tapped my fingers on the steering wheel. My heart was full of love. Medha's smiling face flooded my mind and I smiled. The feel of her satiny body and intoxicating smell were still wrapped around me. Last night had fulfilled me in a way hitherto unknown to me. Medha had surprised me. There was a rawness in the way she had made love to me, coalesced with tenderness. Medha had not only surrendered to me totally but had given me unheard and unfelt pleasures. I experienced a hard-on just thinking about her. I yearned to have her in my arms right now. The music played and I hummed the song aloud.

My thoughts returned to Priyanka after a while.

When I had met her for the first time, after my parents had arranged our meeting for matrimony, I had found no reason to say a no to her. I was already thirty and I knew if I did not get married now, probably I never would. And when I had married her, I had never thought that there would be someone else who would take up the special place in my heart. I was sure that my arranged marriage would be like so many thousand others where both people lived together in spite of all odds. Why had the distance begun to creep in my marriage and when had Priyanka and I ceased to be a couple. The question hung in my mind like a web.

The normal squabbles which I thought were common features in every marriage were the ones I should not have ignored. Maybe I should have. I honked at the car in front of me. It was being driven unusually slowly. The car gave way and I sped past it. Medha's entry into my life had been a complete turnaround for me. She made me laugh at myself.

"Don't take yourself too seriously Nik. Take it easy," she would often say.

She was so chilled out and gave me so much space. Where are you? What are you doing? When will you be back? Priyanka had begun to make me feel claustrophobic in our marriage. I guess my life had become too mechanical. I had forgotten to enjoy myself, to laugh aloud without any reason, to hang out with my friends . I paid a heavy price for having a wife who had put an embargo on the very things that made up the core of my personality. But Medha had fuelled my enthusiasm and my passions. She would always talk of things that I liked to do in my spare time–dancing, photography, hanging out with my friends.

I realized I was home. The lights were still on and that meant Neha was still awake. I rushed to be with my only child.

I entered her room stealthily, careful not to make any noise. Neha was reading and the table lamp lit up a corner of her room. She was totally engrossed in the book.

"Hi sweetie," I whispered in Neha's ears.

Neha was startled but her face broke into a huge smile.

She leapt to hug me. "I was waiting for you… you are so late."

I hugged her tightly "I wanted to surprise you so I didn't call. How's my sweetheart?"

Neha had grown into a fine girl for her twelve years. Tall and slim with a good complexion, straight, silky brown hair, an almond shaped face that cracked up with a smile very often, highlighting a set of pearly white teeth every time her lips parted shining like gems in the dark. Most of my friends had remarked that she had all the trappings of a beauty queen in the making.

"So how was your trip, dad?" Neha asked.

"Oh! Great. When are your exams starting?"

Neha huddled close to me. "They start next week."

Bano entered the room with two mugs in a tray. She greeted me and put the tray on the table near Neha's bed.

"How are you, Bano?" I asked.

Bano replied in a barely audible voice. "Fine saab."

She hardly talked and having a conversation with her was a challenge.

"How's Salim miyan?"

"He is fine, sleeping."

I took out a few currency notes from my wallet and gave them to her. "Salim had asked me for an advance before I left. Here is three thousand rupees, just give it to him", I said.

"Shukriya", she said as she took the money and gave a wide smile.

"You are welcome. You go and sleep. We will manage," I said.

Bano gave another smile, ruffled Neha's hair and disappeared. Neha picked up her mug of Bournvita milk and handed over the mug of coffee to me.

I stretched myself in the chair. "Is Mom asleep?"

"She said she was going to sleep an hour ago."

"Great. So what did you do these two days?"

Neha's eyes shone. "We had loads of fun. Mom and I went shopping, watched a movie and went to Masi's house for dinner."

I watched her as she spoke animatedly.

"Can I ask you something Dad?" she asked abruptly.

I smiled. "Of course darling."

"You and mom... ?"

"What Neha?"

"You guys–are not the same anymore."

My eyes widened. "What made you think so? Did mom... ?"

"Nopes, Dad. You guys hardly talk as you used to. Mummy sleeps before you. You don't even party together or call friends over."

I held her hands. Looking into her eyes seemed like a big challenge.

"We are absolutely fine, sweetie. It's just that the work pressure is a bit too much and your mom's got a new job too. We are trying to work a way out of this soon," I said, even though I knew it was a lie.

Neha looked at me, doubtful.

"Trust me, sweetheart." I looked down at her clasped hands "It's all fine." I lied again.

Neha seemed to be thinking over something.

I shook her gently. "Are you with me?"

"Yup dad. It's just that I find it a bit..."

"Strange that things are not appearing the same between us?"

"Yes dad, I want to see both of you the same way as you were earlier, laughing, having fun, even having little arguments."

I drew her close and hugged her. I did not know what to tell her, what to promise, what to lie to make her feel better? I only knew one thing: I could never break Neha's heart and hopes. She was just too precious. I would have to talk to Priyanka about this.

I let myself into the bedroom quietly. The gray moonlight sneaked in through the parting of the curtains. I changed into my pajamas and fumbled my way to my side of the bed. Priyanka was fast asleep and the soft murmur of her snoring filled the room.

As I wrapped my arm around the soft pillow, I longed to have Medha with me, to feel her breath on my face and to feel her body under my fingers.

The summer sun was less harsh in the morning but not tempting enough for me to sit under the shaded swing and feel the soft grass under my feet. I settled for the huge window near the dining table and watched the sunlit lawn.

Life seemed so perfect except when I thought of my marriage. The house was quiet except for the chitter chatter of Bano and her husband in the kitchen. Last night's conversation with Neha had shaken me terribly. I had to talk to Priyanka about this. Rajan, my closest buddy was in town and I was meeting him for lunch the next day.

Rajan had been a very lively and boisterous kid in school. Very unlike me, he was the livewire of the group...the eternal joker who used to make everyone laugh. We had become attached ever since we had begun sitting next to each other in class, more by default than by choice. Our class teacher, Mr. Hari Dixit was a strict teacher and since I was a shy, quiet child, he made sure that Rajan sat with me most of the times. Our friendship grew.

I had wanted to share Medha with Rajan for a long time but every time my courage failed me. The fear of being judged always weighed heavy on my mind. I had never thought of confessing my feelings even to my best friend. He was not even aware that Medha meant so much to me.

I had feigned a severance of ties with Rajan for the sake of peace in the house. And now I felt I had diminished myself through this act. If I could not even stand up for my friendship what was I worth? I had confided this to Medha. Her words had disturbed me.

"You have to give importance to relationships that matter to you Nik. Why blame Priyanka? If Rajan is your best friend, you have to stand up for him. Whatever is done is past…look at it as a learning experience... Courage comes from within and can't be bought. It's never too late to make amends…"

I had shared my deepest , dark secrets with Rajan; my first crush at fourteen on my geography teacher, whose beauty was the talk of the school; my affair with Kaisha after I left college, which lasted for three years, my subsequent heartbreak when she left me for another man. It had broken my heart and convinced me that I would never be able to love again. My arranged marriage to Priyanka was the only way out, to restore my sanity. I had felt that having a family was sure to salvage my life somehow.

I shifted my attention to the newspaper and scanned through the headlines with the agility of a professional and sipped tea while it was still hot. Somehow I felt an inner peace. I reminisced how Medha had looked at me when I had given her those roses. My mobile rang and I picked it up with a smile.

"Why are you smiling?" Medha asked.

I took off my reading glasses."How do you know? Can you see through the phone or what?"

"I know you better than you know yourself."

"You bet and how are things?"

"I am just floating. You have made everything so beautiful. I feel I am in a trance."

Her voice grew soft and sensuous and I felt her right next to me.

I whispered, "Get used to these trances. They are going to be a way of life for you."

"Don't spoil me Nik…"

"Why not? You deserve to be spoiled and if you wish, I can come over right now?"

I felt her sigh.

"How's Neha?" she said.

"Neha has not been fine," I admitted.

"What happened?"

"She asked me last night if everything was fine between me and Priyanka coz' we no longer talk or party. I am home late and Priyanka sleeps much before I do."

"Shucks."

I sighed. "And I lied to her that all was well."

There was silence on the phone. All we could hear was the sound of each other's breathing.

I let the words hang between us for a while, before Medha spoke. "You need to be more sensitive to this Nik–I guess you should talk to Priyanka about it. Kids are very perceptive. They can sense things very fast," she said with a lot of concern.

"Yes I need to talk," I said.

I focused on the sunlight that fell in my lap in an interesting pattern. I had to change the conversation.

"Guess what? Rajan is here and I am meeting him for lunch tomorrow."

"Guve him my regards," Medha said.

I smiled "I will. I want you to meet him too."

"Even I want to meet him–I have heard so much about him from you."

"Let me fix up something."

Medha chuckled, "You never know I might like him more than you."

"Then I am not introducing you both."

Medha laughed out. "I love this when you get jealous."

I cleared my throat. "Don't test me too much– I can be bad."

"How bad baby?" Medha teased.

"When I meet you, you will know," I whispered.

I could hear Medha sigh at the other end.

❧❖❧

Priyanka's voice was cold. "Tell me."

"It's something about Neha."

"What? Is she alright?"

"Yes she is. May be it will be better if we speak face to face about it."

Priyanka spoke evenly. "No tell me now, I will be home late."

"Neha feels something's going wrong between the two of us. She was very curious to know that if all was well in our marriage," I said.

There was silence on the phone. As if we both were trying to adjust to the weight of the moment.

"So what did you tell her?"

"I couldn't have told her the truth so I lied."

"As usual," she muttered under her breath.

"What did you say?"

"Listen I have to go, talk to you later" and the phone went dead. I felt a weird knotting in my stomach. Why couldn't she confront me straight instead of spinning the words in loops?

It had been two months since Priyanka had picked up that job and she seemed at peace. She left the house by half past eight in the morning and was back usually by half past six. I realized over a period of time that she enjoyed her work and although I was happy for her, I sensed that in the process of finding her own way in life, she was probably abandoning the path on which we both had been together. Marriage was not her priority anymore. She didn't really care when I came home or left? What I said and what I didn't? The complaints had stopped and also the demands to spend more time with the family. She seemed to be content in her own world and all that mattered was Neha. She had shifted all her attention to her and Neha had become the centre of her universe.

The conversation never got resumed.

I approached her a week later.

"Come on Pri, talk to me," I said.

Priyanka put up her feet on the sofa "There's nothing to talk. I guess we are both aware…"

"I agree but it will be good if we know what to expect from each other."

She stared at the cup of tea in her hands "That won't make things easier, in fact that will complicate matters."

"What makes you think so?"

"I know you well Nikhil. There are certain things which are just beyond you."

"Now that's being too presumptuous. Unless you tell me how would I know?"

Priyanka took a sip of tea. "I don't feel a part of your life anymore."

I let the words settle between us.

"You are a part of my life Priyanka, you know that."

"It's not something you have done but it's something you don't even realize you are heading towards."

"Please don't talk in riddles. Tell me what it is?"

Priyanka rested her eyes on my face "It's everything Nikhil; the way you talk to me, you treat me, the way.you spend or rather do not spend time with your family, the way you are drowned in your work–it's everything."

"Oh my God," I turned away from her.

"Do you want to hear more?" she dared me.

"I have tried to give you and Neha my best... all my care, all my attention, all my time..." I seemed lost for words.

Priyanka attacked me. "Yes, fulfilling your duty as a father, as a husband perfectly."

"Tell me what to do? How to please you then, your Highness?"

"I wish I knew," she said and walked out of the room.

࿇

The Mantra bar was not too crowded but the music was deafening. The black and white graphic interiors of the place lent it a charm and neon lights in blue, red and yellow flashed all around. The smell of alcohol permeated the air. Rajan sat opposite me. Medha was to join us in half an hour. I had been keen for both of them to meet. I was sure Rajan would warm up to Medha instantly. I had known him for too long to even try hiding my thoughts or feelings from him. Even after Rajan had shifted to Turkey to join a leading Oil Company, we had been in touch- through a text message, mail or a phone call. He was conncted to me and the physical distance was merely incidental and inconsequential. Even Priyanka's cynicism had not affected our bond.

Rajan turned towards me after placing the order. "Saale how serious are you about Medha?"

I smiled. "Damn serious yaar."

"What's up with you and Priyanka?"

I formed my hands into a steeple. "Nothing, my marriage is over."

"What are you talking?"

"I have not told you but things have been falling apart for a long time. It seems it is the end," I said.

I stared blankly at the table "We have been growing apart for more than a year now."

The waiter arrived with two cans of Heineken Lager Beer and kept them on the table with a plate of Seekh Kebabs and salted peanuts. Rajan reached for a kebab. "It's going to be a big mess buddy–think before you leap."

I took a swig of the chilled beer. "It's too late for that. I have already leapt."

"You love her?"

"Yes."

Rajan opened his mouth and then closed it. The look in his eyes was one of disbelief. He knew that I was a big hit with girls back in college but to imagine me ending my marriage for love came as a bit of a surprise to him, I guess.

"Shocked?" I enquired.

"To be honest, yes."

I looked at the beer mug. "Trust me, even I am. Meeting Medha and falling for her was not a planned thing. It just happened and I couldn't stop myself."

Rajan put his arm around my shoulders. "I can understand. We do not plan to fall in love."

I checked my watch and looked towards the bar's entrance. Medha was still not in sight.

I took a bite of the kebabs. "Enough about me ... what about you?"

"Things seem to be going a little haywire between me and Malvika too."

"Why?"

"Something seems to be going wrong. It's been there for some time now."

"Talk to her."

"I have but it doesn't seem to work. You know after my divorce, I had put everything in this marriage to make it work but there is this boredom which seems to be creeping in."

"You mean you are no longer excited about this relationship?" I asked.

He hesitated, "Sort of."

"I understand. Try something new…go for a holiday, a quiet dinner somewhere…or."

"Have tried all this but nothing seems to be helping. If a person's attitude is a problem then one can't do much."

I could sense the faint bitterness in his voice. We both seemed to be connected by this common thread of pain somehow and it was so uncanny.

"Give it some time. Sometimes we have to let go of things."

He looked away. "May be…"

"Oh! by the way I met Radhika," Rajan said.

"What?" my jaw dropped.

"You had sworn you would never see her face again."

Rajan drew in his breath. "After our divorce, I know…I was so hurt but I guess I moved past the hurt and bitterness. One has to."

I watched him. "So how come?"

"We just met through some common friends. We are going out for dinner tomorrow."

I noticed the spark in his eyes. He had been madly in love with

Radhika before their marriage fell apart.

"Dil hai ki manta nahi," I joked.

Rajan's face burst into a big smile. "It's good to reconnect with her. She's a divorcee now and has an eight year old daughter too."

I looked away. Attachments were scary.

My gaze returned to the entrance again and I saw Medha walk in. She looked lovely in her knee length black top pulled over her fuchsia tights and ankle length boots. I got up to receive her. As we hugged and kissed, I noticed the fondness with which Rajan watched me. I introduced both of them and gestured to the waiter and ordered more drinks, chicken lollies and crispy sesame spinach rolls.

Rajan smiled at Medha. "At last we meet."

"Yeah! been looking forward to meeting you. Nik keeps talking about you."

Rajan gave a short laugh. "Does he? I heard you are a writer? That must be so exciting."

Medha settled down. "Writing is a very lonely profession. You are alone when you are creating…"

"I can imagine but it must be so fulfilling to create characters."

"Yeah! When they come alive and you get into the mind of each character and explore them."

Rajan asked. "How do you do it?"

The waiter arrived with the drinks and snacks. I passed on the drinks and we raised our glasses and cheered.

Medha took a sip of her scotch. "I make notes about them-their physical characteristics, likes, dislikes, the way they talk , words they use, their fears, doubts, insecurities…although each writer has his or her own way of working."

"Wow! That's so interesting."

"Absolutely," Medha replied.

"And who inspires you?" Rajan asked.

I smiled.

Medha slipped her arm in mine and kissed me tenderly on the cheek. "Nik is my muse now but it could be anybody or anything that you feel connected to."

I realized why Medha was so special for me and would remain. The music was loud and foot tapping and soon Medha and I were on the dance floor while Rajan watched us. She looked happy and contented. We returned to the table after about fifteen minutes and resumed our drinks.

"You guys dance well," Rajan mentioned.

A smile lit up her face "Oh! I love dancing."

"Nik's a natural dancer. He was a rage in school. Girls used to woo him to dance with them." Rajan winked.

"Aha! That's news. He never told me about the school bit."

"About the girls or the dancing?" Rajan said.

"That's one of my best kept secrets," I said, with a laugh.

"Now I am curious to find out the rest of your secrets."

I tucked a strand of hair behind her ears. "You know all my secrets babes."

We all laughed.

Rajan continued, "So what's your next book all about?"

Medha helped herself to the sesame rolls. "Adultery."

Rajan's eyes opened wide. "Wow! What's your take on it?"

I looked at her.

"You see the laws of divorce are only five thousand years old. There was no marriage system in India earlier. Anyone could sleep with anybody they desired."

Rajan wrapped his arm around my shoulders and quipped, "That's cool. Why wasn't I born then?"

I smiled.

Medha smiled and continued, "In traditional societies like Himalayan Garhwali tribe, the Garo and Khasi tribes of north east, Bastar tribe of Madhya Pradesh, Mewati tribe of Rajasthan- adultery was and is the norm."

"Oye Nik- let's join one of these tribes man," Rajan said.

"Is it possible to join them?"

Medha fixed her eyes on me. "I said with a smile. So the book takes a liberal view of infidelity. It talks about open marriage. I believe there is no such word as adultery or infidelity. Words are so powerful that they bracket us or judge us and overtake our lives completely."

I swirled the scotch in the glass. "Good point. I feel that the monotony in a marriage can kill it, so why not try and save it if one can."

Medha's eyes shifted towards Rajan. "But then open marriage requires tremendous trust, strength, and honesty. In fact closed marriages can suffer from emotional, sexual, economic, psychological abuse and…"

"What do you mean by open marriage?" Rajan interrupted.

Medha took a swig of the whiskey and pulled her hair back before she spoke, "Seeking gratification outside your marriage with the consent of your partner."

"Sounds impractical to me," I argued.

"Again depends on what suits whom. It works for some because they feel it makes their marriage more transparent with no fear of emotional blackmail or suffering."

Rajan listened intently to Medha and swallowed the last of his drink. I rested my cheek on the palm of my hand. "But it defeats the whole purpose of marriage–of togetherness, bonding, sharing, commitment…" I said.

"Marriage means different things to different people. Men and women come with different expectations Nik, so you can't judge it harshly. It can mean comfort for one, love for another, security for someone..."

Rajan reached for the fresh refill of his scotch.

"I think happiness is most important- what makes both the partners happy. Screw the rest of the world," Rajan added.

I slapped Rajan's back. "That's not easy as it sounds dude."

"Nothing is easy, least of all marriage. The more I try, the tougher it becomes. I wonder what it is that a wife really wants from her husband?" Rajan said and looked at Medha.

Medha traced the mouth of her glass with her fingers. "Depends. It's not about a man or a woman but about the person."

Rajan tilted his head. "But surely there is something that every woman wants specifically from a man. What do they want damn it?"

"I guess some needs are universal–understanding, love, care, compassion," Medha said, pondering.

"All they want is a man who gives them a comfortable life and is ready to dance to their tunes…."

"Come on now Rajan, that's not fair," I countered him. I could sense that the alcohol was slowly overtaking him.

Rajan stood up. "What's not fair? That's all they want and if we ask for sex then we are called sex-maniacs?"

"Why don't you find out what a woman wants?" Medha said.

"As if that is easy–Men are simple, straightforward whereas you women are damn complicated," Rajan continued.

Medha snorted with laughter. She looked at Rajan as if she could understand his dilemma but couldn't do much beyond it. Rajan was on his sixth drink now.

I reasoned. "You can't generalize. Each person is different and comes with a …"

"Tu saale, you lucky dog- you got Medha. What else do you want?" Rajan blurted. His voice was fairly woozy now.

Medha looked away, clearly embarrassed.

"Rajan let's go," I announced.

He held on to my arm. "Ye-s let's go...I ha-a-ve to g-oo," Rajan drawled. "It wa-as grrr-eat meeting you Medha."

"Same here," Medha said.

Soon I was driving Rajan to his hotel.

Medha

I was meeting him after two long weeks. The past fortnight had been very hectic for both of us. I had been busy with submission of a short story for Anthology of Indian writers to be published soon, while Nikhil had been travelling to Bangalore and Mumbai for various presentations and client meetings.

The breeze was cool and carried a hint of rain in it. The Met office had already announced the arrival of monsoons and I hoped today was the day of the first rain of the season.

We had barely been able to talk to each other except for a few minutes in a day and I had been missing his presence acutely although writing kept me busy most of the time. The time gap had only whetted my passion. I longed for our intimacy.

I had specially chosen a lemon chiffon sari printed with purple roses, matched with a low cut blouse for the occasion. I wanted to dress up differently this time, just to surprise Nikhil. And I had been longing to wear a sari for a long time now.

Nikhil was as usual in his dark blue jeans with a crisp white linen shirt that he had not tucked inside his jeans. I couldn't tear my eyes off him.

We were at the Grand Hyatt's Angeethi restaurant. There were candles lit everywhere. The candle lights flickered and the live band played the song which both of us loved–do lafzon ki hai dil ki kahani–ya hai mohabbat–ya hai jawani...(the heart's story is just about two words–either its love or its youth) I was enthralled by the ambience of the place. Nikhil ordered a bottle of champagne and when it was served, I couldn't help laughing.

"What happened?" His eyes opened wide.

"Oh! remember my book launch party ?"

Nikhil's forehead bunched in a knot.

"You have a bad memory. You emptied almost the entire bottle of champagne on me which Rishi had bought for the occasion," I said, laughing.

Nikhil smiled. "Yes, of course."

"That was really cheeky I must say. I was shocked. Shakal se to shareef lagte ho,"

"Really! Did someone say something?"

I fixed him with a soft gaze. "Of course everyone noticed it including Rishi."

"Did he say something?"

"He didn't but I am sure he must have felt the vibes between both of us."

"That day I was very happy for you and I just wanted to show my fondness for you; how proud I felt."

We both raised our stemmed glasses–a toast to the beautiful times in our lives and tasted the champagne.

Then he led me to the dance floor. The champagne had done its bit to remove any inhibition that I might have nursed. He held me closely as our bodies swayed to the music. He was a natural dancer, moved well and the last day of college flashed in my memory.

I felt sensuous just being with him. The way he looked at me made me feel desired and beautiful. He and I moved with a gay abandon. We danced as if no one was watching. By the time, we were through with dinner; we were both drunk on each other. I did not question him when he booked a room in the same hotel where we were dining.

It was pouring heavily and the sound of the first rain of the monsoon filled my heart with a deep longing. As soon as we were inside the room, all desires broke free. He took my face in both his hands and kissed my lips. I responded with the same hunger. He moved his hands over my body ripping away my sari with an exigency which I had not felt in our earlier encounters. He felt me all over with his lips and made love as if I was all he had–his only treasure in the world.

The rain lashed at the windows of the room.

I was left craving for more. When he entered me this time, it was smooth and I felt seamlessly fused with him.

Frankly, I had thought this one will be a quickie but it turned out to be exactly the opposite. His surrender was complete.

"Why are you so good Nik?" I whispered in his ears.

Nikhil smelled my soft hair. "Coz' you are so good…"

"It's what you bring out of me sweetie."

Nikhil turned me around so that he could look in to my eyes. "So, we both bring out the best in each other?"

I smiled. "It's so strange Nik that different people unleash different things in us."

He met my gaze. "What have I unleashed in you?"

"Tenderness, gentleness, and compassion, sensitivity and more sensuousness," I said.

"You had all this in you always. Maybe I just got you connected to that side of yours," Nikhil said quietly.

"You have unleashed a lot in me too," he continued.

I rolled down. "Tell me... I want to hear..."

Nikhil arched his eyebrows. "I am clueless."

"You are such a dumbo?"

"And you fell in love with a dumbo? The writer, Medha Nanda fell for..."

"Shush…" I said.

Nikhil murmured, "You have made me less shy."

"And bolder?" I asked.

Nikhil kissed me on my lips. " Yes and you have taught me how to love unconditionally, something Priyanka could never do."

My ears burned when he uttered her name. How could he be so naïve to mention her now? I drew him closer. "You have taught me how to fly baby," I said, and buried my face in his chest.

❧❖❧

I got up the next day fresh as the morning itself. I sat down to write, to work on the book in progress. It was a good day.

I wrote non-stop for an hour and a half and felt refreshed. The words just flew out of my pen. The room was washed with loads of sunlight that peeped through the windows and the view of the lawn outside was delightful. I kept writing. There was so much inside me that needed expression. I wrote,

…Prashant gulped down the last of his fifth drink and staggered to the bedroom. Sujata was fast asleep and the soft sound of her snoring filled up the silence of the room like a murmur. He stealthily slipped into bed, next to her, almost like a thief on a robbery mission. It'd been ages since he had touched her, felt her smooth skin. His fingers began to caress her crèam satin nightgown. He moved closer to her and inhaled the fragrance of her hair. He touched the soft flesh around her neck. Sujata

stirred. Prashant traced her back with his fingers, but Sujata remained unruffled…

As my pen caressed the white sheet of paper, thoughts of Rishi hit, shattering the silence of my creativity. A band of sunlight seemed to freeze the framed picture of Yash with his arms around me. The painting on the wall showed a beautiful forest on fire. The gruesomeness of the painting with animals running to escape the fire, birds flying away was at once vivid and painful. My thoughts flashed back to the time when things had begun to go wrong in my marriage. The black smoke rose in the air and the deep orange flames seemed to consume whatever came in its way. I knew the same was happening to my life as well.

I snapped my mind shut by returning to my writing.

"No snowflake in an avalanche ever feels responsible."
— *Voltaire*

I walked towards the kitchen. The winters were officially in and the smell of green leafy veggies floated in the kitchen. I had planned pizzas for dinner. Yash was back from Muscat, happy and bright.

I put on the apron and some music before I began the preparation. It was cold but working in the kitchen was more enjoyable now than in the hot, sweaty summer.

It was a beautiful day. Last few days with Nikhil had been the most wonderful days of my life till date. And I was still in a state of euphoria that refused to subside or abate. It just seemed to be swelling with the passage of time.

Yash came back home hungry and tired from play after about

an hour to the delicious smell of hot pizzas. I remembered not putting in so much zeal in cooking a meal since a long time. I was quite pleased with myself for making that kind of effort.

Yash smelled the pizzas. "That looks awesome."

I took off my oven mittens. "I hope it tastes great too."

Within seconds we both were at the table devouring the pizzas.

"This is too good," Yash said. He could hardly contain his excitement.

"I am happy that you like it. I can now try some new recipes I have been wanting to."

"Dad would have loved it too."

The words collided with something inside me and I gave a dry smile. Yash was close to his father and they shared a bond but he had been torn between the two of us when I had decided to shift to India.

"Is there no way that you can stay back?" Yash had asked me one day.

"No sweetie, I need to be back for my writing–simply for the energy that, that place gives me."

I caught a glimse of pain in his eyes. "I know you need to go back but how will dad manage alone?" he said.

"Then maybe you stay back with him."

"And how will you manage alone?"

I looked at him with tenderness. "I will… don't bother about me."

"No way am I going to let you live alone." Yash had declared like an adult.

I had felt my heart squeeze. Rishi had not strongly battled Yash's going away although I was sure he wanted his son to be with him.

So it was decided that Yash would stay with me.

I had wanted to be all alone in India, to experience my relationship with Nikhil without the guilt of motherhood weighing on my mind. But it was not meant to be.

"Yes dad would have loved it too…" I replied, without looking at him.

I kept my focus on the pizza and ate slowly.

It was so strange that day. I felt the happiness in my heart and the mention of Rishi did not bring up any resistance or the need to ignore his thought.

Could love do all that? Was it capable of so much transition? Was it that I was so happy that I could look at Rishi differently or rather with a tinge of compassion today?

That night as I lay in bed, content with myself, I relived the nights I had spent with Nikhil over and over again. I kept turning and tossing in the bed. How I wished to call up Nikhil at this time and be with him? It was eleven already. I stretched my tired limbs and longed for Nikhil; to be in his arms. Sleep came, teasing me. It came to me slowly and deliciously and before I knew, I was sucked into its folds like a child in a mother's lap. It had been a good, fulfilling day; one that I knew would remain tucked inside me like the fragrance of a thousand flowers.

I am in an unknown place and running through the streets and alleys. The night is dark and there is hardly any light to show me the way. I struggle to find my way but all I encounter are more alleys, more passageways, and more narrow lanes. I am scared as I run, my white robe whipping at my body. The robe is torn and shredded in places but I run careless of my naked feet and flowing hair. I finally see Nikhil far away, several alleys away and a smile appears on my face. He stretches his arms and calls out to me. I can see him but don't know how to reach him. There is relief in my heart that I have finally found him but Rishi's face looms large somewhere, I tremble. I am desperate to reach Nikhil as fast as possible and I run faster. My heart is pounding. I am tired, exhausted but I know I can't stop. I am running with sheer madness, trying to find a way to reach Nikhil... I am running towards him or away from him, I don't know...

ঔ❖ঔ

I slept like a baby and when I got up the next day, the dream was still fresh and lucid in my mind. I was clearly shaken. There was a distinct heaviness in my head that refused to ebb even as the day progressed.

Yash had been insisting on seeing a new movie with his friends and I dropped him off for the morning show. The desire to meet Nikhil was growing and I decided to check myself whether I could resist meeting him this morning? I came back after dropping Yash but the restlessness continued.

I sat down at my writing table, restive and determined to fight this.

The words appeared on the blank paper.

Nikhil called and I picked up the mobile with trembling hands. Why was it that whenever I thought of him, either he would call or message me?

"Where are you?" he asked as if he knew what was going on inside me.

"At home... just left Yash for a movie."

"I have to meet you Med," Nikhil said in a drunken voice.

"Not now Nik. I have to work," I said, determined to push him away.

"Please baby. I need you."

"Nik please don't, not now. I can't," I murmured.

"You can, you know it. Don't be heartless. Let me come baby."

The longing in Nikhil's voice warmed me up. "Come home,"

I whispered.

"I am on my way."

And when we met our eyes mirrored the desire of our hungry souls, yet again. It was no surprise that we both were soon in bed. The encounter this time was wilder and longer. We were not able to tear our eyes from each other even when we made love. I felt I could be with him all my life. I felt fulfilled and satiated.

"I've not felt like this ever in my life," I whispered as I brushed my lips against his.

Nikhil merely smiled.

Words were superfluous. Silence was a gift that seemed to equip us to feel the immense beauty of the moment. It was not important where the relationship was heading. I knew Nikhil would not leave his family and I did not want him to either. So many lives could not be sacrificed for our love. So much pain and suffering could be avoided if we just remained content with whatever was coming our way and didn't ask for more. Wasn't it a blessing that we could find love in the midst of our lonely, loveless marriages?

Nikhil regarded me with a tenderness which I was now familiar with.

We moved closer to each other, the hunger satiated but still lingering. It was hard to let go off each other. It had already been two hours.

Nikhil's face was buried in my hair and he held me close.

I murmured, "I have to go and pick up Yash, baby."

"I know. I love this smell of green apples in your hair. It's exactly the way Priyan…"

I went still for a moment.

"I didn't mean it that way, sorry sweetie," he said

I tried to wriggle out of his embrace. "Let me go…"

The mobile rang. I reached for it. It was Yash.

I rearranged my voice. "How was the movie?"

"Super cool; wish dad was with me; he would have freaked out," Yash chirped.

I felt a pang in my heart.

"Ma, can you come a little late. We are going for bowling. I'll call you when I am through," his voice suddenly sounded hasty and pre- occupied.

"But how long will you take?" I asked.

"Another hour and a half. I'll call you, and then you can leave the house."

I couldn't believe what I had just heard. It meant more than an hour with Nikhil.

"So?" Nikhil said tracing the outline of my breasts with his fingers.

"So what?"

Nikhil's hands were cupping my breasts now. "How much more time do we have?"

The light of the day filtered through the sheer orange curtains.

I gave him a smile.

"How much more time you need?" I said, reaching for his lips.

"All my life," Nikhil crooned before he sealed my lips with his.

Rishi

I looked outside the window of my office. The wide, clean road below was gleaming with sunlight and my mind raced back somehow to the narrow lanes and by lanes of Kanpur where I used to run and play. So much water had flown under the bridge. It seemed like ages ago. A small town boy had managed to make it on his own in a big city outside India and become an NRI. I smiled. But then life never gives you everything. It took away my family and my peace of mind in return for my dreams. I let out a sigh. I had never felt so lonely before. I decided to call Medha.

"Hi, are you still sleeping?" my voice spilled over. I was calling her after about a week.

"Yes I was. Tell me?" Medha said rigidly.

"So how are things?"

"Things are fine."

"You don't seem to miss me at all Medha and here I am waiting… forget it."

I felt the bitterness in my voice cracking open the wounds of my heart. I was still nursing my wounds as if they were the most precious treasure I had.

"Anyways I can't force you to miss me," I continued.

Medha sighed and I felt the discomfort rising inside her. Any show of affection from me made her restless. It felt as if I was an intrusion in her personal space with Nikhil and she wanted to guard it fiercely.

She hedged. "How was your appraisal?"

"Oh! It went well. How is Yash? Can I talk to him?"

"He is fast asleep. Can he call you back once he is awake?"

The conversation seemed hard to sustain and I found it better to abort it rather than hurt myself more.

"Please do. I haven't spoken to him for a week," I was pleading.

Medha replied coldly, "Yes sure."

There was silence on the phone. We didn't know what to talk or rather how to talk to each other.

"How are things with you," I asked.

"All good," she replied crisply.

"I'll wait to talk to Yash," I said.

I wanted to end the conversation. It was too painful.

I heard the click of the phone being kept and felt an arrow pierce my heart.

Her coldness was in fact pushing me to introspect myself more. Where had I gone wrong? Why was there no warmth left in her? The questions kept plaguing me constantly and shattered my peace of mind. I hoped I would find the answers soon.

Medha

I surveyed the clear water of the pool as I sat next to it.

Sonal had agreed to meet me and we had chosen the Nirvana Club. The breeze was cool and I watched the kids playing in the pool, laughing, splashing water at each other. I shifted my gaze towards the other side and watched Sonal walking in. I got up to meet her. We hugged each other and it didn't seem as if we were meeting after months. There was no awkwardness or stiffness. I wondered why some relationships refuse to breathe their last even after a part of them had gone numb?

"It's good to see you after so long," Sonal said.

I smiled. "I have just been so busy and you also..."

Sonal folded her shades. "You have been busy darling not me."

I noticed the bitterness in her voice but chose to ignore it. "Whatever."

"Tell me how are things with you and Rishi?" she asked matter-of-factly.

"I don't feel connected to him at all," I said and waved to the waiter.

"You are still married to him remember and you need to sort this out. I told you, you are getting into a whirlpool and will get sucked into it- Nikhi?"

"It has nothing to do with Nikhil."

"Fool yourself if you want to." I felt the sting in Sonal's voice.

"I now wonder how could I remain married to him for so long? I can't fathom anything." I reflected.

The plants swayed to the gentle breeze as I gathered my stole around my neck. I caught the remains of the dying sunrays skim the blue waters of the swimming pool.

"Whatever it was, you were happy all these years; at least that's what you projected." Sonal said tightly.

I felt a blow on my heart as she uttered those words.

The waiter arrived.

"Two Coffees and a plate of pakodas," I said and returned my gaze to Sonal.

"Yeah! As long as I didn't know what love was, I was happy in my marriage...call it naivety, stupidity or whatever. But now that I know-" I lost track of the words somewhere.

Everything was getting lost–my marriage, my sixteen years with Rishi. Where was it all disappearing? In the fog of lovelessness, pain and coldness. Everything seemed to be getting blurred.

Sonal looked at me. "Are you sure you love Nikhil?"

Will she ever know what I feel deep inside?

"Do I need to prove it?" I asked.

Sonal crossed her arms over her chest. "No, just ask yourself. You need to answer this one seriously."

"It's a crazy feeling. I think about him all the time. The world is so beautiful-I sing and dance…"

Sonal looked at me with a feeling of disbelief and wonder. Maybe she noticed the sparkle in my eyes. I circled the embroidered flower on my kurta with my finger "I find myself beautiful and desirable. I never felt like this before."

"The daily grind of marriage sucks out the romance from one's life, especially after the kids arrive," Sonal reflected as she fiddled with the menu card.

"I agree."

The crisp and steaming hot pakodas arrived. Sonal reached for one. "It has to be revived and fed on a daily basis otherwise…"

"I wonder what's happening."

Sonal's eyes softened a bit. "You know exactly what's happening."

"Yes… maybe," my voice cracked open.

The carpet of moss green grass around the pool reminded me clearly of the twists and turns of my own life.

"Are you talking to Rishi?" Sonal asked.

"He keeps calling but I don't feel connected to him at all. I just don't know how to deal with him."

"First gain clarity on your own, only then will you know how to deal with him or the situation."

I looked at Sonal. There was an ocean to be covered and I did not know where to begin.

"I love Nikhil, Sonal and that's the truth," I came out of my thoughts to confess the truth once again.

Sonal took a sip of her coffee. "But Nikhil is a married man. How's he going to deal with this?"

"The way he is dealing with it now. He has his own issues with his wife and I am sure he will deal with all that. The challenge is to find a comfort zone where everyone is happy."

Sonal glared at me like a school teacher at a child, who had come to school without finishing his homework.

"But that's not going to happen. You would want some commitment from him once the relationship grows." She said.

I smoothed my hair gently. "I don't know but as of now I am

content with what I have got."

"You won't be content for long. I know you."

"What do you know of me?" I spat back. I loathed her for judging me all the time.

"That you can be very demanding when it comes to emotions and relationships."

"That we all can be and..." I felt the break in my thoughts.

"And I know Nikhil. He's a coward. He doesn't have the balls to love you, even if he knows that you love him madly."

I felt her words stab my heart. Was she trying to make me realize the futility of my relationship with Nikhil? I hated her for it. She had tried to be my moral compass ever since I could remember. But I could no longer appreciate it. Friends could be so inadequate at times, even the closest of them.

Sonal continued. "Give it some time; that's all I am saying. Falling in love is a big step in your life at this stage. Don't forget the reality that is staring you in the face. You can't be selfish and do what your heart says."

I found myself short of words. I listened to her and felt the mishmash of my emotions wrenching my heart. I had hoped that meeting Sonal would clear my mind, give me some clarity and make me feel better. It had done none of the above.

Nikhil

I kept calling her but Medha seemed busy with her book. The weather had turned absolutely wonderful. I wanted to sit with her and soak the warmth of the sun in her garden with some tea and pakodas. I wanted to go out for a long drive, somewhere outside the city and stop over at a dhabba for tea. The cold was irresistible but she was unavailable.

"I can help you with your writing if you want." I insisted one day over the phone.

"C'mon Nikhil, there's nothing to help," Medha said.

"There is. I can sit with you, be your assistant, wipe your sweat, make tea or coffee and get water for you."

Medha laughed.

"It's only been five days since we met," her voice softened.

"Five days means a hundred and twenty hours. I want to hold you, feel you, take you in my arms, and look deep into your eyes," I murmured.

"And?"

"Feel your lips, breathe in your fragrance and touch you…"

I was already feeling her in my arms.

"Umm," Medha whispered.

"And talk about the impact of global economic meltdown on Indian economy," I said in the same vein of seduction.

Medha burst out laughing. The rings of her laughter spread in the air around me. We both laughed.

"You are impossible Nikhil!"

"Come on now, I have to meet you today."

I heard her take a deep breath.

"I am too deep into the book right now. Why don't you come by at seven? Yash has to go to a friend's place," she said.

"Wait for me," I said, before disconnecting the phone.

I couldn't wait to meet her. The passion was just swelling like a river in spate. It was very hard to resist her. She was certainly growing on me like moss on a tree trunk, covering my vulnerable self with a softness that left me feeling safer and more secure.

Medha

I felt the goose bumps on my body as I kept down the receiver. I had wanted to be away from him for a while- to let the giddiness of this love subside. Sanity was becoming a lost proposition for the craziness had to be tamed before it turned wild and unmanageable. There was both a boy's pleading and a man's authority in his voice when he had insisted on meeting me today. How could I have refused?

I stretched my arms and cast a look at the clock. It was half past two. The quietude of the winter afternoon was all over the place. I went back to my writing with renewed energy. The lure of meeting him in the evening kept me going. We had of late found it difficult to meet at a public place. The intimacy that we shared was too sacred to be revealed and broadcast in front of the entire world. And it was becoming hard to resist each other. Even if we didn't end up having sex, the joy that we felt by just being in each other's arms no place could make us enjoy that intimacy except my home.

I got back to my book, the evening date looming large in front of me.

***

I chose a long blue flowing skirt with a sleeveless, white, embroidered top with a slightly deep neckline which amply hinted at the cleavage and dragged myself for a bath. Once ready, I sprayed the perfume that he simply loved. The doorbell rang and I felt my face flush with happiness.

I could still get excited at the very thought of seeing him, almost like a teenager. I was relishing every bit of this. He appeared fresh and inviting like the dew on the morning grass. He looked yummy in his pale pink t-shirt. The smile on his face lit up his eyes. He took me in his arms. There was an urgency in the way he held me close and buried his face in my hair, inhaling its fragrance. I could sense my defenses crumbling. However hard I tried to exercise control over my emotions, the moment I came face to face with him, it all seemed futile. Love could render one so powerless. We kissed each other hungrily. Nikhil's hands were all over my body and I reciprocated. Suddenly I felt myself stiffen. I removed his hands gently.

"What?" Nikhil was astounded.

"Not now..." I sank on the sofa.

"But why?"

I hugged myself tightly. "I feel so intoxicated when you are around Nik, sometimes I wonder if it's real?"

"What makes you think it's unreal?" Nikhil touched my bare arms.

I trembled. "It's so beautiful...too perfect to be true."

"And you think you don't deserve all this?"

I dropped my eyes. "Don't know. Maybe I am judging myself too much. Maybe I have not felt like this ever."

"Then why are you stopping yourself?" Nikhil leaned closer to me and kissed me lightly on my cheek.

"No I am not nor do I want to."

I clung tightly to him as if I would never let him go. I looked into his eyes and found the same pain. Nikhil held me close. I felt safe.

I had been edging Rishi out from my life and it would not be easy to bring him back except if a miracle happened. I had always believed in miracles as a little girl -when I watched my parents fight and tackle the challenges of a middle class household. I had believed that my own marriage would never be like this. When things had begun to grow sour between Rishi and me, I believed somehow, that one day this bickering would stop and we would live happily ever after, like the couples in movies who were so much in love. But the miracle never happened but my faith survived. I had thought that my marriage would be happy and beautiful unlike my parents'. Suddenly I was in a crumbling marriage, unable to understand whether to live life waiting for miracles to happen or to live as if they would never happen.

And then Nikhil had entered my life...the biggest miracle of my life; and my faith in miracles was restored.

The evening was beautiful. I realized that just being with someone you love could be so magical. We decided to cook a meal of chicken stew and garlic bread as if we were a married couple. We had mundane exchanges like a married couple–Can you pass me the onions? Switch off the gas, will you? Chop the garlic–I felt elated. It was a space that would never be open for both of us forever, I knew.

After coffee, we both sat on the sofa. The taste of food still lingered in our mouths. Nikhil caught hold of my hand. His fingers trailed my face, the nape of my neck and the hollow space on my throat. Suddenly he seized my mouth with his lips. He smelt of coffee and cologne. Our bodies locked in a passionate embrace. I realized our bodies had now grown familiar to each other's touch and there was a comfort which was so essential to good sex. When he entered me this time, it was different. It was almost like he was healing me. I felt at peace and fulfilled.

The rising moon's reflection glinted on the hood of Nikhil's car. The breeze was pleasant and the starry sky seemed to know what we had just experienced. He had just stayed in my heart for the last twenty years like the prayer on the lips of a devotee. I watched Nikhil drive away. I hugged myself. I felt alive.

Nikhil

The December fog hugged the morning like a cloak, masking the sunlight. I felt the buoyancy missing in my limbs. Damn! I was already late for a client meeting. I had been on the phone since morning, leaving me with little time to get ready. There was a pardonable lethargy all around because of the weather and everything moved slowly. Priyanka had already left for office.

My mobile rang. I rushed out of the bathroom wrapped in my towel to pick up the ringing phone.

"Hey monkey where are you?" Rajan yelled from the other end of the phone.

"At home but leaving for work. Where the hell are you?"

"Have been travelling a lot and lots has been happening. Let's meet up for dinner tomorrow."

"Are you in town?" I asked, surprised.

"I am coming tomorrow morning for a conference...dinner suits you?"

I shivered in my towel. "I have to check but should be fine. Give me a buzz when you land or when you get over with the conference."

"Done. See you," Rajan said.

I found my teeth chattering as I kept down the phone. I smiled. Rajan had that effect on me. It had been a long time since we had met.

I shrugged out of my brown corduroy jacket and hung it over the blue, high chairs at the bar counter. I sat down on the leather sofas of the Park Premier Hotel. I had come directly from my office in Lado Sarai and was looking forward to having dinner with Rajan. The bar was warm and dimly lit and exuded a distinct coziness.

I waited for Rajan, wondering whether things were better in his marriage. Rajan walked in. He looked handsome in his dark grey jacket which hinted at his pot belly. He ran his hands through his grey hair which was swept back revealing his broad forehead. His angular face had grown a bit thinner and his features seemed sharper somehow. I wondered whether I had observed him more clearly last time than I did now. When we hugged, his five feet eight inch frame seemed to get lost in my six feet two inch body somehow. The smiles on our faces could surely light up a few bulbs on the street.

"You look different; new hairstyle; skin is glowing- the paunch is visible- what's happening?" I teased him.

Rajan smiled back. The waiter arrived to take the order. I ordered a coke and rum while Rajan opted for a single malt whisky with soda, as usual. Rajan fished out a Benson and Hedges cigarette and lighted it with his musical lighter. "How's Medha? What have you guys thought of?"

"Thought of what?"

"About your relationship?"

"Medha is still in a bad marriage. She needs to sort that out and I need to sort out mine." I put on my reading glasses to order the appetizers.

Rajan billowed out smoke from his mouth. "But are you sure of what you want?"

"It's all very chaotic right now. It can't go on like this forever. Medha and I are happy with the way things are...so I don't know…"

Rajan narrowed his eyes, "But Nik you have to take a call man-sometime."

"I know," I said and waved to the waiter. "How's Malvika? Are things better?"

"Worse."

The waiter arrived with the drinks.

I looked at Rajan.

"Order whatever you like yaar," Rajan said.

He looked around the place to soak in the ambience while I rummaged through the menu.

"Popcorn Chicken, Stuffed Italian fried peppers and a spicy bacon bean dip," I suggested looking up from the menu.

"You still remember…"

"Of course Popcorn Chicken has always been your favourite-

Is there something wrong?" I closed the menu card and looked at Rajan. There was something that he wanted to share. I just knew it.

"It's Radhika." Rajan blew out faint rings of smoke from his mouth.

I looked at him, not at all surprised. "I knew it was coming."

"I met her last time I was here–you remember?" Rajan took a sip of the whiskey.

I sat up straight.

"We slept," Rajan spoke softly.

He continued. "We have been together ever since. I could not resist her. It's a beautiful relationship. We have got connected."

I surveyed the interiors of the bar, buying some time to respond to what Rajan had just said. I drained all expression from my face before I spoke.

"Does Malvika know?"

"She found out one day–and there was a big show down." Rajan tapped the end of the burning cigarette in the ashtray.

The instrumental music in the background somehow seemed to ease the discomfort on Rajan's face.

"Now what next? Is Malvika…?" I asked.

"She created a furor and just wouldn't listen. I know she is in a lot of pain- and I am the reason for it but it just happened Nik." Rajan's eyes searched mine.

Maybe what he was looking for was some approval, some validation that it was alright. That looking for love and happiness outside one's marriage did not mean carrying the baggage of guilt, one's whole life.

"So have you confessed everything to Malvika?"

"Yes I have. What's the point of being dishonest? Our marriage has been going downhill from such a long time. I had told her we need to work on it but somehow she never took it seriously…"

"You could have made the effort." I said.

"Yes, maybe but even she needed to…"

The waiter arrived with the appetizers. Rajan stubbed out the remaining cigarette in the ash tray. He served the chicken and the frying peppers to me and then dug into his plate as he talked.

He spoke of all that had been going wrong the last few months and how he had tried hard to work things out. He talked of Malvika's insensitiveness, her callousness and arrogance. He spoke of his own inadequacies, his irritability, and his total lack of understanding of Malvika at times. He confessed how he had booked a hotel room for five days where he stayed with Radhika and how he had been careless enough to leave the credit card statement in his bedroom drawer. That's how Malvika found out.

I listened as he poured his heart out to me. I could sense a deep longing and desire in him to be understood and to be loved for what he was something which Malvika had somehow not been able to do. There was loneliness somewhere which I too had felt in my marriage and which had pushed me towards Medha when she had entered my life with love in her heart.

"I have told Malvika that I cannot break off with Radhika," Rajan continued.

"What does she say?"

"She obviously doesn't agree. She wants me to disconnect with her completely- no phone calls, no text messages, and no meetings."

I took a bite of the popcorn chicken. "I don't blame her Raj. She is obviously insecure now."

Rajan took a swig of his drink. "But I can't think of a life without Radhika. We have become very close."

My eyes widened. "You mean... Are you planning to divorce

Malvika?"

"No I don't want to do that. Kids will be shattered."

"Then what?" I surveyed his face.

"I have told Malvika to give me two weeks in a year to be with Radhika for a holiday together."

"Are you nuts? Do you even know what you are saying?" What was Rajan planning to do? He wanted to have both the women, like having one's cake and eating it too.

"You think it's selfish and heartless of me to even suggest this to Malvika but believe me this is the only way to remain in this marriage," Rajan said and looked away trying to gauge the impact of his own words.

He was clearly in pain.

"But this will lead to more pain."

"All I am talking about is an open marriage man. It will give the much needed impetus to our dying relationship; perhaps make it more exciting and interesting. I will remain committed to Malvika but I also need my emotional sustenance."

I tried to grasp the implication of his words. Medha's conversation with him last time at the bar resounded in my mind.

"Are you sure it will work out? I mean won't you feel divided between the two?" My tone was tentative.

"One can make it work. I love Radhika; you know that. We did get divorced because we grew apart but I have always loved her. Malvika is the mother of my kids and I want to be fair to her as well."

"But she has to be ready to accept Raj...it's not easy."

Rajan's voice cracked. "It's not but she is not ready to even understand the situation; she won't move an inch."

I marvelled at the clarity of his thoughts.

"Give her some time. She is hurt and feels cheated right now." I gulped down the last of my drink and waved to the waiter for a refill.

"Frankly speaking I don't care. I am very sure I want Radhika back in my life. Malvika will have to understand. If she allows me to be with her, our marriage survives otherwise..."

"Have you lost it? How can you expect a woman to accept another one in her life as if nothing has happened? Would you have accepted?"

"Maybe I would have if I was desperate to save my marriage and if my marriage gave me all the security."

"C'mon Raj, you also know it's not as black and white as it seems."

"I do not know what I would have done in a similar situation; maybe I would have walked out of my marriage. I have suggested we stay apart for a while and deal with this but she obviously doesn't find this a very good idea," Rajan took out another cigarette from the box and lighted it.

"So what have you decided now?" I asked.

"I don't know. Malvika wants to come back to India and stay here but the kids are not too hot on the idea. I don't want to push her for anything. I don't want to be in an emotionally dead relationship either..."

I watched him with resignation. I could never have imagined Rajan to be so unconventional and defiant of the norms that bound us to behave in a certain, prescribed manner. These norms reined us in and also made us compromise with people and situation. Perhaps this was the biggest cause of unhappiness. Everyone had the right to be happy and lead the kind of life they wanted so why not Rajan? If he and Malvika could have an open marriage then what was the harm? Who was I to judge him?

We ordered the food and I steered the conversation towards his work. Rajan was only too happy to talk. The evening was pleasant and the effect of liquor was slowly showing effect on both of us. There was an underlying sense of deep comfort and letting go off one's emotions.

By the time, I dropped him at his hotel, I was extremely tired but the exhaustion somehow did not seem to trouble me at all. I had felt strange after talking to Rajan. I had never spoken about Medha to anyone or shared our relationship, except just a little with Rajan. Something seemed to hold me back every time. I wanted but I never could gather the courage to share her with someone close. Was it because I myself thought of it as morally wrong? Or was I afraid of Priyanka finding out about it and feelings hurt? I still had feelings for Priyanka and this distance that had crept between us was something I was not able to deal with.

The chill of the night was all encompassing, as I drove back home. The roads were almost deserted except for a few hand carts serving hot tea and boiled eggs, with a few people huddled around it. At some places one could see a bonfire by the roadside with a few people warming themselves, huddled together in worn out blankets. There was a faint mist in the air which rendered the winter more seductive than usual.

I entered the bedroom. Priyanka was fast asleep. The air was diffused with a faint smell of eucalyptus oil. I drew in my breath as I watched her sleep. Why were we faking our marriage when there was none? For the sake of Neha? It made no sense. Maybe I should talk to Priyanka and sort this out. But my lightheadedness was getting the better of me and I decided it was best to discard these thoughts for the time being.

Medha

I adjusted my purple bindi and smoothened the plum coloured

kurta and the ivory colour cutwork, Patiala salwar with my hands. I wrapped my pashmina shawl to beat the biting cold and looked at the clock on the wall. It was time already. The doorbell rang and I ran to open the door. Nikhil smiled as he stood there with a bunch of white roses in his hands, even as his eyes felt me all over. I felt my skin tingle with a soft warmth. He handed me the roses and we hugged. I felt his hands igniting my flesh. Our lips met in a ravenous union. It took immense effort for both of us to tear our hands away from each other when the door bell rang again. I opened it to find Yash standing there. He was returning from his friend's place. I felt my heart beat get quicker and the heat rise on my skin. I straightened my shawl and kurta instinctively and pushed my hair back from my face. Yash's face lost a bit of colour when he stepped inside the house and saw Nikhil sitting on the sofa.

I smiled nervously. "Nikhil...remember?" I licked my lips.

"Of course we met at your book launch," Yash recalled.

Nikhil smiled weakly at him. "So how are you young man?"

"I am good."

"Are you enjoying yourself here?" Nikhil asked.

Yash's eyes lit up. "All my friends are here and I love this place but I miss dad a lot."

I wanted to get out of that space as fast as possible. There was discomfort rising inside me which I wanted to stifle. Yash sat down besides Nikhil and I felt the ground become shaky.

"What do you do Nikhil Uncle?"

Nikhil cast a quick glance at me. "I own an Advertising Agency."

"That's cool."

I interrupted. "I am going out for dinner sweetie. Your food is in the microwave. I will be back by ten thirty or eleven."

"Chill mom. Let me talk to him," he cut me short.

Nikhil looked at me and said calmly, "Medha...let him."

I sat on the sofa, next to them. Nikhil shifted his attention to Yash.

"It must be an exciting field...Advertising," Yash asked.

Nikhil weaved his hands together. "Well not as exciting as it seems from the outside."

I had a strange feeling in my stomach as they both conversed.

Yash wiped the sweat on his face with the sleeve of his T shirt. "Why?"

"Running after clients, bagging accounts, presentations, shootings, media management, and production...phew! It's not as glamorous as you think," Nikhil explained.

"So how easy is it to become a model?" Yash asked.

Nikhil smiled. "You want to be a model?"

"I am just wondering, maybe."

I opened my mouth and then shut it. Yash had never ever shown his inclination to be a model to me earlier and I wished Nikhil would end this conversation soon.

"See it depends on a lot of factors–looks, height, personality and tons of hard work." I stared at Nikhil and motioned him to get up.

"Yash we have to leave. I don't want to be too late in the night," I announced, rising to my feet.

"No problem," Yash said. I saw his face fall. He was enjoying his talk with Nikhil and I had played spoilsport.

Nikhil patted him on his back, "Nice meeting you Yash. We will talk about it in detail some other time. See you soon."

Yash shrugged. "Cool, next time."

"Take care and have your food on time," I said hurriedly and hugged him. I quickened my steps to be out of the house. I heaved a sigh of relief as I settled down in the Chinese restaurant which was about twenty minutes drive from my place.

There was a faint fragrance of Chinese spices that drifted in the air and we found a secluded corner where the noise and crowd, both were negligible. We ordered a clear noodle soup to be served before the main course of Chicken in wine, succulent baked lobster in clear broth and vegetarian pot stickers along with shanghai stir fried noodles. The red and white décor looked pretty and matched well with the elegant rosewood furniture. I admired the painted carved murals, the huge decorative wall fans and the bright red and gold lanterns which hung from the roof. The air was suffused with the smell of soya sauce and sea food. I was waiting to hear about his meeting with Rajan.

"I tried calling you last night," I said.

"I was busy with Rajan," he replied.

I observed him. He appeared distracted.

"I was waiting for you to call me."

He looked away. "I was too tired after dropping him at the hotel and..."

"And?"

"Chuck it; you don't need to know everything," Nikhil grunted

I felt a hurt somewhere inside me and looked away.

"I am sorry sweetie." He held my hand.

I gazed back at him, hurt.

"You are free not to tell me Nik. It's your life and..."

"No, I want to tell you everything. You are the only one I can share this with."

The food arrived. Nikhil began once the waiter had left. I listened with rapt attention as he revealed the details of his conversation with Rajan. His eyes sparkled and his voice dipped and rose. I sensed a different energy as he shared his thoughts and views on life, that had strangely joined these two friends with a common thread.

"I never knew that Rajan was such an open minded person. I mean he was always outgoing and bindaas but ..."

I cleared my throat. "But why are you surprised? He seems a very practical man and selfish too as I can see... wanting his cake and eating it too."

Nikhil bunched his forehead. "At least he has been honest and knows what he wants."

"I agree at least he is being honest..."

The waiter arrived with two vermillion red bowls of hot steaming soup. The faint ginger, parsley fragrance rose up in the air.

Nikhil shifted his gaze to me. "I know what you mean."

I spread the striped red and white napkin on my lap and looked at Nikhil.

"I never said it; you admitted it Nik."

Nikhil opened his mouth and then shut it. I watched his expression change.

Nikhil said. "I wonder if Malvika will agree to such an arrangement. I mean no woman would, although he is adamant..."

I reasoned. "It's not easy and requires immense understanding and trust between the couple and that, as you said, is missing in their relationship so I don't think it's a viable option in their case."

Nikhil licked his lips. "I think you are right, but Rajan is very insistent and hopeful that it will work Malvika may have no option but to agree."

"Tell him a woman's mind works differently. He should just focus on rebuilding his marriage if it's important for him, and if not, then he should move on with Radhika. Malvika will never accept another woman in their life."

"But you have accepted Priyanka in my life without any resistance."

"I am no one to accept or reject Priyanka. I look at things differently, Nik. I never came into the relationship hoping or wishing you would leave your wife. I confronted my feelings and dealt with them," I paused. "I followed my heart, unafraid of where it will lead me, ready for the pain that would come as a result; not many can do that."

The air was soft and the winter chill made the soup taste more divine.

"Sometimes I am simply amazed at your clarity, Medha."

"I guess love empowers you. It makes you look beyond yourself and yet it's not easy."

Nikhil caught the fleeting pain in my eyes.

"It requires conviction and courage but their marriage is shaken right now," I continued.

Nikhil threw his head back. "Yes, but Rajan is hopeful that it will work out."

I gave him a lazy smile. "Hope is the only reason we survive , isn't it?"

Our eyes met for longer this time and I could feel my heart thaw.

"Tell me how are things at home?" I asked.

The question was deliberate.

"It's the same but I wonder for how long. I have given up," Nikhil said with a faint resignation in his voice.

"Why Nik? Don't do that to yourself. You can't live in this state forever." I said a bit irritated.

"I guess so. Neha is a major reason and I think peace is very important. I can't lose it even if it means living like this all my life. Priyanka and I have no marriage but there is at least peace in the house and I don't want to disturb it."

The pain in his eyes flashed for a millisecond and then died away. I knew he was not capable of confronting Priyanka with his relationship with me and it weighed on my mind most of the time. It made me mad too. But I guess it was his call and I was clear that I would never push him. It was foolish to test the frailty of human emotions sometimes.

Nikhil said. "Let's not talk about it. I am here with you, I want to talk about us."

I could not relate at all to this trait of his, evading issues that required urgent attention. Why couldn't he confront his problems head on? I sighed.

"You are my ticket to the fantasy world," he murmured.

I smiled. "Ticket or escape route?"

"Don't play with words. You know what you are for me," he said.

I peered into his eyes. "Sometimes I wish I knew for sure."

He kept gazing at me till I dropped my eyes. The music in the restaurant switched to instrumental now and I found my feet tapping to the music. We ate in silence.

I loved him immensely and wanted him to be free to fly. There was no condition I would apply to love him. None whatsoever.

The stillness of the winter night consumed me and the questions surfaced one after another like bubbles in boiling water. They seemed to be born out of the same stillness, ripping my world apart, threatening to make me look into myself and find the answers. I felt the cold sweat break behind my neck even though my blue flannel nightie was warm and clung close to my body. I wrapped the quilt tightly around me.

Had I been fair to Rishi?

Why such a question and why now, when everything was falling into place? When my life with Nikhil was at its most beautiful; when I shared this incredible intimacy with the man I truly loved; when I had experienced what I had always dreamt of. Oh! The irony of getting your heart's desires....wasn't that the biggest tragedy as well?

With Rishi, the sex was good but the intimacy was only on the surface. But then good sex is not always a clear indicator that all is well in a marriage. I stared at the pale moon visible through the parted curtain. The chirping of crickets drifted in the air. They seemed to share my loneliness somehow. And I realized I was fearless at that moment. I remembered reading somewhere that whatever one wanted; one had to give to themselves first. I clung closer to my quilt.

Love, compassion, kindness, respect...I had to give it all to myself before I could even begin to expect it from anyone else. Maybe I had not given myself enough love and respect. Maybe I had become too flexible and adjusting in my marriage, so that Rishi had let me down completely. He had not been able to give me what I had not given to myself. I felt the prick of goose bumps all over my body. The realization dawned quicker than lightning. Going away from Rishi had created the desired space needed, to let our marriage be suspended for the time being, without getting choked under the pressures of daily life. The mobile rang. It was Nikhil. My breath thickened merely on hearing his voice. I felt sensation rise like wild fire between my legs and overpower me. We talked for an hour and by the end of it I felt exhausted and spent. It was as if we had made love over the phone. But I still had to find answers to the questions that were beginning to cause unrest in my heart.

***

I looked at my watch to check the time again. It was probably the seventh time I had checked the time in the last fifteen minutes. Ever since Yash had left for a school excursion to Jaipur for five days, I had felt the desolation descend on me. The house was silent and empty and the worst was that Nikhil was travelling too. He was away to Goa for an Advertising conference. Five days without Yash and Nikhil seemed impossible. I realized how dangerously close I had come to rely on Nikhil to fill up my life. The mobile rang and I was thankful for the intervention.

"Hi, how are you?" Rishi's voice asked.

"I am fine. How are you?" I replied slowly.

It had been many days since he had last called. I had been cold with him every time he had attempted to strike a conversation. But Rishi had been persistent in calling regularly.

His voice was soft. "I am ok. You seem to be a little low?"

I flinched. "Why? I mean....what makes you think so?" This was unexpected. It seemed he had been able to peep inside my heart and understand my feelings.

"I know it Medha even if you don't talk to me. You are so cold … but I still care for you."

I felt my heart squeeze. Ever since Nikhil had been away, I had not been able to talk to him and it had been five days now. I was missing him terribly. In fact I was mad at him for not calling me up all these days even if he was busy.

"I am really fine," I said rather quickly.

"We can be friends at least. Is that not possible?"

It had been more than eight months since I had walked out of that house in Muscat and the pain of the broken marriage had surely dulled with time. Dulled or shifted, I could not decide. But was it possible to live with a wounded relationship even if I was happy with Nikhil? The pain would somehow seep into my subsequent or existing relationships without my even realizing it. Sixteen years of marriage was a long time to easily discard and walk off.

"Yes Rishi, I'll try," I said, surprised at myself.

Rishi heaved a sigh. "Thanks a lot. I have been thinking about you, our marriage and where I went wrong. I've been unfair to you Medha."

I listened. The stillness of the house seemed to submerge me.

"Ever since you have gone away, I realized how much you mean to me, how much you have adjusted with a man like me for sixteen years. How I must have let you down when you needed me. How I could not understand you in spite…" Rishi's voice broke into pieces. I heard a sob rise to his throat.

I felt a wave looming large over me, ready to drown me. I felt an intense pain pricking the back of my eyes and soon my eyes were moist. The tears trickled out. There had been so much pain in our relationship, so much anguish but somehow at this juncture, we both seemed to at last recognize it.

"Are you there?" Rishi collected himself before he spoke again.

"Yeah! I am here," I responded.

"Don't go that way Medha; There's a lot of pain there."

I felt a lump in my throat. Of late I had been feeling some vagueness; a kind of tentativeness in my relationship with Nikhil. I had not expected any commitment from him but this lack of expectation somehow was (not the reason but) a catalyst in the overall feeling of strangeness. I had tried to decipher many times what it was but could not put my finger on it.

I cleared my throat. "Maybe that pain is my destiny. I need to go through it."

"But I can't see you in pain."

"It's inevitable. Sometimes one can't avoid it. It's like stopping the rush of water. If I close one way, it'll eventually force its way through some other way. So let it be."

Rishi was silent.

He couldn't take me away from my destiny. Could he? If he could, I would not have left him in the first place.

"Promise me that you'll talk to me as a friend," the childlike pleading in his voice reached out to me somehow.

I remained silent.

"Where's Yash? I am missing him," he asked.

"He's gone for a school trip to Jaipur for five days."

"So you are alone. Must be feeling low without him."

"Yes- the house is so quiet, it seems so unreal. I am missing him."

"Imagine how much I must be missing him?" Rishi's words sliced through me like a knife. I felt a stone hurled at the glass of a window through which I had been looking out. I had been so engrossed in my pain, wrapping it around me so securely that this reality had escaped me somehow. For the first time, Rishi's loneliness jolted me.

"I know it must be tough," I admitted.

"Yes it is. A foreign country, no family....You know better."

I shifted in the chair I was sitting on.

"It really doesn't matter what you do, how well you are at your job. Nobody cares. A foreign place makes you feel more alien when you are alone. It seems to mock at you…"

I was at once aware of the pain I had gone through back in Muscat. The doorbell rang.

"I have to go Rishi, someone is at the door. Bye," I said hurriedly.

"You take care," he said.

"I will. You too."

I felt confused as I disconnected the phone.

Medha

Rishi called me daily and we spoke to each other. We talked about how we had both behaved with each other. Why we had been mad at each other and callous as well? Why our marriage had gone through this maze of pain and suffering? We shared our feelings about the broken marriage, worn out emotions, spent energies. I knew we had to heal this relationship, otherwise we both could not move on in life.

Wounds had to be healed. You couldn't band aid them.

The more we talked, the lighter we felt. I cried at times when we talked about the incidents, that had been the turning points in our marriage... of the child we had and the one we had lost. I was surprised at the reservoir of emotions that had been stored inside me. But it was comforting to discuss all that with Rishi, looking at things from a distance. Sometimes merely viewing the grief from a distance can heal it amazingly.

Rishi had been a part of my life. I had given him so many years of my life and that was not an insignificant thing. He was also the father of my child and that could never change, even if I loved Nikhil with all my soul. Rishi had been in my life for all those years that I had been married to him. I could never dispute that. Nikhil had existed in my thoughts but not in my present when my marriage was alive. But the biggest truth right now was that I loved Nikhil.

Nikhil meanwhile postponed his return to Delhi by another ten days. He was flying to Goa and then to Mumbai for some important work. His agency was pitching for a Fortune 500 company and his presence was essential. He had already briefed his creative team over the phone, discussed and worked out the details, while he himself had decided to visit the client's factories in Bangalore and Mumbai and spend some meaningful time with the CEO. Bagging this account was decisive for the agency and he had mentioned all this in a mail to me. He had also called me briefly on his way to the airport. I felt deflated and lifeless. Maybe I needed to be alone and assess the relationship from a fresh perspective. I was myself surprised at my reactions. Why was his being away bothering me so much?

Once back from the trip, Yash spoke to Rishi and exchanged notes on his cricket practice, studies and living in Gurgaon. I listened with rapt attention as myriad emotions flitted across his face. I felt at peace somewhere deep down, happy that the father- son relationship had not been too gravely affected by this separation. I had no business to colour Yash's opinion of his father and I vowed to myself that I would never do it even if the worst happened between us.

I felt a shift in myself gradually. I had been writing and reading a lot since the time Nikhil left–what with all the emotions surging inside me- the loneliness, the longing to be with Nikhil, getting connected to Rishi, the slow healing of the pain between Rishi and me and the most amazing part–of being able to share Nikhil with Rishi. We had both begun to look at the present situation in our marriage with the prudence of two mature individuals and see it for what it was in the past and what it was now.

Rishi decided to fly down for a couple of days. He had been yearning to meet Yash too.

***

We sat outside in the comfy cane chairs. The sun peeped from the sky like a neighbor from the window. The smell of fresh cut grass wafted in the air. The winters was now nearing its end and the cold had lost much of its sting. There was a pleasant coolness in the air and one could still soak in the sun for a while.

I looked at him. "You know Rishi, he gave me so much attention and care that I just got drawn towards him. You were so bitter and cold," I confessed.

"I know. I realize I never respected your huge appetite for life and writing the way I ought to have; your dire need to be free."

I wrapped a strand of hair around my finger. "And I felt so lonely and isolated and then Nikhil came into my life. What timing?"

His voice softened. "But you just closed yourself to me."

"Of course I did. I felt you were just not equipped to handle my emotions; that you were so full of yourself," I explained.

Rishi was silent, soaking in my words.

I sighed. "You never understood that writing was and is my passion. I always felt that you were taking me away from my own self and I started resenting you for it. I could not allow it."

Rishi listened without breaking my thoughts. Perhaps he was relieved to realize that I was opening up and talking about my feelings as never before.

"I may not have been too expressive but I always realized what writing meant to you."

I protested. "Only rarely-I felt you never really cared about it. You acted as if …"

"Could be. I should have been more expressive of my concern but maybe because you perceived me as a hindrance, I became one. We always perceive things differently Medha and not the way they actually are…"

I had seen him mostly as a selfish, callous, unloving husband and he had turned out to be exactly that, proving me right in the process.

"Remember whatever we manifest, comes back,"

Rishi continued.

I felt the discomfort rising within me. I was keen to round off the conversation here.

Rishi said evenly, "Even I perceived you as insensitive and rude

Medha- as someone who could never love. We were both so negative…we could not see the positives."

"I guess we brought out the worst in each other," I inhaled.

"Imagine we have been so hard on each other," Rishi's said.

That night I reflected on what Rishi had said. I was alone in my room. Rishi slept with Yash in his room. My heart had never been so still. I felt numb. What was happening? Was it Nikhil who had been able to change my life so completely? I had been filled with love ever since Nikhil walked in through that door and that was probably the reason I had been able to look at Rishi's viewpoint and had been able to appreciate it with sensitivity and maturity.

I sat up hugging the pillow tightly. But strangely, I longed to be with Nikhil. He was one of the reasons I had been able to know and discover myself.

It had all escaped me till now.

Nikhil

I waited as the phone rang at the other end. I began to wonder where Medha was. It had been close to ten days since I last spoke to her. The Goa conference had lead to this presentation in Mumbai and another conference in Bangalore. I had been too preoccupied with work and I realized now, how much I had been missing her.

The trees outside the hotel window were flushed with the morning rays of the sun and swayed in gay abandon. The breeze flew in through the open window and circled my body. It felt good. I dialled her number again. She must be upset with me. I hadn't called her in days? I walked towards the window and looked out. Medha's face flashed before my eyes. Her crooked smile, her luscious lips and her curves- I felt the heat rise between my legs.

The mobile rang and I ran to grab it.

"Hi! Where are you?" I asked.

"I was sleeping baby. Where are you?" Medha's sleepy voice was seductive.

"I am in Bangalore...missing you baby," I said softly.

"When are you back? Ten days and no news from you Nik," Medha said with a yawn.

"Oh! I have been busy as hell but I am going to make up for it. How are things?"

"I am fine. Rishi was here for a few days."

"Patching up?"

"Healing. There is so much hurt."

I felt a strange constriction in my throat.

"No wonder you didn't call me."

"Nik, I should be the one mad at *you* for not calling. You told me you would be calling regularly. I tried so many times but your phone was non- reachable or switched off." Medha snapped.

"C'mon now, you can understand. I have been working, not having fun."

"Don't look for excuses Nik. One is never too busy for the ones we love."

I felt a wave of guilt rise inside me.

"You have no idea what I have been through all these days," Medha fumed. "Work is all that you care about."

"I am sorry Med- have been too tied up," I tried to explain.

Medha sighed. "Nik…"

"I agree. Tell me what's my punishment?"

"Wait till you get back," she said.

"Anything you say sweetie and how have things been with Rishi?"

"Generally discussing why and how things went wrong between us. He is a changed man", Medha said.

"That's good. I always told you, you can't be bitter about him," I said.

I had always told her that I could not imagine her feeling bitter about a sixteen year old marriage. Medha had countered me by admitting that she was in pain. That the hurt was too deep and time was the only factor that would decide a lot of issues. I knew one day her bitterness would be flushed out; she would feel warmth for the man she had lived with for so long. But that could not stop me falling in love with her.

"I am missing you Nik," she whispered.

"I am missing you too. I'm back the day after," I murmured.

Medha sighed and I could sense her longing across hundreds of miles on the phone.

☙❖❧

I walked from one end of the hospital's waiting lobby to the other with a strange heaviness in my heart. I dug my hands into my trouser pockets. There was a slight chill in the air and I craved for a hot cup of tea somehow. Rajan had called in a hurry, very late last night and had informed me that he and his family were in Delhi and that I should meet him up in the hospital early in the morning. He had refused to tell me more and I had been unable to sleep the whole night, wondering if all was well. I could sense something was amiss. His number had been constantly engaged since morning.

I sat down on the sofa and looked at my watch. He should have been here by now. I had barely landed back from Goa when he called. I had not been able to even inform Medha that I was back. The lobby was full of people. A strong smell of medicines lingered in the air. I saw Rajan rushing towards me. His face was pale and his clothes were in disarray. His hair was also unkempt.

"What happened? Is everything ok?" I caught hold of his arm.

Rajan trembled. His eyes looked blank.

"When did you come to Delhi? Why all of a sudden?"

Rajan sank on the sofa. "We arrived a week back. Malvika was insistent and I could not say no."

I looked at Rajan. He looked like a man who had lost something.

"Where is she?" I demanded to know.

"Here."

"What happened?"

"Last night, she tried to commit suicide…"

No, it was not possible. I must have heard it wrong.

"What did she do?"

I could sense Rajan forcing the air into his lungs.

"She swallowed about twenty sleeping pills. Luckily I found out and rushed her to the hospital. She has survived but …."

"Raj," I held his hand firmly.

The morning sun had flooded the hospital lobby and I saw the plants in their huge planters sway in front of my eyes. I focussed hard to find a spot to rest my eyes on.

Rajan seemed to have lost his voice.

"How did this happen? I never meant…" he squeaked.

"Just calm down Raj. It's too much of a shock for you. Where are you guys staying?"

"At her sister's place. I even told her I won't see Radhika again. I know I have hurt her. She is the mother of my children but she is not ready to trust me now?" Rajan wailed.

I tried hard to keep my voice under control "Trust will come with time. You can't force it. She feels betrayed. You have to give her time to deal with it."

"The kids are traumatized. What do I tell them?"

"Be with them. Explain that although she is in pain, she will be fine."

Rajan laughed nervously, "The kids are not fools. They can see how bad she is."

"Raj, I know but you can't tell them the truth. They will be devastated."

Rajan got to his feet and moved about restlessly. "Malvika's sister is taking care of them. I'll talk to them once all this settles down."

"I want to see her," I said.

"It's not a pleasant sight...not now, maybe tomorrow," Rajan said. I saw the pain in his eyes.

"I want to Rajan," I insisted.

He nodded and we both walked towards the lift.

"How did this happen?" I asked.

Rajan fixed his gaze on me. "She started snooping on me, reading my mails, chats, text messages."

"But how?"

"My mistake- I gave her the password to my mails."

" WHAT?" I almost shrieked.

"I had to. She was after my life for it," he admitted.

I could feel my head spinning like a top.

"She has even hinted to the kids that their father was having an affair and he might leave them! I hate her for this man."

"And then she wanted to be in India for a few days- with me and the kids. We came and that day there was a big showdown at her sister's place and later she swallowed..." his voice died down.

We entered the room. The nurse got up and left. I cast a look at Malvika- Rajan's wife whom I had met many times before. She was a thin, fair woman but now her skin was dark and pale.

Rajan moved closer and sat down beside her on the chair. Just then the doctor entered, followed by two junior doctors and a nurse. He checked her medical report and instructed the nurse to take her blood pressure and check her fever. Rajan stood like a guilty child who was about to be punished.

"We are observing her for any infections that she might have contracted. She seems fine as of now," the doctor explained.

"The pills have been flushed out totally doc?" Rajan enquired.

The doctor rearranged the stethoscope. "We did clean her stomach but we have to monitor her closely for another twenty four hours to rule out any other complication."

"Fever is 102 *C doctor," the nurse spoke.

"I want a temperature record every two hours," the doctor instructed.

He turned around to face Rajan. "I don't see much of a complication now but still the next twenty four hours are a bit crucial." And he left.

Rajan slumped on the chair.

Suddenly I felt alone as if stranded on a long, lonely road all by myself.

Medha

I spread myself on the carpet and snuggled close to Nikhil. The morning sun peeped through the lace curtains and there was a calmness in the morning. Since the winter was bidding us goodbye, there was a lingering chill in the mornings and late evenings which felt nice and cozy. Nikhil had arrived at my place by half past nine and we had a breakfast of upma and poha. It was eleven now.

Nikhil narrated his meeting with Rajan and his visit to the hospital. For the first time I felt there was a deep remorse in him somewhere for the way things were in his marriage. His concern and attachment to Priyanka didn't come as a surprise to me. I had sensed it even when we had been together. Priyanka had somehow loomed large like a shadow over our relationship. A small part of him still belonged to his wife. Although he had surrendered completely to me in moments, somewhere the failure of his marriage had become a tiny pebble in his heart that I knew would never melt. It withheld a part of him from me and that was strangely the beauty of our relationship...the completion in this incompleteness; the consummation in the unconsummated part of our bond; the finished in the unfinished part of love.

I also realized that his feelings for Priyanka were primarily borne out of his attachment to her being the mother of his child. He needed to heal his relationship with Priyanka just as I needed to heal mine with Rishi, before we could think of moving ahead together.

Our relationship could never blossom, if we both were not healed.

Two incomplete souls could not make one complete relationship. It was just not possible.

I kissed him tenderly on his lips, caressing his face with my fingers. Nikhil kissed me back with searing passion and I felt drunk instantly. But his mind seemed preoccupied with other thoughts.

"I don't know how Priyanka would react if she found out about you and me." he said.

I combed his hair with my fingers, "What do you expect?"

He lifted his eyes towards me. "She will be shattered."

His concern hit me.

"So you don't want her to know?" I asked gently.

"No. If speaking the truth causes pain to someone, it's better not to tell the truth. What one doesn't know, can't hurt."

I drew in my breath. "Yes, what she doesn't know won't hurt

her but the truth is truth Nik, whether you say it or not. You can't bury it and walk off. If you had the courage to love me, have the guts to admit it too."

He just looked at me perhaps aware of his limitations.

I continued. "I am not asking you to marry me or leave your family for me Nik. But have the balls to accept me for what I am for you; for what I mean to you at least."

Nikhil did not reply. He chose silence and I realized he was not yet ready and probably would never ever be, to take responsibility for what he felt and for what he had done. He was not the kind to act on his love. He loved me but would never admit it openly or express it to the world. He couldn't.

It was not just the paralysis of will; it was the hypnosis of social conditioning.... Where we put our relationships within brackets and tagged them with names for our convenience and for the succour of the society we live in. Nikhil could live in that hell he called marriage but he did not have the courage to walk out of it or to even make efforts to save it. Nor did he have the nerve to announce his love for me as a truth of his life to people close to him. It hurt me but then I had walked ahead, aware of his limitations. Maybe somewhere I was content to have the love he had given me. It was enough for me.

I kissed him till I felt the tightness leave my body. And then we made love as if we were reuniting to be whole and complete with each other.

I drew aside the curtains of the study and settled in the swivel chair next to the writing table. The sun had still not risen. I inhaled the early morning breeze and sat down to work on my book. The book was halfway through and I was happy with its progress. I preferred to write long hand and the feel of the pen in my hand and the sight of the blank paper was enough to set my thoughts rolling. The hush and the freshness of the morning, coupled with the solitude, was a potent aphrodisiac to activate my passion to write.

It was four a.m. As I poured myself deeper into the lines that kept forming one after the other, I felt myself emptying and sensed this infinite space around me.

"So did you sleep with her?" Prashant's eyes are full of fire.

Anjali trembles and walks off towards the kitchen.

"Did you both do it?" He raises his voice.

"Yes," Anjali whispers, staring at the marble counter.

Prashant bangs his fist on the wooden table and mutters an abuse. He is like a wild horse that has lost his direction.

"How was it?" he yells, hungry to know more but Anjali is in no mood to oblige. She starts to walk away but he grabs her by her arm.

He stares at her coldly. "Did you come?"

Anjali glares back at him, trying to gauge the working of his mind.

"Don't do this please," she pleads.

But it falls on deaf ears.

Prashant holds her tighter than before and his nails dig into her skin like needles. She knows he wants to know the tiniest details. As if knowing about it would save him from it somehow.

"Did you come?" he thunders.

"Stop it ...will you?" Anjali screams and the room echoes her shriek.

"Did you come?" He is relentless.

She pushes him away. Her eyes are glimmering with tears but she tries hard not to let them threaten her composure. Prushant persists.

"How did it feel?"

The rain thunders outside and Anjali realizes that her world is slow-

ly being ripped to pieces. She trembles with an uncanny fear and rushes up the stairs to her bedroom. Prashant follows her. Anjali huddles herself in a corner of the bed. The clouds wail and she feels the rain in her eyes.

Prashant comes closer to her and caresses her arm. Anjali pushes him aside.

He gives her a slow smile. "Did you come, sweetheart?"

Anjali feels the anger seething "You are so sick," she spits the words and stares at him through her teary eyes and walks out into the balcony. The rain is pouring hard and the darkening clouds look menacing. Prashant gets hold of her arm and twists her around.

"Tell me NOW," he shouts.

Anjali looks at him blankly.

"Yes I did and I loved it. He was so amazing and sensuous that I could sleep with him a million times more…"

Prashant lets go of her arm and suddenly his burning red eyes lose their rage. He keeps looking at her as if she is something he has lost forever. He feels an emptiness engulf him from head to toe and he shivers. He walks away, crushed. Anjali shudders. She had not wanted to kill the hope in his heart with one stroke but he had asked for it. The clouds rumble louder and Anjali can hear their echo clearly inside her empty heart.

I looked out of the window and stopped writing. I needed a break- maybe a coffee. Nikhil's face loomed large in my thoughts. I brushed it aside ruthlessly. Ever since I had made an effort to thaw the ice between Rishi and me, I had felt a heavy weight lift off my chest. It had been like the opening of a rusted window closed for years, to let in the fresh, refreshing breeze. I was glad for this breeze.

I made myself a hot cup of coffee and sat down to complete the chapter. It took me an hour more and by the end of it I was exhausted and spent. I closed the journal and shut my eyes. My mind travelled far and wide. I remembered the house I grew up in and my brother Siddharth. We had gone to the same school, played, fought, laughed and cried in that house. I remembered Sonal visiting me so often; how we had sat for hours chatting. I did not remember seeing my parents hug each other or even hold hands. I had grown up hardly experiencing any expression of affection between them or with me or Sid. It had seemed absolutely fine then. It seemed to make no difference to me until I got married.

Rishi was over expressive or that's what I thought. His affection and caring found its release in daily dose of hugs and kisses and squeezes…I had been surprised. I was not used to so much affection in my life. Maybe if my parents had been a little more expressive, I would have accepted it as a normal part of my life.

I felt a shiver run through my body. My eyes were now fixed on the dew laden leaves outside the window. I had resisted Rishi and how. He had been aghast. And when things went wrong between us, I had resisted him even more.

I watched the paleness of the sky get ambushed by the pink and golden hues of the early morning. The sun was still shrouded but its light had begun to overpower the leftover darkness of the night. I opened the window and breathed the fresh morning air into my lungs. The nip in the air was refreshing. I dug my hands deep into the pockets of my oversized cardigan. I felt connected to the universe like a baby to the mother.

The truth dawned on me slowly and stealthily.

I had not surrendered totally to Rishi. I never had. I did not know what it was to surrender and love. Tears sprang into my eyes as this truth unravelled.

And Nikhil had taught me to surrender, to give unconditional love. I had been unable to love Rishi all these years. I had withheld something inside me whenever I was with him. I had always kept a part of myself with me and not given away myself completely. Yes I had lived with the father of my child and yet I had not loved him enough or probably loved him in bits and pieces.

The realization came as a sweep of a huge wave. I looked at the sky. The sun was rising slowly in all its majesty and grandeur. Did I owe him all the love that he had given me but never got back? It was all making sense now.

❖

It was the end of March and the winter had melted into spring. Days were much warmer. The flowers had started to bloom and there was a new energy all around. The winter clothes were being washed and aired before they would be tucked away inside suitcases or trunks. T-shirts, shorts, skirts, sleeveless tops were what greeted the eyes now.

I finished my cooking and sauntered out of the kitchen, wiping the sweat and loosening the string of my apron. I had made Yash's favourite Chicken Lasagna and was waiting to see him enjoy it..

I walked into his room where he was busy studying, his head bent amidst a heap of books,the ear plugs of the iPod in his ears.

He took out his earplugs when he saw me.

" Dinner's ready Yash," I announced.

"Gimme a minute mom."

His voice sounded weaker than usual.

I looked at him. "What's wrong?"

"Nothing mom…"

There was something weighing on his mind.

"Are you sure?" I said touching his shoulders.

"Yup! Just missing dad," Yash's voice quivered and suddenly his face bunched up as it never had.

I saw his tears. I shuddered and quickly hugged him and felt the tears in my own eyes.

I wanted to say, this too shall pass but the words had frozen inside my mouth. I just wrapped my arms around him gently and rubbed his back. Warmth was the only consolation I could offer as a mother. That night, I could not sleep. The silence of the darkness came to haunt me as never before. Was I being unfair to Yash? He needed both his parents. What about Nikhil? But what had Nikhil got to do with Rishi? What I felt for both of them was distinct and different from each other. One could never feel the same for two people ever. I trembled inside the quilt and snuggled closer to myself.

Nikhil

The evening was a bit warm and the sun had disappeared leaving the day to merge with the night. The summer breeze caressed her hair that hid her face partially. I moved it aside.

"All fine Med?" I asked.

Medha gazed into my eyes and hugged me tightly. The breeze moaned.

I felt her body against my chest.

"What's wrong?" I murmured.

Medha clung tighter to me. "I love you Nik."

"I love you too Med but..."

She withdrew from the embrace and faced me, her eyes glittering with tears. I took her in my arms and kissed the tears which had trailed out of her eyes.

"Is it Rishi?" I asked.

"I don't know but..."

I could sense her restlessness. Ever since she had reconnected with Rishi, she had been lost.

"Did he say something?"

She placed her head on my chest and clung to me.

"Nothing."

I moved my hands down her back and felt her spine relax "Then why are you restless?"

"It's just that I can't think of being away from you, I can't," she whispered.

"Who's asking you to? You can never be away from me you know that- even if we are miles apart."

I let her be with me, twined like a creeper.

"Life is strange Nik. It tests us more severely than we can imagine."

I looked at her kindly. "Yes it does, but that's what life is all about, isn't it?"

Medha ran her hand through my hair. I loved the softness of her fingers. "Why did you come into my life and stand in front of me like a mirror? For the first time I saw myself clearly in you."

I remained silent.

I held her close. The warmth of my touch soothed her and she put her head on my shoulder.

"I came because you needed me, the same way that I needed you," I whispered. The wind blew on our faces. Our lips met again and I felt her softness inside my mouth.

She had the right to choose whatever she wanted. I would never force her. I couldn't.

I had to just flow and be in the present moment. And let life happen.

Rishi

I had been talking regularly to Medha now. There was a growing sense of comfort between us and I felt it was now the right time to be together.

"Let's go for a holiday. It'll be a good break for you and for both of us," I suggested.

The sun was hot and harsh outside but the insides of my office were cold.

"I don't want to go alone with you Rishi," Medha said bluntly and I could feel the discomfort raising its ugly head again. I felt my heart break silently. I knew there was a long way to go before Medha would feel safe and comfortable to be with me alone. It was not as easy as it sounded. The silence over the phone was almost deafening. I feared we had hit a dead end.

"Let's all three of us go as a family," I suggested "It'll be a good change for Yash as well and he will feel good. The child has been through enough…"

"Don't know."

I stared at the blank wall after she kept down the phone. Maybe she was not ready yet to open up? But then Yash deserved a holiday with his family. He needed to see both of us together as friends even if we were not a couple anymore.

I moved through the office documents I was checking on my laptop but my mind was entangled with thoughts of Medha and Yash. I pressed the bell for an office boy and ordered a hot coffee.

It was the least that we could do as parents; to assure Yash that things were getting better between Medha and me. I would request Medha to do this for the sake of our son if not for our marriage. A holiday together would act as a balm on his wounded soul and help him recover from the trauma of our separation at least. Just to see both of us together would be good for him.

Medha called after a few days.

I picked up her phone quite excited. In the last few months she had rarely called except when Yash was in Muscat for a short break.

"I think we can take a trip for Yash's sake. It will do him good," she said.

I felt my heart swell with joy. She had said what I wanted to hear. This was incredible.

"I am so happy you took this decision. Any particular place?" I could barely conceal my happiness.

"The place is not important Rishi. It's a trip we are taking for our son, so choose anyplace," she said.

"Let me know the schedule of Yash's holidays. I am thinking of Koh Samui Islands in Thailand for about ten days. What do you say?"

"Make it a week. I can't be out for more than that. Just speak to Yash about the dates that suit him. He has a project to complete during the holidays."

The anticipation of the joy of being together superseded any other emotion right now. I looked out from the window. The day was bright and sunny and so was my heart.

Nikhil

I listened as Medha told me about the plans for her holiday with Rishi and Yash. I had parked the car on a lonely road that lead to her house. There was hardly any traffic on the road and I pulled down the windows of the car to feel the breeze. Her words were hard to swallow and accept.

"I owe this to Yash, Nik; he misses Rishi," Medha said as she held my hand in the car.

I kissed her hand. "I understand. It's no fault of his. Why should the child suffer?"

I looked at her tenderly. There was no commitment in our relationship. We had kept it open. We both knew that breaking away from our families was not an option we even wanted to consider. Yet we had gone ahead to pursue the beauty of a nameless relationship.

We both also knew that the intimacy between us would throw open an entire world of unbridled passion and still we had dared to sail too near the wind, strangely confident that our understanding, empathy and compassion for each other will see us through this storm. It was the unsaid in our relationship. And what was unsaid was much more powerful than what was said.

Medha looked into my eyes. "I don't want Yash to see any more mess between Rishi and me. He needs to see us together, even if it's a sham. No arguments, no fights, he has seen too much of that already."

I looked at her...trying to find my girl in this mother.

"I don't know how it will pan out." she reflected.

"Just go with the flow."

She gave me a dry smile. "It's not as easy as it sounds."

"I know it's tough but then we chose this path, didn't we? Kids don't deserve our mess. I look at Neha and feel the same loneliness in her, although she is very brave about it."

"I don't blame them Nik," her voice broke and I felt tears in her eyes.

I held her close. "Family is important Med. We as adults can find our own ways to deal with unhappiness and heartbreak but for kids, family is the only security. How can we let them down?"

She remained silent. "Let it be. You don't have to know all the answers all the time. You have lived with Rishi for sixteen years and that's a long time. It's not easy to just forget everything."

I hugged her and stared at the, potholed, broken road outside and knew my life was beginning to look the same.

Medha

This was making no sense to me and yet it made sense somehow. I was a little wary of going for this holiday. I knew it would break down a lot of walls and I was not ready yet. I was sure Rishi would make advances and try to lure me towards him. I had come a long way and worked hard to move away from him and now I couldn't let it all slip from my grasp.

When the plane landed at the small, quaint airport of Koh Samui, a far cry from the sprawling big airports, I soaked in the sheer wide spaces and the greenery of the place. The freshness of the cool crisp air filled my lungs. I feasted my eyes on the spectacular view of the green hills in the background and the sparkling, cobalt blue waters of the sea that stretched before me. There was a delicious warmth in the place that seemed to draw me to it. We reached the resort to the welcome of a fragrant white and pink string of frangipani and a welcome drink. The beauty of the resort was arresting. I realized that Rishi must have researched a lot, before deciding on this place for a holiday.

Our room overlooked the sea. There was a huge bed in the middle of the room made of carved wood. I checked out the chic restroom which was lined with pebbled stones in the bath area. I cast a long look at myself in the mirror overlooking the two basins as a beam of light fanned out of the empty coconut bark hanging from the roof. My eyes gazed at the glass roofing to catch a view of the tree's branches.

The view from the bed was surreal. As I lazed on the bed, I could see the sea spread out. I had this sudden urge to write and took out my travel journal. The thoughts came flooding and I started to pen them down. I had not been on a holiday for more than two years.

This was heaven.

Rishi

I watched her walk up to the bed in a conservative, printed nightie. The weather was very pleasant and the sea breeze brought the faint sound of the sea right into our room. She slipped under the quilt quietly and I could smell her body fragrance. It had been many months since I had inhaled that fragrance. I felt the hotness between my thighs.

The awkwardness of this whole arrangement was dawning on her I guess. I had booked an adjacent room for Yash who was more than thrilled to be on his own. I could feel the discomfort rising in Medha again. She had agreed to come only for Yash so why was she miserable now? Had creating this hunky-dory picture of our marriage started taking its toll?

That night as she lay next to me, I found her shrinking into her quilt. I remembered the first time when I had met her, a typical meeting for an arranged marriage at my cousin's place.

She had walked in wearing a pale pink churidar kurta, which highlighted her slimness superbly. A thin waist, tall frame and long flowing black hair; she had smiled at me and I had seen her eyes light up.

"So what do you do?" she had asked me.

"I am a marketing professional. I work for In- style appliances."

"Selling is an art I guess, not everyone's cup of tea," she remarked.

I smiled. "It's a lot of hard work and persistence."

She tossed her thick, glossy hair and I saw her complexion glow faintly under the dull lights of the room.

"Convincing people must be a task I am sure- ask me," she had said, laughing.

"You write articles so you know. The only difference is you use words and I talk."

"I write ads too sometimes, so I know how hard it is to sell. At the end it's all about being convinced yourself. Once you are, convincing others is easier."

"Impossible is nothing," we both blurted out together. We laughed, a bit surprised at the unanimity of our thoughts.

I had taken an instant liking to her. We had talked endlessly as if we had known each other for a long time and when it was time to say goodbye, we had been surprised that we had been chatting for more than an hour. The subsequent meeting had only confirmed my attraction and liking for her. We were soon engaged.

Was it possible to bring back the warmth again? Medha turned her back towards me.

***

Three days passed by. The holiday was turning out to be enjoyable. Medha was indulging herself. We went for sightseeing to the sunrise point, the Chewang beach side, the big Buddha temple, the grandfather and grandmother rocks, sea safari, the viewpoint climb, the mini tour. We ate Thai food at roadside pubs and eateries and went for a soothing Thai massage. Yash was enjoying himself thoroughly and to watch him smile and be happy was all that mattered to me. The cruise was the highlight of the trip.

***

I looked back as the cruise boat revved up its engines. Torrents of water erupted at its tail as the boat pushed forward. I watched the green mountains shifting away from my view and the blue sea emerging till there was only a seamless blue around us. We were going on a cruise to another island near Koh Samui.

"This place rocks," Yash beamed.

I looked at him fondly and smiled. "I am so happy you are enjoying yourself."

"This has been my best trip so far," Yash chirped.

Medha ruffled Yash's hair and smiled. I caught the joy on her face. She looked out at vast sea and was soon lost in her world. Yash opened the shutter of the camera and trained it towards us.

"Dad, closer to mom, I need a pic," he insisted.

I shifted closer to Medha

"Say cheese."

He clicked the photograph and gave a wide grin. The boat cruised along and the clear waters glinted like jewels kissed by the rays of the sun. The island was a piece of heaven. The breeze was cool and the summer sun seemed less harsh and we all freaked out as we attempted snorkeling, canoeing, and mountain climbing. We came back to our hotel room, tired and spent but full of joy. I wondered if this was all a dream and could I ever have Medha back in my life?

***

Yash climbed the stairs leading up to the huge statue of Buddha. Medha and I trailed him. He had the camera in his hands and I could sense the thrill in his steps and joy in his heart. How I had missed all this? The weather was warm and the sun pierced through, burning the ground below our naked feet. Yash was unmindful of the heat though. A Thai woman called out to us. We turned around to see her with a medley of cages with tiny birds in them. Fascinated, Medha walked up to her.

"Please take madam, good luck birds."

Medha smiled. "What do you do with them?"

"You buy five birds in a cage- go up, near the statue and release them."

Medha inspected the cages. The birds were cute and small.

"But why?"

"They bring you good luck madam- you release all negative

energy when you let them fly away."

I stepped in. "Let's take it."

We all climbed up together and when Yash opened the cage and freed the birds, I felt a strange relief descend on me.

Medha

Sleeping in the same room with Rishi after so long seemed strange.

I cast a look at the sea outside. It roared softly and the sound lifted in the air spreading itself like the wings of a bird. I had forced Nikhil out of my heart and mind before I tied the knot with Rishi. I was sure Nikhil would fade away with time. I had presumed that the passage of time would at least dull the shine of my memories. I wondered whether things would ever get to a state of total comfort between Rishi and me. It seemed impossible.

The soft bed sank with my weight. I longed for a human touch. I wanted to scream from the rooftops that I loved Nikhil. Why couldn't I get him out of my mind? I closed my eyes...maybe the thoughts would go away. But they didn't.

I turned to see Rishi fast asleep. It had been a long time since I had closely looked at him. His features seemed flattened and more spaced out. His face looked calm. His slight snoring filled up the room and the faint smell of white and purple orchids kept in the room floated in the air.

I had not looked at him like that for a long time.

I found myself doing the same, the next day too.

As I retired for the day, I found Rishi tucked in bed, reading a self-help book. Ever since we had met, he had kept his distance physically and had respected the aloofness that I had wanted to maintain. We had been sleeping on the same bed but the dignity had been maintained.

I had anticipated Rishi to be the same, insistent on getting his own way but I had been pleasantly surprised. Maybe when he had told me that he had changed, he really meant it. I had of course not trusted him, the past coming in my way. I had waited to experience it myself rather than believe his words. And now I could sense the change quite emphatically.

I watched him from the corner of my eyes. He was focused on the book. He appeared alone and vulnerable. I had Nikhil but he had no one. He never had anyone, no close friend, no one. He had been waiting for me all along. He had lived without me for all these months, lonely and miserable, like a man lost in the jungle while I had been soaking in the warmth of Nikhil's love.

I shifted in my bed and returned to the book which I was finding hard to concentrate on. I had found an oasis in the desert of my life but he had been all alone, fighting the battle of our broken marriage, wondering whether he would ever have me back?

Rishi closed the book he was reading, took off his glasses, wished me good night, lay down and closed his eyes. I watched him sleep. There was a look of acceptance on his face. It disturbed me somehow.

Stealthily, I walked out of the room to face the still blackness of the night and sea. I smelled the damp air as I sat down on the chairs. I could see some twinkling lights far away. I let my tears flow out as the dark sea roared and shattered the hush of the night. There was so much inside me that needed to come out.

Had I been unfair to Rishi? I had not been able to love him completely all these years; had never been able to return what he had felt for me. We had good sex all throughout our marriage whenever I had wanted it. Whenever he had wanted it, I had termed it as lust; was that fair?

That guilt would remain forever in my mindscape.

Yes, there had been something missing but I had realized it

only after being with Nikhil. I had not been able to surrender to him as I had to Nikhil.

I focused my eyes on the moonlight that kissed the surface of the sea. The truth dawned on me more rapidly than I could keep pace with.

I looked heavenwards and cried.

I had chosen to be with Nikhil and had allowed my emotions to take me where they could. I had wanted to know how far I could go with him. Maybe I was destined to reach Rishi through Nikhil. If Nikhil had not come into my life, I would never have known or realized what love meant and Rishi would not have worked on himself and realized how much I meant to him.

My marriage could never be the same without him.

I had confronted my deepest desires-to discover, to explore what constituted me. I somehow knew it would be worth all the pain.

The sea breeze hugged me; after a while I returned to the warmth of my bed–tired.

I am looking for a place to take a bath but am not able to find it. The house is big and unfamiliar. It has a huge verandah, many rooms–finally I find a bathroom but it has glass walls. I take off my clothes and realize that people would be able to watch me from the street below. I quickly cover myself with my towel… I am roaming aimlessly to find a place to take a bath, wrapped in a towel. A lady guides me to a place in the middle of the verandah but there are many people. I am anxious… why can't I find a place to take a bath…?

I woke up from my dream, sweating, with my heart beating fast.

I sat up in bed and looked around. Rishi was fast asleep. The night was still dark, the dawn was far away. I closed my eyes-thankful that this was just a dream.

That night when Rishi retired for the day, I lay down beside him, wondering what was bothering me now. Why was it that I felt that I should just flow with the energy that God had given me, without questioning it.

I wanted to put myself and Rishi back together as a whole, assimilating the pieces that we both had become over the years. To somehow sew the frayed seams of my marriage, stitch by stitch.

The night was hushed just like my marriage. And if the hush was not broken now, I doubt whether it would ever be.

I moved closer to Rishi and touched his face with my fingers. Rishi shivered; someone had touched him after a long time. I traced his mouth with my trembling hands.

I had not touched him for the past fifteen months and right now I felt as if he was still mine. Rishi stirred. I moved my hands through the kurta, over his chest and waited for him wake up.

He slowly opened his eyes. I suddenly noticed his cinnamon coloured eyes...they were the same colour as Nikhil's.

He looked at me and I noticed the mist in his eyes. How long had it been since we had looked into each other's eyes and reached for each other. He reached for me, his appetite shimmering in his eyes and embraced me tightly. I held him close, closer than I ever thought I would.

The night was still and the fragrance of the fresh orchids wafted inside the room, as if in celebration.

Suddenly Rishi was kissing me all over with a hunger that only he and I recognized. His hands ripped apart my nightie and for the first time in months, *he touched* my bare body and I quivered. I moaned as his hands moved on my body. He made me arch my body the way only he could. I began rising, rocking. He closed his mouth on my breasts and I opened my legs wide and felt his hardness between them. I was soon rocking more rapidly, faster than he could handle. He kept looking at me, trying to keep pace with my desire. I was fully aroused and ready to come. He knew.

I felt myself loosening up and rising like froth in the ocean.... He was inside me now and I was gasping to hold on to something that would save me... and then suddenly there was this wave that took me higher and higher to the highest mountain peak...the dizziness was mind blowing. I trembled like the earth during an earthquake. I felt as if I would break up into a million pieces, never to be formed again. I was flying like a bird. I was merging, breaking into countless pieces, drowning, sinking and laughing and Rishi knew what he had given me. Rishi had reclaimed what he had lost.

I realized that in those few moments, my broken marriage had begun to heal and join together; that the hollow trenches of my slowly disintegrating marriage had started to fill up again.

When we had spent ourselves and were lying next to each other, I felt a calm descend in the room.

I realized that we both had shed our old skins forever and had become new for each other. The old Medha and Rishi were no more.

I cast a look at Rishi and noticed a lonely tear at the corner of his eye. I wiped it off with my fingers, burying his face in my chest and in that moment we were aware of the fact that we had reconnected. And that life would not be the same anymore. There was no need to celebrate or own this moment. It was destined to be this way...planned by God to the last detail...the place, the time.

❖

I got up the next morning and noticed a band of sunlight drifting in through the sheer curtains of the room. I looked around and realized Rishi was not in the room. I looked at the unmade bed and recollected what had happened at night; the night that seemed to have bridged the chasm between me and Rishi; that among the twisted sheets of the bed, our marriage had somehow straightened itself.

I rose slowly and moved towards the bathroom.

When I stepped out of the room after taking a shower, I saw Yash and Rishi enjoying in the pool.

The breeze was cool and fresh.

"Hey mom, come on in," Yash shouted

I smiled. "No way, I just had a bath."

Rishi said, "C'mon Medha, be a sport."

I looked at Rishi a few seconds longer and said, "No way."

"It's been ages," he sighed.

I nodded and sat down on the pool chair.

Yash came out of the pool, dripping.

"You look happy mom," he said wiping himself dry.

I gazed at him. "Do I? You mean I have been unhappy all this while?"

Yash dried his hair. "No I mean, it's different today; you and dad; I don't know."

"Then maybe it's different after all."

His face had the happiest smile I had ever seen. "That calls for another lap," and he dived back into the pool.

I watched him splash his arms and legs with a renewed excitement. Rishi and I exchanged a warm glance. Suddenly there was so much peace and beauty around us. Yash noticed the change in us with relief. For the next four days, life was a roller coaster ride. Rishi wooed me with the ardour of a new lover. We made love in the day even as the waves crashed outside our room. We made love as the night sky was filled with a million stars. We made love as if that was the only thing that could save our marriage from falling apart.

And Rishi made love to me as if I had not been touched by anyone else ever. That I was all his and not an iota of me belonged to anyone else.

I realized that Nikhil had completed me for Rishi, so that I could go back to Rishi as a whole and not in bits and pieces. I also realized how deep I had grown within myself.

Rishi

I looked out of the glass doors of the restaurant and saw the blue sparkling ocean. I had gotten up early and had sneaked into Yash's room, to surprise him. To my surprise, he was awake and we both got ready for breakfast and landed at the resort's restaurant.

I had decided not to wake up Medha.

"I'll have a *Khanom chin namya* with this drink, Krating Dae-ng," Yash ordered.

"*Khao khai chiao* for me," I said.

The Thai waiter smiled. I turned towards Yash, "A few more days and I'll be gone."

Yash looked at me. "Is there no way you can stay on in Delhi?"

I laughed. "It's not as easy as it sounds dude...jobs are hard to find these days."

"I guess then we should be visiting each other at shorter intervals."

I caught the longing in his voice.

"Let's click a few photos," Yash suggested.

I handed him the camera.

We clicked many photographs- in the restaurant, besides the pool, next to the big Buddha statue kept at the entrance, till the waiter arrived with the breakfast. The smell of fresh green peppers, fish sauce, cucumber and rice drifted in the air. I watched him dig into his food and was overcome by emotions. I still couldn't believe it had happened; that I had been able to break the wall between me and Medha; that we had been able to reach out to each other.

In the days following that night, Medha had told me about Nikhil. How they had grown closer emotionally; how she had been drawn towards him and how she had gone with the flow, unafraid and without a doubt. I listened to her without questioning her much. Her eyes had the stark honesty of a child and she spoke without remorse or guilt.

"I went ahead, being aware of everything Rishi and I have no regrets," she confessed.

I kept looking at her.

"We love each other and what we have experienced is so divine and pure that I can never forget him nor do I want to."

"Then where do I figure in your life?" I questioned her.

Medha knitted her hands in her lap. "You are the father of my child Rishi, something that Nikhil can never be. But just because Nikhil exists, doesn't mean you don't."

I took a deep breath. I was sure my love would help her untangle the knots of her heart, but for that she had to come back to me.

"You can come back to Muscat as and when you feel the need. I will wait for you," I said softly.

Her eyes softened.

She reached out to embrace me and I felt the warmth of her hug.

I left after two days. My holiday was over but I knew the celebration had just begun.

Medha

I was at peace.

It was not so much the relief of the fact that I had been able to reach out for the first time in my marriage but the release of guilt had left me at peace with myself. I had been able to liberate myself from my own self.

I could sense how happy Rishi was. It showed in his eyes. There was a lot which was left unsaid and I knew only time would take care of that. I needed some time to be with myself, although I knew deep down that my security stemmed from Rishi.

I recalled my conversation with him in Koh Samui.

"I still wonder what you found in him that you didn't in me," Rishi had asked me.

We were having coffee outside our room. The blue ocean spread out in front of us, wide as a smile.

I took a sip. "It's not about finding something that I didn't find in you- maybe it was that unfulfilled desire to have him which just got triggered. I just got pulled towards him and it was such a strong pull, I couldn't do much."

"And to top it all we were not getting along. Our marriage had turned ugly and this was beautiful."

Rishi said. "You never thought even once how it would affect our marriage...I mean you threw caution to the winds and went ahead…"

I looked past him to the sea. "Maybe deep down–subconsciously I was sure you would help me deal with this chaos…that our marriage could withstand such a storm," she paused. "It was something I had to do to know what I was made up of, like dismantling myself into pieces to join the pieces again."

Rishi cradled the coffee mug in his hands. "But it could have gone the other way too…I could have freaked out and…"

"You did, didn't you?"

Rishi kept silent.

"You mean you would have left me, divorced me?"

"No I mean..." Rishi faltered.

I smiled. "Those are presumptions and at that point I was not thinking too much ahead. It was all about that moment..."

I scooped the froth of the coffee with a spoon and put it in my mouth.

"I realize it now Rishi, that you are the soil in which I had held myself securely and Nikhil has made me fly. You are my roots and he is my wings."

"That's the biggest truth of my life and I hope you can understand it," I added.

"I am trying to Medha...and I am touched by your honesty and clarity, I really am."

I drained the last of my coffee.

I needed them both. Probably I had been able to get out of my marriage, aware somewhere that Rishi would pull me back from this storm.

Rishi was a treasure I could not afford to lose and Nikhil had paved the way for me to reach that treasure. But in the process of finding that treasure, I had fallen deeply in love with Nikhil...the bridge between the seeker and the sought. Our relationship had blossomed like the wild flowers that spring up when the monsoons set in, carefree and spontaneous.

I had not imagined that life would spin around so fast. I could see things more clearly now. I could now read the omens that God was sending me and wondered what had made our marriage so strong as to survive such a hurricane.

Nikhil

I looked at my watch again and wondered how much more time before she would arrive? It was pouring heavily and the rain beat down the glass panes of the Costa coffee outlet at the Greater Kailash II market. It was a place we often had met before. The coffee house was full and the aroma of coffee was mixed with the smell of rain today. I had arrived before time. The road outside was choc a bloc with traffic and the cars honked as my eyes looked for her in the crowd. But all I could see was the rain lashing on the road, beating on the roofs of the cars and whiplashing the trees and plants. The low rumble of thunder echoed in the air.

Medha arrived in her dark blue jeans and a rose coloured, low neck chiffon blouse, almost drenched. My eyes lingered on her wet hair, her damp face and her wet blouse that clung to her curves. We both hugged each other. It was so hard to resist her. I knew a part of being attracted to her was that she was not mine and could never be. She was Rishi's wife and the mother of his child. What could not be attained or was forbidden was always seductive.

We settled on the sofa and ordered two cappuccinos. Medha took out a napkin and wiped her face and arms.

"What awful weather? It was so tough driving," she lamented.

" But you love this rain- don't you?"

She laughed. "Of course I do. I had always wanted it to rain when we met."

"Looks like your prayers have been answered."

"How was Thailand?"

"Koh Samui is a beautiful place, you must visit it."

"How was the holiday?"

"Good. Yash was super excited and enjoyed thoroughly..."

"And you?" I cut her short.

Medha's eyes lingered over my face. "I reconnected with him."

My heart sank. My eyes searched hers for an explanation but

my tongue felt like gravel.

"You mean…you…." I faltered.

"I-I could reach out to him Nik. It's something I have not been able to do all these years." I could see her tremble. "And he had been waiting…"

I had dreaded this. I knew this the moment she had told me that she had consented to go for the holiday.

I persisted. "How was it?"

She stared back at me. "It happened…I didn't have to try you know and I …"

"Don't justify or explain anything Med," I murmured.

Medha lifted her gaze to me. "I never knew that I could- you know…"

I could sense her restlessness

"You don't owe me any explanations Med; you did what you felt right. It's just that–I don't know what to do with us," I swallowed hard.

Medha reached for my hand and held it.

"You have lived with him for sixteen years…that's almost one fourth of one's lifetime," I tried to smile.

"Nik, I love you and will always, you know that," Medha said.

"I know that. No one has loved me the way you have."

Medha looked deep into my eyes. "And no one will. No one can love you more than I."

I reached for the coffee and took a long sip.

"Are you happy?" I asked.

Medha's voice shook. "Sometimes love is an answer, not a question. He never gave up on me Nik, in spite of everything, in spite of knowing I fell for you, that I love you deeply. I owe him sixteen years of lovelessness Nik."

I felt something break inside me again.

"Please Nik, you have to help me take this journey back," she said. "And only you can," I heard a sob rise inside her throat.

"I will. I have to, I know."

Medha stared at the coffee mug. "I have to go back. I don't know if it makes sense to you or not but…"

"It does. What doesn't make sense is why should you go away from me?" I said.

"I can never go away from you Nik. We will always be connected through our hearts and souls, you know that."

I drew in my breath. "You are all I have. How can I let you go?" I almost cried.

Medha looked at me. The mist clouded her eyes as well.

Medha

It has been two weeks now since Rishi left. Nikhil and I had resisted each other, afraid of going back to the paradise which we both had decided to pass by. I ruffled his hair as he sat next to me in the car. "You don't want to ask me anything?"

He smiled at me. "What is there to ask? You never asked me anything when you reached out to me; I never asked you anything when I reached out to you, why now?"

He held my hand and reached for my lips. He kissed me and the sensuousness and gentleness moved me. I fluttered as a bird about to take a flight.

"I want you to be happy Medha, that's all I want," he whispered.

We embraced each other and I broke down in his arms. He held me close.

"I will meet you whenever you want to Med. Just call out and I'll be there," he said.

He wrapped me in his arms again like a gift. I closed my eyes. Moving away from Nikhil was tough. With him, I felt whole and complete. I had never felt so much love inside me. He was the one who had saved me from the chaos. He had brought out the best in me. He was the passage through which I had passed to reach Rishi.

As we withdrew from each other, I gazed at his face. I wanted to remember each line and contour, the glow in his eyes, the softness of his lips, the kindness that flooded his face. I wanted to keep these alive forever. I knew he would eventually submerge into my subconsciousness, taking up the space that he had created.

By the time we parted, I felt like two parts of the same, ready to part but still attached. We had been two souls who had been able to walk in and through each other's lives with freedom. There were no barriers, no expectations from each other.

"Never cut what you can untie."
— Joseph Joubert

Rishi

I picked up the phone. It was Medha. I had not seen her for three weeks now but strangely, I wasn't restless. I was at peace. The weather had begun to turn cooler in Muscat and the flowers were beginning to bloom all over the place.

"Rishi, I am coming back," she announced.

I felt the joy explode in my heart like fireworks. I did not know what to say to her. I wanted to cry.

"Rishi, did you hear me?"

It took me a few seconds to find my voice. "I knew you will be back home one day. I knew it," my voice finally broke through.

Medha sighed.

My eyes were moist. "It's gone. The worst is over between us Medha."

"Yes, I know," she admitted.

"I have been waiting for you all along."

"I know Rishi. It's your faith that has brought me back but I couldn't have if Nikhil hadn't shown me the way. He is the reason I found you."

I knew what she meant.

And once she was back, my life took a turnaround.

As she opened herself and shared Nikhil with me, I realized the biggest truth about knowing her was to know Nikhil. Her eyes sparkled when she talked about him. There was an exceptional honesty about her which I had never experienced. She seemed like this child- woman to me, at once lovable and childlike. I realized that if she could share Nikhil with me, she was sharing a part of herself that no one knew or would ever know. To know about her relationship with Nikhil was a passage to knowing her and understanding her. The more she confided in me, the deeper I fell in love with her.

"I had zero tolerance for snapping and insolence Rishi," she told me.

"Why?"

"Because I had seen enough of it while growing up, when papa snapped at ma, was insensitive and rude with her most of the time. So I guess when you showed even a slight degree of it, I reacted."

"And Nikhil was the opposite," I said.

"Yes, he was all tenderness, warmth, attention, finesse."

"I found you emotionally inadequate most of the times as well..."

"But I always tried my best to reach out to you?"

"Yes you did, but you came to me as a needy, little boy while I was looking for a loving man."

"My body shut down sexually to you because I did not find you erotic anymore."

"You found my need for sex…"

"Gross," she completed my thought. "Yes I did. I hated to *mother* you."

"You were craving for my attention and love and I couldn't give any," she continued.

"I know it must have ripped you to pieces but I just couldn't…"

Medha held me close and hugged me tightly. I hadn't realized how much I loved her and was ready to go any distance for her love.

Medha

I looked outside the window of my house in Muscat. It was the end of January and the breeze was soft and mild, carrying with it the fragrance of the man I had always loved and could never stop loving. The flowers swayed gently, and the breeze ruffled my hair. My eyes admired the purple, pink, white flowers circling the huge roundabout overlooking the window. Muscat was indeed beautiful this time of the year. There was a slight chill in the air and the sky was bluer than ever and the white buildings looked like a marbled kingdom against the backdrop of mountains with their myriad shades of sepia, cocoa, and rust. I was aware of a deep longing in me.

I had just come back from a trip to India where I had met Nikhil for coffee. We had met after three months and there had been so much to talk about and to share that I had realized that time and distance had been powerless in taking him away from me. The meeting was etched in my memory like it happened yesterday. He had walked towards me, his long steps quickening. I moved towards him, my heart hammering inside me. As we stepped closer to each other, his eyes spread over me. We hugged and he kissed me gently on my lips. I felt his tenderness.

"Your hair has gone whiter," I teased him.

"And you have gone slimmer."

We settled on the plush sofas of the Costa coffee outlet.

"I guess you have been missing me."

A slow smile lit up. "I guess you too."

We laughed.

Nikhil walked up to the counter to order coffee. I looked around. The place was so familiar as if we had just met here a few days ago.

"So how are things with Rishi?" he asked, settling down.

"Calm, peaceful and beautiful. He is a changed man. He amazes me most of the time."

He gazed at me closely. "I guess that's the reward for saving six lives."

"I couldn't have done it on my own- you saved them with me."

Nikhil gave a wry smile. "C'mon you have always been the brave one, I am still a coward."

I felt my heartbeat quicken. "All's well between you and Priyanka- Nik?"

He looked away.

"Nik," I called out.

"It's the same as it was. I tried reaching out but I guess she has moved on," he sounded deflated.

"Sometimes marriages can survive on neglect," I said.

"What did your marriage thrive on Med?"

The coffee arrived.

"I guess mine thrived on faith, trust, fearlessness and also Rishi.

Its only when I reconnected with him, did I realize what he meant to me- that I couldn't lose him."

Nikhil sighed. "And you could lose me?"

I felt a pang sear my heart.

"No Nik.... I can never lose you because I found myself through you."

I took a sip of the coffee. "And I found my way back to Rishi also because of you...your presence has glued my marriage forever, how can I afford to lose you?"

I saw his lips quiver. "I miss you Med."

I felt the prick of tears behind my eyes "I miss you too Nik and we have each other. What we feel for each other is something no one can take away...not even Rishi."

Nikhil drank up his coffee slowly.

"You need to pick up the threads of your life,Nik," I said gently.

He merely nodded his head.

"You know Nik, love is enough to get someone out of the grave. Priyanka is still around you, living with you don't let her go."

Nikhil smiled. It was the same million dollar smile that had enchanted me back in college.

"I'll try- can't promise though."

"Do it for yourself Nik, do it for Neha. You deserve to be happy," I said.

We had sat at the coffee shop for a long time, feeling the warmth of the spaces we had both made in each other's life. I realized that my love for him was like an iceberg, only one small part visible above water. I myself didn't know how much I loved him.

I had wondered how I would be able to cope with this extraordinary affection I felt for both Nikhil and Rishi.

I had felt a major shift in my feelings for Rishi when he had understood my relationship with Nikhil like a true friend and a compassionate man.

My eyes watched the cars zipping past as I stood on the balcony. It was a fairly windy day and rains were expected to lash Muscat. A cyclone was fast approaching the coast of Oman. It was all over the news on the radio and television.

I felt the winds whip my body.

I realized that Nikhil and Rishi both had got what they had been able to bring out in me.

Nikhil had brought out the tenderness, gentleness and the compassion and all the love and sensuality in me while Rishi had given way to my wild, free self.

The fact that Nikhil and I had never made any promises of love, of loving each other till the moon spins out of its orbit or till the oceans run dry–it had become easier to surrender and love. There was no weight of broken promises, no guilt of believing in the truth of words that lovers cloak around each other. It had made everything very simple. It had made my going back to Rishi–possible.

Suddenly I felt a hand on my shoulder.

"You seem to be lost, Wifey," Rishi's voice fell on my ears.

"It's so strange that I feel whole and complete with you and I also feel whole and complete when I am with Nikhil," my voice trembled.

Rishi squeezed my shoulder.

I looked at him. " I don't know whether you will be able to understand..."

He caught hold of my hands. "I am trying to, that's why I am standing beside you."

"I know it's been such a long journey and I don't know..."

"You have already reached me, isn't it?" Rishi kissed me gently on my cheek.

I looked him in the eyes. "I don't feel guilty Rishi. I have no regrets."

"I had seen the chemistry between you two on the day of the launch and I guessed where you were headed the day you left for India. I had seen it in your eyes."

Words can fail us so miserably at times. I didn't know what to say to him. He had made it so easy for me. I was grateful.

Rishi took my face in his hands. "I know what it is to feel whole and complete with someone. I feel that with you. As long as you are happy, that's all I want."

I rested my head on his shoulders and gazed at the mountains. They no longer seem cold and heartless.

Nikhil had rekindled the spark in me and Rishi was there to sustain, protect and nurture it.

It was perhaps this leap of faith that had helped me close the yawning chasm of my marriage forever and seal it.

"You know Rishi I realized something–you are my strength," I said tenderly.

Rishi looked at me, his eyes same as Nikhil's.

"And Nikhil is my weakness, my first love. I go weak in the knees when he's around me and one can't build one's life on a weakness–I need you to build me," I slipped my arm around his waist and cuddled close to him. The breeze twirled around us and I felt his breath on my face.

"You have me, Wifey," Rishi said .

Sometimes there are no answers to questions. We do not choose love, love chooses us. I knew Nikhil's memory would always remain an inseparable and strong part of it. Maybe that was what it was meant to be.

I stood with my arms around Rishi. I had found a close friend in him, something I had always craved for in my marriage. And it had taken me sixteen years and a Nikhil to discover him. Rishi and Nikhil, both were a part of my seamless and sacred sky. Yes, I did feel divided somewhere inside me and whether this would turn out to be a curse or blessing or both, I knew only time would tell.

Epilogue

Longing is the cross nailed to my soul
I carry & will carry all my life
Longing is the sky I fly across
like an eagle searching for its home
Longing is the earth I walk all over
covering the seamless distance that never ends
Longing is the ocean I swim far far away
losing sight of the shore
Longing is the mountain I climb high,
higher
till I can see the world spread out below
dwarfed
like a miniature kingdom
smaller than itself
A bonsai view...
Longing is looking for you
but never finding you

Its you flowing inside me
& making me move
Longing is the fire that sets me aflame
without burning me out
Longing is the rain that soaks my heart
drenches my soul
yet leaves me thirsty
Longing is the sunshine that warms my heart
but leaves me cold with desire
Longing is the road that leads me to you
and then takes me away from you
Longing is me aching to have your soul
Longing is you aching to surrender
Longing is both of us, with that shining light within us
That soul ache
which belongs to both of us
& nourishes us
leaving us both, full to the brim
for all times to come...

Glossary

Yaar	:	Friend
Saab	:	Sir
Rajnigandha	:	Name of a white, fragrant flower
Rehne de	:	Leave it
Galat Jawaab	:	Wrong answer
Abaya	:	A long, flowing black gown worn by Arab women to cover themselves.
Dishdasha	:	Long white shirts worn by Arab men
Saket	:	Name of a colony in New Delhi
Bread Pakoda/Pakodas	:	Names of Indian snacks
Miyan	:	Sir, as addressed in Muslims
Jama Masjid	:	Name of a major mosque in New Delhi.
Parantha	:	Round wheat cakes made with loads of oil, an Indian dish.
Dhabba	:	Modest, road side eating joint
Langoor	:	Leaf Monkey
Beta	:	Son

Cheez	:	Thing
Shakal se shareef lagte ho	:	You look decent by face
Khana lage de	:	Lay down the food.
Bindi	:	Round adornment worn on forehead by Indian women
Patiala	:	Name of an Indian trouser worn specially by Punjabi women
Tu saale	:	You, scoundrel!
Dil hai ki manta nahi	:	The heart doesn't listen